Cross Roads

Cross Roads

Fern Michaels

WHEELER
CHIVERS

This Large Print edition is published by Thorndike Press, Waterville, Maine USA and by BBC Audiobooks Ltd, Bath, England.

Sisterhood Series.

Wheeler Publishing, a part of Gale, Cengage Learning.

Wheeler Publishing Large Print Hardcover.
The text of this Large Print edition is unabridged.
Other aspects of the book may vary from the original edition.
Set in 16 pt. Plantin.

LIBRARY OF CONGRESS CATALOGING-IN-PUBLICATION DATA

Michaels, Fern.
Cross roads / by Fern Michaels. — Large print ed.
p. cm. — (Sisterhood series)
Originally published: New York : Zebra Books, 2010.
ISBN-13: 978-1-4104-2931-5
ISBN-10: 1-4104-2931-8
1. Vigilantes—Fiction. 2. Large type books. I. Title.
PS3563.I27C74 2010
813'.54—dc22 2010025452

BRITISH LIBRARY CATALOGUING-IN-PUBLICATION DATA AVAILABLE
Published in the U.S. in 2010 by arrangement with Zebra Books, an imprint of Kensington Publishing Corp.
Published in the U.K. in 2011 by arrangement with the Kensington Publishing Corp.
U.K. Hardcover: 978 1 408 49261 1 (Chivers Large Print)
U.K. Softcover: 978 1 408 49262 8 (Camden Large Print)

Printed in the United States of America
1 2 3 4 5 6 7 14 13 12 11 10

For my friends, Bob and Sara Schwager

Chapter 1

Even though every light in the old farmhouse was on, it did nothing to dispel the gloom that seemed to shroud the house and its two occupants. Fragrant peach candles flickered on the dinner table, the crystal sparkled, and the delectable meal on fragile bone china sat basically untouched. Outside, a summer rain pounded on the roof and battered the ancient smoky windows.

"Myra, we need to talk," Charles said quietly.

"Hmmm, yes, I suppose we do. What would you like to talk about, Charles? It's raining outside. I always hated thunder, but I hate lightning even more. But then, you already know that, so there's no point in discussing it. Dinner is wonderful."

"How would you know? You haven't touched a thing on your plate. Close your eyes, Myra, and tell me what's on your plate."

"Roast beef," Myra snapped irritably.

"Wrong! It's pork tenderloin. You've always loved pork tenderloin."

"I used to love a lot of things, Charles. I'm sorry. We should just have had sandwiches and soup, or even just the soup."

"You wouldn't have eaten that, either," Charles snapped in return.

"What do you want me to say, Charles? I'm not trying to be difficult, it's just that . . . I miss my family. You know what else, Charles? I'm sorry we got those pardons. I was happy on the mountain with the girls. I cry every time I think of them. I would give anything to have yesterday back."

"That's rather cavalier of you, Myra. The girls wanted their old lives back. They didn't want that outlaw life anymore. They wanted to get married and have families. Surely you can't fault them for that."

"Of course I don't fault them for wanting their old lives back. I was speaking for myself. It's been a year and a half, Charles! Do not, I repeat, do not tell me to get a hobby. I do not want a hobby."

"I never thought of knitting as a hobby, old girl. I'd love a hand-knitted sweater."

"Then go to town and buy one! I am too old to learn to knit, and I have arthritis in my fingers. Why are you deviling me like this? Why can't you just let me be miserable?"

"Because I love you, that's why. You're starting to act the same way you did when Barbara died, and you're scaring me. I can't go through that again, Myra, I just can't."

"Oh, Charles, no, that isn't going to happen. I'll get a handle on it, just give me some time. Just a little more time."

"Myra, a year and a half is a lot of time. We need to make some decisions here. We need to join the living, to get on with our lives. We can't keep marking time like this."

"No one needs me these days, Charles. Not even you. Somehow, you manage to keep busy helping the boys with Global Securities. There are just too many hours in the day to fill. I now know how Annie felt. There's nothing worse than not being needed.

"Those old, supposedly dear friends of mine from my other life have cut us dead. Nellie spends almost all day in therapy for her two hip replacements, and even when she's home, she's too tired to do anything but sleep. Pearl is out there somewhere doing her thing with the underground railroad. I volunteered my services, and she said that if she needed me, she'd call. Well, guess what, Charles, she hasn't called once. I don't want to be a pest where Lizzie and her new baby are concerned. She and Cosmo are so happy, they don't need me fussing around them even though they said their door is always open to us.

"I love it that Lizzie is just doing consulting work these days, and Cosmo is just on call in case some emergency crops up. They're such wonderful parents to Little Jack."

"Speaking of Little Jack, tell me again why we didn't go to Lizzie's baby shower at the White House?"

"Because it would have stirred things up, and I didn't want to ruin Lizzie's day. And it's the same reason we didn't go to Little Jack's christening. Isn't it wonderful how Lizzie and Cosmo donated all the gifts to Babies Hospital and to families who need all that baby gear? They've set up so many foundations for baby care, I can't count them anymore. I can't wait for them to come back to town. Just a few weeks, and we'll get to see Little Jack again."

"You're done with dinner, right?" Myra nodded. "Get your slicker. I have something I want you to see. If you don't come with me, I'm going to pick you up and carry you. Move it, old girl!"

Grumbling, Myra followed Charles out to

the mudroom and donned her slicker and Wellingtons. She held his hand as they made their way to the barn. Inside, light blazed. The horses whickered softly at the intrusion. Somewhere deep in the barn, a dog growled. "Be quiet, don't make any fast moves or loud noises. Just stay with me.

"It's just me, Charles, Little Lady. I'm coming in. Remember what I said, Myra. Look!"

Myra looked down into a mountain of straw where a warm blanket had been spread. "I don't know what her name is or even how she got here, but here she is with her newborn pups. I found them this morning. I call her Little Lady — not that she's little, because she isn't."

"Ooooh, Charles!" Myra dropped to her knees in front of a magnificent golden retriever, who eyed her warily. She made no move to touch the mother or her pups. "Did you feed her, Charles?"

"I did, and she gobbled it all down. I'd like to bring her and the pups into the house if you don't mind. You know, just to keep an eye on her. I already called a vet, and he came out earlier this afternoon. Aside from being undernourished, Little Lady is fine. He gave me some nutrients and vitamins to give her. Like I said, it will be a lot easier to take care of them in the house."

"Of course it will, but you said we can't touch them. How will we get them into the house? Will Little Lady allow us to pick them up?"

"I don't know. I think that's up to you, Myra. She trusts me, but she doesn't know you yet. You have to make friends. Talk to her, see if she'll let you pet her. Touch is very important, so be gentle."

"It's so damp in here, Charles. That can't be good for the puppies. Find the wagon, the one we use to wheel in firewood. If you lift Lady and put her and the pups in it, we can cover them with a tarp and scoot right back to the house. We can build a fire in the living room even if it is July and make a bed for all of them. That's a good idea, isn't it, Charles?"

Charles beamed. "Splendid idea, old girl. Now why didn't I think of that?"

"Because I'm a mother, and you aren't," Myra said as she stroked the golden's head. "I don't think there's anything more beautiful in the whole world than a new baby or a new puppy or kitten. What are you waiting for, Charles, Little Lady is shivering."

Forty minutes later, the air-conditioning in the house was turned off and a fire was blazing in the humongous fireplace. Old, worn, soft blankets were spread close to the hearth but not too close, in case a spark eluded the fire screen. Mother and pups were settled within minutes. A bowl of real food was set out for Little Lady, who gobbled it down within seconds. When she was finished, she used her snout to move the bowl away from the blanket, then she offered up her paw to Myra, who dutifully shook it.

"I think you have your family, old girl," Charles said.

Myra looked up at her husband, her eyes misty with tears. "Whatever would I do without you, Charles? You always make it come out right somehow. But what happens when these little creatures don't need me?"

"An animal always needs a human, Myra. That's a given. And for your help, you get undying love and devotion. They'll never leave you until it's their time. Can you handle that?"

Something sparked in Myra's eyes. "I'm a mother, Charles, and mothers can handle anything that comes their way."

Charles turned away to hide his smile. "Well then, there you go. If you have the situation under control, I think I'll head back to the kitchen to clean up. And then I have some work I need to finish. If you need me, just give a shout."

"Before you head down to the dungeons, I could use some coffee. It's going to be a long night, and I have a lot of stories to tell Little Lady, so she'll feel she belongs. She is ours, isn't she?" Myra asked anxiously.

"Damn straight she's ours, and so are those pups," Charles said. He didn't see any need to tell Myra the vet had brought Little Lady and her pups out to the barn yesterday. He'd called ahead when Little Lady's elderly owner passed away two days ago and asked Charles to take the dog and her pups. Sensing this was the solution to Myra's problem, he'd jumped at the chance, hoping his few little white lies to Myra would never come back to haunt him. He whistled now as he started to tidy up the kitchen.

It was so nice to have a family again.

Three thousand miles away, Annie de Silva was walking around the floor of the Babylon Casino. The customers ignored her as they feverishly dropped money into the slot machines or plunked down chips at the tables. Not so the casino staff. They imperceptibly straightened their shoulders, stood a little taller, their sharp-eyed gazes wheeling around the floor like random ricochets. Everyone learned from day one that Annie de Silva was hell on wheels, that she kicked ass and took names later. They learned it because Annie de Silva herself told them so and warned each and every one of them not to bring it to a test.

From time to time she would stop at a table or slot machine and, if the customer seemed amenable, strike up a conversation. She liked to know the people who frequented Babylon and loved hearing the nice things they said about the establishment she and Fish owned. She especially loved the seniors who came on bus trips for the free luncheons and the twenty-five dollars in chips her people handed out. The business never made any money on the little groups, but the casino counted on the goodwill the program generated.

As she ambled about the floor, Annie's mind wandered. How much longer was she going to keep doing this? It was so old hat that she could do it in her sleep, and the thrill had been gone for a long time now. She felt her eyes start to burn as she thought about Myra and the girls, and wondered if they felt at loose ends the way she did.

She was sick and tired of lying to Myra and the girls about how happy she was, that she loved working in the casino and being with Fish. Well, she did sort of love being with Fish, more or less, but she was just as happy when he took off for days, sometimes weeks, at a time to work for Global Securities. Plus, she was starting to think there was something a little screwy where that organization was concerned. Well, one of these days she'd figure it out, but not right this moment. Homecomings with Fish were rather nice but a real letdown at times, too. The bloom, if there had ever been one, was definitely off the rose these days. There just wasn't one damn thing about this new life of hers that was exciting or spontaneous. Not a single damn thing.

Sad to say, owner or not, the staff here at Babylon merely tolerated her, and that was the bottom line. It was time to take a crack at sticking her nose into the *Post.* Maggie probably wouldn't like it, but then, Maggie was expendable, just like everyone else. Annie owned the damn paper. She'd stay just long enough to stir up some trouble, screw things up, then take off for other parts. That was her life these days.

Annie stopped now where a gaggle of seniors were arguing over the slot machines. She sat down on one of the chairs and listened to the heated exchange. Half of the group wanted to cash in the chips for money so they could put it toward something or other at the group home they lived in, and the other half wanted to play with it.

Annie looked enough like some of the members that she felt she could stick her nose into their business and offer some advice. Without stopping to think, she started to chat up one of the women with a tart tongue who wanted to cash in the chips.

"Before you make a decision," Annie said to the sharp-tongued woman, "you should all play the only slot machine on the floor that actually takes a chip." She craned her neck to see that machine, standing apart from all the others. The bells and whistles emanating from it were earsplitting. She pointed to it and watched all the little old ladies and stoop-shouldered men staring at it. One of the men, who claimed to have exceptional eyesight, bellowed that it cost ten dollars a turn. His partner with two hearing aids shouted that the jackpot was $1.8 million.

These startling declarations started a whole new round of arguing. "We have to pay tax on it if we win!"

"What would we do with all that money?"

"We could prepay our own funerals so our kids don't get stuck with the bills."

"How will we get all that money back to Culpepper, Virginia, without getting mugged?"

"Then everyone will want to be our new best friends and borrow money from us."

"Who's going to manage the money?"

Annie wanted to swat all of them. "Come along, ladies and gentlemen, you can watch me play. I'll warm up the machine for you."

"Who did you say you were again?" someone asked.

"I'm a gambling addict," Annie said cheerfully, leading the way to the machine that promised untold riches. Cell phone to her ear, Annie whispered instructions, then quickly turned off her phone. She looked upward and nodded in slow motion to the unseen eyes that saw everything that went on down below.

"Hit it!" the man with two hearing aids bellowed. Annie hit it with a chip from her pocket. Nothing happened. "Bummer," the man said.

Annie dropped another forty dollars before she turned the machine over to the members of the group home. Another hassle ensued as each of them kicked in a dollar. With two dollars to spare, it was decided that the group had to sign off on a scrap of paper that if they won, the money would be divided equally. Everyone signed their name, but it didn't solve the problem of the extra two dollars. Annie settled it by snatching the twelve dollar bills and shoving them in her pocket. She handed out two ten-dollar chips.

By this time, to Annie's dismay, a small group started to form around the famous slot machine as the seniors started to argue again about who was going to press the button that might or might not make them rich. "You all need to just shut up for one minute here!" Annie screeched to be heard over the bells and whistles. "You!" she said, pointing to a mousy little lady wearing a shawl and carrying a string bag. The lady stepped forward and flexed her fingers.

"Shouldn't we say a prayer or bless ourselves or something?" the man with two hearing aids queried.

"Absolutely!" Annie said through clenched teeth. She wished she was sitting in an office at the *Post* writing a grisly story about something or other, one that would win her a Pulitzer Prize.

The mousy lady dropped the chip into the slot and pressed the button.

"Well, so much for that!" someone groaned.

"You still have one more chip!" Annie shouted.

The mousy lady flexed her fingers, sucked

in her breath, and pressed the red button.

Pandemonium broke loose as Annie backed off and headed away from the fast-approaching crowd descending on the famous slot machine.

Annie's private cell phone rang. She clicked it open and drawled, "Yes?"

"I heard what you just did, Countess de Silva!"

"I bet you did. What are you going to do about it, Fish? Not that I give a tinker's damn what you think."

"Nothing. I just wanted you to know I know. And to tell you I won't be home until next week."

"I'm fed up with this place. But I have to tell you, that was the best and worst ten minutes of my time since I've been here. I'm going to Washington tomorrow."

"You gonna screw up the paper now?"

"I am. I'm going to write op-ed pieces, cover the crap no one else wants, then I'll move on to exposés and win a Pulitzer, and by the time they kick me out, it will be time to come back here and start all over again. I-am-bored, Fish!"

Fish laughed. "You could start planning our wedding."

Annie started to sputter, but Fish clicked off in midsputter.

■ ■ ■ ■

Maggie Spritzer sat behind her desk and thought about going home, but she really didn't want to do that. The house in Georgetown was empty, with only Ted's cats, Mickey and Minnie, in residence. She'd moved them into her house while Ted was away working for Global Securities. God, how she missed him.

She looked down at the ring on her left hand, then at the new acrylic nails she'd had put on once she kicked the very bad habit of chewing her nails. She hated the nails because they interfered with the keyboard when she was typing. She even had a French manicure that she had to keep up with, which also irritated her. The only alternative was to stop wearing the ring, remove the acrylic nails, and go back to the hateful habit of chewing her nails.

Maggie's door opened, and her secretary stuck her head in. "If you don't need me for anything, Maggie, I'd like to leave a little early."

Maggie roused herself enough to reply. "No, go ahead — things are quiet, it's summer, no news, politicians are going on recess, and we're good. Sometimes I like it when nothing is going on in this damn crazy city. I'm thinking of leaving myself. See you in the morning." She waved listlessly before the secretary closed the door.

Maggie looked down again at the sparkling ring on her finger and her beautifully polished nails. They weren't the only thing that was new in her life these days. She was no longer obsessed with food; her metabolism had somehow magically fallen back into the normal range. She wasn't sure how she felt about that, because there were days when she barely ate at all. "Crap!" she said succinctly.

Maggie heaved herself to her feet, looked around for her lightweight suit jacket, kicked off her heels, and slipped her feet into Velcro-strapped sneakers that she didn't bother to fasten. Maybe when she got home she'd putter in the weed-filled garden or go for a run. She knew in her gut she probably wouldn't do either of those things. She'd pour herself a glass of wine and park her butt in front of the television set and watch one of the twenty-four-hour news channels until she dozed off for a few hours. Result, she'd be sleepless the rest of the night. "Crap!" she said again.

Maggie turned off the lights and closed the door just as she heard the ping of the elevator. She looked up in time to see Annie de Silva step out and look around. She dropped her bag and ran squealing to greet Annie. "Oh, my God! It really is you, Annie! I can't tell you how happy I am to see you! Oh, Annie, I missed you so," she said, crushing the older woman to her chest in an agonizing bear hug. She held her so tight, Annie had to gasp to draw in any oxygen.

"I don't think I've ever had a greeting like that in my whole life. I'm happy to see you, too," Annie said, struggling to find the breath to get the words out.

Maggie released her grip and stood back, alarm bells sounding in her brain. "What's wrong? Did something happen? Why are you here? Tell me everything. Do you want to go in the office or go somewhere and get something to eat? A drink? Everyone is okay, aren't they? Oh, God, Annie, I missed you so much. I miss everyone. Nothing is the same anymore. I . . . I just hate the way it is now."

Her breathing back to normal, Annie wrapped her arm around the younger woman's shoulder, and said, "Tell me about it. Everything is fine, no problems. Let's walk over to the Squires' Pub and tie one on. By the way, I decided to try my hand at running the paper. That's one of the reasons

I'm here."

"Do you know anything about running a newspaper, Annie?"

"No, but I can learn. I didn't know anything about running a casino, either, but I learned as I went along. The best thing you can say about that is, they can't fire the owner. I'll stay here just long enough to screw things up, then I'll find something else to do. I promise not to get in your way."

They were outside by then, the heat like a furnace after the air-conditioning inside the building.

"I forgot how hot it is here. It's hot in Vegas, but it's a dry heat. You can keep this humidity," Annie grumbled. "I like your nails."

Maggie wiggled her fingers. "I hate the maintenance. You have to go every two weeks to get them filled in. They show off the ring." A second later, Maggie burst into tears.

"That bad, huh?"

"Yeah, it's that bad. I can't get a handle on anything anymore. Every day is like the day before, and nothing is going on. I feel as if I'm just marking time. Before . . . well, before I just thrived. Life was a constant challenge. I never knew from one minute to the next what was going to happen. Now I can tell you what's going to happen seventy-two hours in advance. Nothing." She sniffled. "Absolutely nothing."

"I know exactly how you feel. Yesterday I gave away $1.8 million to some seniors from a group home. I let them win it. That's why I'm here — figured it was time to get the hell out of Dodge. Fish was on the horn the minute the slot paid off. I really don't like him much anymore."

"You didn't! Wow! Do you have someone else on the string?"

"I did. I'm not sorry, either. No, on someone else on the string. That's what I meant about screwing up. It should give you some idea of what I can do to the paper."

"I'll keep my eye on you," Maggie said, dabbing at her eyes. "Okay, we're here. Are we drinking or eating? We can drink all night, and my driver will pick us up and carry us to the car and take us home. It's like win-win. I have never been really, really drunk. Have you, Annie?" Maggie asked fretfully.

"A time or two," Annie drawled. "Let's play it by ear, dear."

They gave their order to a snappy little waitress dressed in shorts and a bolero top.

"The food isn't even here and I can hear my arteries snapping shut," Annie said peevishly, referring to the everything-loaded hot dogs, french fries, and onion rings. And the margaritas.

"We'll eat pomegranates tomorrow, and the seeds from them will flush out our arteries," Maggie said.

"Is that true?" Annie asked.

"I read it in the *Post.* We printed it in our health section, so it has to be true." Maggie laughed.

Four margaritas later, Maggie started to cry. "I miss Ted and Espinosa, Annie. I miss the girls. Myra doesn't leave the farm; she said all her old friends thumb their noses at her. That made me so mad, I did a piece on climbing socialites and friendships that brought in so much mail I had to hire people to read it. Then I did another piece on all the boards and foundations Myra used to sit on, all the monies she pledged, and how, after she was treated like a pariah by these same climbing socialites, she withdrew all the pledges. The amount of money was staggering, and it brought another avalanche of mail. It was all I could do, Annie."

"I know, dear. If I'm not too hungover, I'm going out to the farm tomorrow to surprise Myra and Charles," Annie said, holding up her glass for a refill.

"Life is not fun anymore," Maggie boohooed. "I don't mean life should be fun, but fun has its place. I am bored out of my mind."

Her eyes crossing, Annie had a hard time bringing her glass to her lips. She leaned forward and whispered, "It was the danger, dear. We all thrived on the danger, and we liked pitting our wits against all those crazy alphabet-soup groups that run this damn town. I heard the FBI has had so many screwups since Bert left that they had to ask Elias to come in and help them out. He, of course, pleaded ill health and told them they were on their own. I had a good laugh over that when I heard about it. Supposedly, they are revamping the entire Bureau."

"Do you care, Annie?"

"No-I-do-not!" Annie said emphatically.

"I think we should go home, Annie. I have to feed the cats. Good thing my driver is number three on my speed dial because I can't see the numbers to dial."

"Well, don't look at me, dear. Just do your best. This has been a very interesting evening, don't you think?"

"I hope we remember it tomorrow, Annie."

"You have a point, dear."

CHAPTER 2

Myra blinked, then blinked again when she saw the fur on the back of Little Lady's neck stand on end. She shivered at the low growl deep in the golden's throat. Someone was approaching the house! She ran to the security monitor in the kitchen, Little Lady on her heels. A car was approaching the electronic gates, an arm outstretched to press in the security code. Friend? Foe? So few people had the code, it almost had to mean a friend. "Shhh, let's wait and see who it is. I'm sure Charles can see the monitor in the war room." Little Lady made a sound deep in her throat again, but she remained still at Myra's side.

Myra marveled that, in less than twenty-four hours, Little Lady had appointed herself Myra's protector. She smiled. It was the mother in the golden, ready to protect and do battle. She leaned down and hugged the beautiful dog.

Myra heard the high-pitched whine of a powerful foreign car as it raced through the gates and skidded to a stop. The door swung open to reveal a pair of legs whose feet were encased in rhinestone cowgirl boots. Annie did love those boots. Myra burst out laughing as she thrust open the door and raced out to the compound to greet her lifelong friend, Little Lady right behind her. "My God, Annie, what took you so long?" she said, crushing her friend to her so tightly that Annie gasped for air.

"That bad, eh?" Annie finally managed to say.

"Worse," Myra said, refusing to let Annie out of her embrace. She finally let go when Little Lady barked, a signal she wanted to be introduced. Myra obliged. "This is Little Lady. She is the new mother of four adorable pups, who are sleeping at the moment. It's a long story, Annie. I am so glad to see you. There are no words to tell you how glad. A telephone call once a month isn't what we agreed to, Annie. I know you couldn't wait to get out into the world, so you could set it on fire, but I thought . . . I wanted . . . expected . . . Oh, hell, Annie, I just plain old missed you. Come on, let's go inside and get out of this heat."

Little Lady stepped back and barked, then

stepped forward and held out a paw, which Annie dutifully shook. She ruffled the fur on the back of the big dog's neck. "She's gorgeous, Myra. I can't wait to see the puppies."

Linking her arm with Annie's, Myra led the way to the kitchen door. The new mother barreled through the door and headed straight to the pen Charles had fashioned in the living room for the newborns. "Come along, Annie. Little Lady is just like all new mothers. She wants to show off her offspring. Two boys and two girls. I'm relying on what Charles said, and you know how he knows everything. So, two boys and two girls. Be effusive, Annie."

Annie dropped to her knees and peered at the four little balls of fur all nestled together. Her eyes misted with tears as she looked at the big dog and said in a choked voice, "They're too beautiful for words, Little Lady. You take good care of them, you hear?" She held out her arm for Myra to pull her to her feet.

Both women watched as Little Lady stepped into the pen and lay down. "Her world is right side up, so we can go into the kitchen now. Do you want coffee, tea, a soft drink?"

"Hell, no, Myra. I want *a drink.*"

"Name your pleasure, my friend. By the way, that's a pretty fancy set of wheels you arrived in."

"Bourbon on the rocks, and I'm test-driving the car. I don't know yet if I want to buy it or not. It's built for speed, and I'm all about speed these days."

"You don't say," Myra drawled as she poured bourbon into two squat glasses and added ice cubes. "Is this a social drink, or are we going to get schnockered?

"Let's just take it one drink at a time, Myra. Talk to me, tell me things," Annie said, clinking her glass against Myra's. She took a great gulp of the fiery liquid, her eyes watering.

"Annie! See that dog in there? That's my life. I am in such a funk I can't function. Charles rags on me constantly. I have never been at such loose ends. I can't sleep. I argue with Charles over nothing. My friends . . . well, the less we say about them the better. Your turn. Tell me about the trail you blazed when you left the mountain. I want to hear everything. Don't leave a thing out."

"Everything?" Annie said as she finished off her drink.

Myra poured again. "Everything."

Annie sucked in her breath and let it out

with a loud swoosh of sound. "Well, when Fish picked me up at the airport in Raleigh, and we don't need to discuss the fact that I was headed back to the mountain in Spain, we went to Vegas to get ready for a surprise trip. That didn't happen for a week because Jellicoe needed him for something or other, so I hung out in the penthouse till he got back. I have a hate on for that man — Jellicoe, that is. The surprise was a trip to Tahiti. It was wonderful.

"In my quest to set the world on fire, I had this vision of myself as a smoking-hot babe, so I took it to the casino floor, picked up one of the employees, and went on a three-day sex binge. You know, to get myself ready for Fish's return."

Myra gaped at her friend and somehow managed to say, "Continue."

Annie sampled her second drink. "I think it's safe to say I got out of Vegas by the skin of my teeth. I did manage to create a bit of havoc during the year and a half I was there. No one but me seemed to think my ideas were any good," she sniffed. "That didn't stop me, made me more determined to leave my mark." Defensiveness rang in Annie's voice when she said, "I own half the joint, Myra. By the way, before I forget or get too drunk to mention it, I read in the paper on the plane that there's a bike rally going on in Florida next week for the benefit of the Juvenile Diabetes Foundation. I thought you and I could go, make a nice donation, and get out of this rut we're in. What do you say? Do you want to go with me?"

"Absolutely I want to go. What . . . what ideas did you have, Annie?"

"I wanted to tone down the outfits the cocktail waitresses wore. They fought me. Skin sells, did you know that, Myra? Their outfits coincide with their tips. To prove my point, I duded up and went out on the floor. I made sixteen dollars for a six-hour shift. The girls average four to five hundred per shift. I had to back down."

"It's okay to retreat now and then, Annie. You were new to the game. How could you possibly know how a place works and the rules they have right off the bat?"

"That's very kind of you to say, Myra. I fired a lot of people."

"I'm sure they deserved to be terminated," Myra said soothingly.

"The staff lived in fear of me, Myra. I mean that. The minute they saw me they cringed. It was like, 'Oh, shit, here she comes.' I did not like that one little bit. I initiated work-related fireside chats that the staff slept through. Everyone more or less loves Fish, but he hasn't been there too much with all the work the boys have been piling on him. He thrives in a crisis, and there's always a crisis somewhere. I was left to my own devices, so I started trouble. What would you have done, Myra?" Annie asked, peering across the table at her friend.

"I would have done the same thing," Myra said spiritedly. "Is there more?"

Annie looked down into her empty glass, then at Myra's glass. Taking the hint, Myra upended hers. "A little."

"Well, spit it out, Annie."

"They said I was too generous with the seniors who come to the casino by the busload. Too many freebies. I thought there weren't enough. We locked horns. I fired the lot of the dissenters."

"Good for you! Seniors need all the help they can get, and they also deserve to have fun. I would have fired them, too."

"Well, we did have a slight employment problem after that. It was . . . eventually solved."

"How?"

"I just went to the other casinos and pirated their people by offering to pay them double. It wasn't one of my smartest moves. I will admit to that."

"Lesson learned," Myra said, pouring from the bottle. "Do you have more to share?"

"Well, there was this . . . incident. I was told, mind you, the key word here is *told.* I have absolutely no recollection of the . . . incident, but they said I showed my tattoo on the casino floor. At 12:36 on New Year's Eve. New Year's Day, to be precise.

"Oh, Annie! Do you think you did that?"

"Hell, yes, Myra. I was nuts back then. I decided to mend my ways, so I went out to the desert to see Rena Gold and visit the Institute. I wanted to be a volunteer. You remember the place down the road from Fish's place? The one we hid out in that had all the rattlesnakes. Well, I lasted a week. They said I was too aggressive. So, with my tail between my legs, I went back to the casino. Where just the day before yesterday I had the guys rig a slot so this group of seniors could win a big jackpot. Fish was on the phone minutes after the group hit it. I knew all hell was going to break loose, so I split, and here I am. Myra, I have never been so miserable in my life."

"Join the club, my friend." Myra reached across the table to take Annie's hands in her own. "I'm in the same place you are. I am bored out of my mind. When Charles isn't around, I cry. I miss the girls, I miss the mountain. I miss all of our missions. My God, Annie, what happened to us?"

"We got old. We can't accept change. No one needs us. At least you had the good sense to get a dog. You have to take care of a dog. The dog depends on you. I don't even have a dog."

"But . . . we have Charles and Fish, so in a way that doesn't compute," Myra said.

"Myra, they don't *need* us. They can function on their own. We're talking about causes and missions where we used to make a difference. No matter what you say, we got off on taking matters into our own hands and making things right. I wish to hell those damn pardons had never come through. There, I said it!" Annie cried.

"Oh, Annie, I just said the same thing yesterday to Charles. He said he understood, but he doesn't. He's a man. So now what?"

"I checked in at the *Post.* I'm going to take a stab at screwing that up. You want to help me? You can bring the dogs along. We'll each have an office, and we can text back and forth. We can take turns walking the dogs and writing editorials that will set Washington on its ear! The best part is, no one can fire us."

Myra started to laugh and couldn't stop. Finally, gasping for breath, she said, "Let's go for a walk and work off this liquor."

Annie grabbed the bottle of bourbon and headed for the door. The two old friends walked aimlessly around the farm, stopping from time to time to sip from the bottle.

Charles, a frown building between his brows, watched the women as they walked toward the barn. He felt an itch settle itself between his shoulder blades. Then he shivered.

With the sun beating down on their heads and necks, Myra and Annie headed straight for the barn, where they walked the entire length of it, stroking the horses and speaking softly to them as they walked along. The barn cats clustered around their legs, purring loudly. Myra led the way to where Charles had left two bales of hay near the door. The women settled themselves.

"So, Annie dear, what part of your dissertation was true and which part was false?"

Annie laughed, but to Myra's ears it sounded forced. "Sad to say, Myra, it's all true."

"Fish?"

"Fish is . . . I don't know, something is off-key there. I care for him a great deal.

No, let's just say I more or less like him. He would like to get married, but I am not ready for marriage. I doubt I'll ever be ready. I don't know . . . I think . . . the second time around someone always gets cheated. I loved my husband heart and soul. I meant it when I said to death do us part. I know he meant it, too. I think he would be okay with Fish. I say *think.* I'm not sure if I *know* he would be okay. That . . . ah . . . one episode, I'm not sure if I regret it or it was just not for me, no one else. I was trying to prove something to myself. Whatever it was, it didn't work. I'm still not sure about that tattoo episode, either. It's all negative, Myra. That's my life, a sackful of negatives. Except for Fish; he's a negative with a little plus sign. I have to be honest, I think he's getting fed up with me, and I know I'm getting fed up with him. I wasn't like this on the mountain. On the mountain, my adrenaline pumped daily. I looked forward to getting up in the morning and never wanted to go to bed at night. I counted for something up there. We all did. It's gone now, and, goddamn it, Myra, I want it back. Do you hear me, I want it back. And another thing. If you think that dog back at the house, and her pups, is your answer, then you are crazier than I am. We aren't crazy, are we, Myra?" she asked fretfully.

Myra burst into tears. Annie followed suit.

"You never called, Annie. Maybe once a month."

"Because I would have started to blubber the minute I heard your voice. You didn't call, either. Why?"

"For the same reason. We have to get a life, Annie. It's been a whole year and a half. Look at us. We haven't moved forward one step. We've regressed. Even I know that is totally unacceptable. Do you see Lizzie much when she's in Vegas?"

"No. She invited me to dinner one night, and I went. The baby was about two months old. She let me hold him. All I did was cry, so I left and never went back. He is a gorgeous little boy, Myra. How many times did you see him when she was here?"

"Twice. But he was asleep the second time. Lizzie and Cosmo have their own lives now. That's the way it should be. I didn't want to intrude. I didn't go to the christening or the shower at the White House. I thought . . . well, it doesn't matter what I thought. I hope Lizzie understands."

"Do the girls call you, Myra?"

"About like you did, Annie. Do you think they're happy?"

Annie upended the bottle of bourbon, took a slug, and passed it on to Myra, who drank deeply. "I would think so. They have their lives, and they scattered to the four winds. I can't believe they forgot about us so quickly. It hurts so damn bad, Annie, I want to cry."

"You are crying, Myra. Are we saying our girls are ungrateful little shits?"

Myra pondered the question. "Yes, Annie, I think so. I tried to be fair in my heart. They have husbands and lovers who travel the globe with the girls at their sides. At this point, I am not even sure who is married and who isn't other than Nikki and Yoko. Then there is the time difference in different parts of the globe. The worst part was when none of them came for Christmas. You didn't come either, Annie. You all broke my heart that day. Charles and I worked so hard to make it all festive. We decorated and shopped and cooked till we were worn-out, and the only guest on Christmas day was Elias. Nellie was recovering, so she couldn't come. It was one of the worst days of my life."

Annie sniffed and blew her nose. Then she sniffed again. "Did you know Yoko has had two miscarriages? I think it's a rotten shame no one saw fit to tell us."

"No, I didn't know. How did you find out? That's awful. Harry and Yoko would make wonderful parents. Where are they? Do you know?"

"Maggie told me last night when I stopped at the paper. They were in Israel. It's that Jellicoe thing. Harry goes to train the troops or whatever. Maggie said she thinks they're back at the *dojo,* but she isn't sure. Said no one answers the phone. She thinks they came back because Yoko was so depressed about the miscarriages, and if she got pregnant again, she wanted it to be here in the States. Because Yoko said she wanted to have her baby in Washington. That's all I know."

"That has to mean they're all in touch with Maggie but not us. What does that tell you, Annie? I don't believe this!" Myra burst into tears again. This time she reached for the bottle and took a healthy gulp. Her throat burning, tears flowing down her cheeks, she said, "Yoko needs a mother figure in her life right now if all that is true. I think we both qualify for that role, Annie. This is unforgivable."

"You're right, it is unforgivable."

The bottle changed hands again. "Where do you think Maggie stands, Annie?"

"I don't have a clue. She seemed really

happy to see me last night. And she didn't get upset when I told her I was going to work at the paper. What could she say? I own the damn place. She's been calling regularly to check in. She said she did her best to help you when all your friends shut you out. But something was off-key. I had the feeling something is wrong somewhere, and she's trying to deal with it."

"She did try to help. She really went out on a limb when she published what she called her personal scoop on all those charities. I adore Maggie."

"Maggie feels as lost as you and I, and she doesn't know what to do about it. We both cried a bit. Myra, do you think it's even remotely possible that the girls were waiting for us to get in touch with them? Like they were taking their cues from us? We did moan and groan about those pardons and what we were going to do with our lives. Is it possible, Myra?"

Myra upended the bottle and gulped. "Anything is possible, I suppose. What do you think, Annie?"

"I would like to believe it. If it's true that Harry and Yoko are back at the *dojo,* all we have to do is pop in and see what's going on."

"I'm seeing two of you, Annie."

Annie laughed. "Ha! I can't even see one of you!"

The cats circling the bales of hay purred as they did their best to rub up against the women's legs.

"The bottle's empty," Annie said.

"So it is. When was the last time you slept in a barn, Annie?"

"When I was ten years old. I loved it. It made me feel so grown-up at the time."

"We're all grown-up now, Annie. And we're old in the bargain."

"Stop raining on our parade, Myra."

"How long are you staying, Annie?"

"Until I get tired of causing trouble."

"That long, huh?"

"Maybe longer."

Myra laughed as she teetered toward an empty stall, Annie and a string of cats behind her.

CHAPTER 3

The sun was just creeping over the horizon when Myra opened her eyes to see her farm foreman staring down at her. Her mouth felt as if she had just swallowed a pint of glue. She struggled to sit up. "Good morning, Mr. Jackson."

"Miss Myra, is everything all right?"

"I don't know yet, Mr. Jackson, I just woke up." Out of the corner of her eye she saw the empty bourbon bottle and Annie sleeping peacefully. The barn cats appeared and eyed the three of them warily. A second later, with the help of her foreman, Myra was on her feet.

"Wake up, Annie. It's a whole new day, and I do think we have things to do. Annieee!!!!"

"What? What? Is the barn on fire! Stop screaming, Myra! What things do we have to do?"

Myra was busy picking straw out of her

hair and off her clothes as the weathered, cranky foreman reached down to pull Annie to her feet. "Take this with you," he grumbled. "And don't be littering up my barn," he added, holding out the bourbon bottle.

The warm summer morning greeted them with open arms as the two women made their way to the farmhouse. "I slept like a baby," Annie said as she brushed at the straw covering her clothes.

"A quart of bourbon will do that to you," Myra snapped.

"You drank half of it," Annie snapped back. "Let's not do that again for a long time."

"That's what you said when we got those damn tattoos on our asses," Myra said.

"Myra, that was forever ago. Are you always cranky this early in the morning?"

"When I sleep in a barn I am. How are we going to explain this to Charles?"

Annie stopped in her tracks and almost stepped on one of the cats. "Do you have to explain your actions to Charles? Well! Who knew you were such a *wuss*, Myra Rutledge Martin Sutcliffe, or whatever the hell your married name is."

"And you think I'm cranky? Ha!"

The screen door banged shut behind the

two women. Little Lady was the first to greet them. She nuzzled Myra's leg, then Annie's, before she held up a paw in greeting.

"She's been out and fed, ladies. Good morning! Did you sleep well?" Charles asked cheerfully.

"We did, dear, thank you for asking." Myra plopped the empty bourbon bottle down on the counter, her eyes defying Charles to comment. He didn't.

"I'll wait breakfast for you ladies while you shower. I thought we would have banana macadamia nut pancakes with melted butter and banana syrup, with a side order of Canadian bacon."

"That certainly sounds better than a bran muffin with decaf coffee," Annie said. "I hate bran; it makes your stomach expand and growl, and you get gas."

"Thank you for sharing that, Annie."

"It's a standard breakfast in Las Vegas. All I said was, I don't care for it. I can't wait, Charles." And off she went to the staircase at the far end of the kitchen that led to the second floor.

"Is there anything you'd like to share this morning, my love?"

"No, Charles, there isn't. I'll be down in half an hour. It looks like it is going to be a nice day, doesn't it? Annie and I are going to go into town to see Maggie. Do you mind?"

Charles's eyes twinkled. "And if I did?"

"Too bad," Myra called over her shoulder as she made her way to the staircase.

The moment Myra was out of sight, Charles's fist shot in the air. "Yessss." This was the Myra he knew and loved. Thank God for Annie's visit. It was just what Myra needed to jolt her out of her funk.

Upstairs, the two women talked back and forth as they prepared for the new day.

"Annie, I told Charles we were going to town to meet up with Maggie. Did I dream that, or did we really make plans to do that?"

"I can't remember, Myra. It does sound like a plan, though. This might be a good time to tell you I suspect Maggie has a secret. Well, maybe it isn't a secret, but I had the feeling she was holding back on something. It might have to do with her and Ted, but then again, she might be onto something and just isn't ready to share. By the way, she doesn't chew her nails anymore, and she has those acrylic things. Her ring is beautiful, and the nails really show it off. She gets French manicures these days."

"That's interesting," Myra yelled as she stepped into the shower. When she got out ten minutes later, she said, "Let's not mention your suspicions to Charles, okay?"

"Okay."

Dressed in summer linen and sandals and smelling like a flower garden, Annie and Myra descended the steps. Little Lady appeared out of nowhere, circled them, sniffed them, then woofed her approval before she trotted back to her babies.

Charles whistled appreciatively as the two women seated themselves at the kitchen table, shook out their napkins, and waited to be served.

Conversation consisted of the weather, with a possible pop-up storm later in the day; the condition of Charles's vegetable garden, which was nowhere near as wonderful as the one Yoko had on the mountain; falling gas prices; and his decision to write his memoir that would never get published but was something to do during his off-hours.

Breakfast over, Charles said, "Since you ladies are dressed so elegantly, I will do the cleanup today. If you'd like to sit out on the patio, I can bring your coffee to you."

"Then we'll have full bladders on the ride to Washington. One must be cognizant of such things at our age, Charles. Thanks, but no thanks," Annie said. Myra rolled her eyes, and Charles just grinned. Annie was so entertaining, even this early in the morning.

Outside, Annie pointed to the flashy car she had arrived in. "What do you think, Myra, should I buy it?"

"It certainly is sleek-looking. What is it?"

"A Lamborghini. I only took it to piss off the salesman. I could see by the expression on his face that he thought a set of wheels like that would be wasted on an old woman like me. And to add insult to injury, I don't think he thought I could pay for it. I even had to have my bank call the dealership and tell them I could afford it. Myra, when that weasel came back, he had such respect for me, or should I say for my money, that I wanted to punch him in the nose. I think I'll take it back and tell him it doesn't measure up to my demanding standards. I do love it, though."

The gates opened, and Annie floored the gas pedal. Myra was jolted backward. "This baby goes from zero to sixty in a second. Whatcha think, Myra?"

Holding on for dear life, Myra said, "I think you should get a Volvo station wagon. *Slow down,* Annie."

Annie obliged. "You are so negative, Myra.

I'm thinking I was built for speed. This *is* speed!"

"Yes, well, you thought you were a smoking-hot babe, too, and where did that get you?"

"Now, that is one thing you are never going to know. Some things are just way too personal to share, and that's one of them. I can tell you about it but not give details. Besides, you couldn't handle the details."

Somehow, Myra managed to look offended. She sniffed. "Details, Annie, do not interest me." Hoping to change the subject, she asked, "Do we have a game plan for today?"

Easily diverted, Annie replied, "Not really. I thought we'd play it by ear. Maggie did say that in the summer, the paper pretty much runs itself. All the politicians head off for summer recess, the socialites head for spas around the country, and there is no news to speak of. I think we're wide open. We could drive to Georgetown, check on Nikki's house, drive out to where Cosmo and Lizzie live part-time and check that out. Go to lunch and try to pick Maggie's brain. We could probably go to her house and just hang out. There is absolutely nothing to do in the District in the summer; you know that as well as I do."

"I'm almost embarrassed to admit this, Annie, but I have never been to the *Post.* I have no clue how a large newspaper works. If you plan on working at the paper, doing whatever it is you were thinking about, it might be a good idea to have some working knowledge of how the paper makes its way to the street." At Annie's grim look, she added, "I'm just saying. You're the one who said you screwed up at Babylon. With that kind of track record, you should give this some thought."

Annie muttered something under her breath that Myra was glad she couldn't hear.

"How fast are you going, Annie? People are looking at us. Are you sure you didn't *steal* this car?"

"I am going seventy miles an hour when I should be doing ninety-five in this vehicle. Not that I would ever drive that fast, mind you. The reason people are staring at us is they are green with envy, because this set of wheels costs over two hundred grand." She ignored Myra's gasp of shock and said, "No, I did not steal this car. I've decided I don't want it, and the price tag is outrageous. You're right, I'm going to get a Volvo station wagon, which means people will still look at us and think we're stupid for driving such a mundane vehicle."

Myra laughed. "I love you, Annie. Please, don't ever change."

"I'll try not to. Listen, Myra, on a serious note here. The universe is out of whack. I feel such bad vibes that I can't even describe them. Something, somewhere is going on that involves us. I can't explain it any better than that. You getting any vibes?"

"Well, now that you mention it, yes, I am. I thought it was all due to my . . . funk, as Charles calls it. What do you think it is, Annie?" Myra asked uneasily. "Do you think it has anything to do with Maggie's demeanor yesterday when you were with her?"

"No, but that capped it for me. I've been feeling this way for about a month. I think that's why I threw caution to the wind at the casino and did what I did, knowing I would have to split afterward. Does that make sense, Myra?"

Myra laughed. "In an Anna de Silva kind of way, it most certainly does."

When Annie stopped for a traffic light, she turned to face Myra and said, "I think, Myra, we are either at a crossroads in our lives right now or fast coming up to it. And it has an ominous feel to it."

Myra shivered at the intensity in her friend's voice. She didn't trust herself to speak, so she nodded solemnly.

"One more block, and we'll be at the paper," Annie said as she cut off a Jeep Cherokee. When she looked in the rearview mirror and saw the single-digit salute the driver offered up, she offered up one herself. "Jerk!"

"Annie, you cut him off."

"He was just sitting there. When you're in a car, you are supposed to drive it, not sit in it and watch the traffic."

This was a battle Myra knew she couldn't win. "Thank you for getting me here safe and sound. Charles will appreciate it. One more thing, Annie. You really have to give up those rhinestone boots. They don't go with your outfit. What happened to the sandals you started out with?"

"Didn't you see me change them? You are not the least bit observant. Those sandals accentuate my bunions. The boots don't. So there. Besides, I like making a fashion statement."

It was another battle Myra knew full well she couldn't win. She waited till Annie turned off the engine, checked everything, then got out of the car.

When Myra and Annie stepped out of the elevator, Maggie's greeting was effusive and lingering. The women gushed, hugged, and linked arms as they walked to Maggie's office. Once inside, Myra and Annie both immediately sensed something off-key. Annie's request for a tour for her and Myra was no sooner out of her mouth than Maggie literally dragged both women out through the newsroom and into the hall. "Just act normal and don't say anything. Just follow my lead," she hissed.

Perplexed, Myra and Annie managed to make appropriate comments along with a few other mundane observations about the stifling heat outside. Maggie picked up and ran with the comment. "Let's do a picnic. We can go to the park and spread a blanket and chill out. I haven't been on a picnic in ages." She babbled on and on, saying she knew of a specialty shop near the park that packed a picnic basket and even provided the blanket.

Back in the office, Annie and Myra were told to wait while Maggie changed her clothes to suitable picnic attire. Thirteen minutes later they were outside and headed to Annie's test car.

Settled behind the wheel, Annie turned around and said, "I think you need to tell us what's going on, Maggie. We aren't stupid — what's wrong?"

"Nothing. Today I had cabin fever, and I was trying to figure out what to do with myself, then you two showed up." *Wait till we get to the park to talk,* she silently mouthed.

Her brain working at warp speed, Annie swung around, turned on the powerful engine, and peeled out of the lot onto the street. "Then we are the lucky ones. Do hardboiled eggs go with the picnic?"

Relief rang in Maggie's voice. "Absolutely. Eggs, fried chicken, potato salad, fresh fruit, cheese, and a bottle of wine along with some to-die-for butter rolls. Soft drinks or ice tea are extra. No charge for the blanket, but you have to return everything in twelve hours. We did an article on the shop for the Sunday section, and their business tripled in a week. Not to worry — for me, they won't hold us to a reservation. Make a right here, then the next left, and follow it out till you see a big red sign. Polly's Picnic Palace is on the right." Annie followed Maggie's instructions to the letter and pulled into a tiny lot behind Polly's Picnic Palace.

Maggie hopped out of the luxury car. She leaned in Annie's open window and wagged her finger playfully. "Now don't talk about me while I'm gone."

Annie and Myra sat like statues, their eyes straight ahead as they tried to figure out what was going on. Don't talk meant don't talk. Both women literally bristled with curiosity.

Ten minutes later, Maggie hopped back into the car, the picnic basket offering up delectable aromas. "The chicken just came out of the fryer. By the time we get to the park, it should be just right to eat with our fingers. They do make the best chicken. I think they put dill in the deviled eggs." She continued to babble about food and her on-again, off-again metabolism, which continued to baffle her doctor but certainly was not life-threatening.

Annie and Myra, twitching and squirming as if they had fleas, couldn't wait to get out of the car once they hit Rock Creek Park. Maggie in the lead, the picnic basket in her arms, galloped forward. Myra carried the blanket, and Annie carried the small portable cooler.

Myra spread the blanket, then dropped to her knees. "What is going on, Maggie?"

"I don't know. I've had this feeling since as far back as January that I am being watched. I think the paper is bugged. I think my house is bugged, and so is the car that picks me up and drives me to work. At first I thought I was being paranoid, but that's not it. It's my reporter's gut instinct. Ted has it, too. No, I think it started before

Christmas. Ted was supposed to come home, then he said he couldn't make it. By the way, that's why I didn't go out to the farm for Christmas, Myra. I went to Delaware to see my grandfather over the holidays.

"When I got back, I noticed a change in Ted. His calls and e-mails took on a different tone. We have our own code when we try to tell each other something we don't want anyone else to figure out. It's not important for either one of you to know what it is, but he let me know something was wrong and for me to stay on my toes. Which I have been trying to do.

"You were parked just long enough for someone to plant a bug or a GPS while you came up to the office. That's why I didn't want to say anything in the car or at the *Post*."

"But why?" Myra asked nervously as she looked around.

"I'm not sure. At first I thought it had something to do with someone trying to find out who owns the paper. That's not it. It's something else entirely. I've had six months to think about all of this. I came up with . . . *something*. That something is what I can't figure out. I want you both to sit here and think about everything that's happened since you all received your pardons. No matter how outrageous, how over the top it is, tell me what you think. It's been eighteen months since you were all freed. Think about how it happened, think about all of your lives and how everything has changed from what it was to what it is now. Think about all the e-mails and calls from our little club, the girls and the guys. Think about the *tone* of everything, the sparseness. We used to be such a tight group. Surely you've noticed a change."

Hearing the desperateness in Maggie's voice, Annie and Myra looked at each other in alarm.

"Everything did change when the pardons came through. But that was to be expected. We missed the girls' weddings, if there were weddings. We didn't go to Lizzie's White House shower or the christening because we didn't want to make a circus out of it for her. I think things might have turned out differently if Henry Jellicoe hadn't stepped into the game," Myra said, her voice cold and tight.

"It was like he stole everyone away from us in the blink of an eye," Annie said, her eyes narrowing in thought.

"Keep going, ladies," Maggie said.

"It did happen fast. He dazzled the boys

with all that money," Myra said.

"Just like that, he decided to retire. I thought it strange at the time," Annie said.

"Did you know that Henry Jellicoe dropped off the face of the earth for a whole year and a half?" At Myra's and Annie's blank looks, Maggie nodded. "He did. I understand he's back at his farm, or whatever it is, in Pennsylvania. It could also be a rumor."

"Did he disappear . . . go away . . . right after he hired all his new help?" Myra asked. The glint in her eyes was like cold ice.

"As far as I can tell, that's what happened. There was a *thing* going on with Jellicoe and the president. In fact, you'll remember, he asked her to marry him and gave her a ring the night of the pardons. No one knows exactly what happened afterward, but there has been a lot of speculation.

"However, the press, the *Post* included, cut her a lot of slack. Engagements and marriage are too personal not to. The president has never made any comments about the engagement or the marriage. In the press photos I've seen of her, she wasn't wearing an engagement ring. That might not mean anything since as a rule she doesn't wear jewelry for photo ops," Maggie said.

"If anyone would know more about it, it would be Lizzie," Myra said.

"Lizzie is wrapped up in her own little world, and rightly so. When we talk, it's about the baby and how wonderful motherhood is. I did try to ask some off-the-cuff questions, but she acted like she didn't know what I was talking about. I really don't think she knows anything to share," Maggie said as she picked up a chicken leg and looked at it as though she couldn't decide if she should eat it or not.

Annie threw her hands in the air. "And all that means what? I think you need to spell out what exactly your concern is, so we can talk it to death."

Maggie laid the chicken leg on a colorful plastic plate. "Am I the only one who is getting this? Ooops, Ted and I are the only ones. Okay, listen up." Maggie crossed her legs Indian style and leaned forward. "First things first. We are having this discussion here in the park, so no one can hear us. Now, do you not find it weird, strange, inexplicable, as to why Henry Jellicoe would turn Global Securities over to our people? And they are our people. It's a given that he knew the pardons were going to go through. The man then practically offers up his company on a platinum platter to Bert and

Jack, who in the blink of an eye resign respectively as director of the FBI and as deputy district attorney for the District of Columbia, jobs they loved. I know the money offer was a little too enticing to turn down. Ditto for Harry and the others. Global Securities is the eyes and ears of the security world. They do not come any better than that company. The whole world knows that.

"It has sixty thousand employees around the world. Revenues are off the charts."

Myra toyed with the food she'd heaped on her plate. "No one is disputing that the firm is solvent. What are you trying to say?"

Maggie picked at the crisp batter on her chicken leg with one of her pointy nails. "What was the urgency in going after our people? And as you know, Jellicoe immediately scattered our guys all over the world. Lizzie and I are just about the only ones left here in the States. Well, Annie was in Vegas. And someone made sure you stayed down on the farm, Myra, now, didn't they? No one has seen hide nor hair of you in the past year and a half. No one showed up at the farm for Christmas. I'm sure you asked yourself why a thousand times. From what I can gather, every place one of our people is stationed, there was some kind of crisis that prevented any of them from taking a trip. Never lose sight of the fact that Global is the eyes and ears of the world. They can do what the CIA, the FBI, and all those other organizations can't. They take the law into their own hands and get the job done. Kind of like the vigilantes, don't you think? Are you starting to see what I'm seeing?

"When you're done asking yourself that, ask yourself why Jellicoe hired Ted and Espinosa. JGS had a newsletter that went out to all employees four times a year. Clients got a slightly different version. There's nothing wrong with that. He had smart people in a suite of offices in New York taking care of the text of both versions. He shut that down and opened offices in Rome, where he sent Ted and Espinosa. All they do is travel the globe, get info from all the group leaders or whatever they're called. Ted puts it all together in a glossy twelve-page magazine that goes out once a month. Espinosa does the pictures. Ted said it's all bullshit. Espinosa agrees. But . . . they're not *here*. Meaning here in the States. Particularly here in Washington. No one is here but the three of us, four if you count Lizzie. And until now, Annie, you were nowhere near the capital."

Annie and Myra both threw their hands up in the air at the same time. Their words were identical when they spoke simultaneously. "What does it mean?"

"I'll be damned if I know," Maggie said as she finally bit into the chicken leg she was holding. "But the reporter in me and Ted says it means something. You can take that to the bank!"

Chapter 4

Myra and Annie looked at each other, their eyes wide. It was Annie who spoke first. "So what you are saying is, Hank Jellicoe did not consider either Myra or me a threat. I'm not sure about you, Myra, but I feel insulted. It's like he thinks you and I don't count. Off the top of my head, I'd say you, Maggie, are a huge threat. He takes away Ted and Joseph Espinosa and leaves you behind. You're the EIC of the *Post.* The position alone should be a threat to him if he's up to some kind of shenanigans."

"Ah, but without my star reporter and star photographer, I just have regulation reporters, greenhorns, guys and gals who don't have that fire in their bellies like the three of us do . . . did. They don't think outside the box. Ted and I were born outside the box. We always took it to the next level with no coaching or pleading from anyone.

"Think about it. In the blink of an eye,

everyone is gone. G-O-N-E! Didn't even one little red flag go up?" At Myra's and Annie's blank looks, Maggie shook her head in disgust.

"How about this? Hank Jellicoe disappears. For well over a year and a half. I can understand you maybe not knowing that, but now you do. That's a red flag all by itself. Then he gets very publicly engaged, and that gets a lid clamped on it. To the president of these here United States!" Maggie drawled. "That's another great big red flag. At least to me it is, and to the reporter in me, too. Jellicoe has gone to ground, and he certainly knows how to do that considering the business he's in. To be honest, I'm not even sure he's at his farm in Pennsylvania. That place is like Fort Knox. Impossible to penetrate. I know because I tried."

"You did!" Myra cried in surprise.

"Well, yes, Myra, I did. When I started getting these weird e-mails and texts from Ted, I knew that's what he wanted me to do. Look, Ted is the best of the best. So is Espinosa. Jellicoe dazzled Ted and Joe with all that money. Ted saw it as a way to get a house for us, some new vehicles, sock some money away for retirement. I can't fault him for that. First, last, and always he is a gut reporter. He smelled it before anyone else did. And he's on it in his own way. I have to admit that I'm more than a little worried. G.I. Joe, as Ted calls Jellicoe, is up to something. Since we three are odd men out, so to speak, I guess it's up to us to ferret out what is going on."

"I can't believe the man thinks you, Annie, and I are no threat to him. That doesn't say much for us, now, does it? I've known Hank for a long time. The man sent Charles and me a wedding present. I'm having trouble with all of this, Maggie," Myra said fretfully. "Charles is . . . I think Charles would have said something if he . . . suspected anything was amiss. They're personal as well as undercover-business friends. They go way back. Who did you send there, and why aren't you sure if Hank is in residence?"

"It's not important who I sent. What's important is that the person had a thermal-imaging camera, and he picked up on three persons in the house. There's a housekeeper and a groundskeeper. Jellicoe would make the third person. Or the third person could be the head of his personal security. My person said he's seen him go into the house and stay for hours. I'm not sure. Like I said, the security at that farm is worthy of Fort Knox."

"But if Jellicoe is up to something . . . illegal or . . . worse, why hasn't whatever he was planning happened? It's well over a year, and nothing particular seems to be wrong anywhere, so what is it specifically that is worrying you?" Annie asked.

"If I knew that, Annie, we wouldn't be sitting here having a picnic in Rock Creek Park away from prying eyes and ears," Maggie snapped irritably. "I just hate it when it won't come together and I can't figure it out."

Myra threw her hands up in the air. "I know the feeling." She watched as a fat squirrel scampered toward the blanket. Two blue jays swooped down, then flew off. Annie tossed some of the breading from the fried chicken in the direction of the squirrel, which immediately picked it up and turned tail back to wherever it had come from.

"What should we do?" Annie asked. "Do you think we're in danger? Do you have a plan?"

"Not yet. But here comes trouble. See that couple heading this way with a paper bag? What do you think the chances are of someone wanting to picnic in this exact spot where we are? Zip, that's what. Come on, we're outta here. There are devices on the market that can pick up conversations half a mile away. Farther, too, I'm told. Do not stare. Let's see where they settle, then we pack up and leave. Act like everything is fine. If either one of you knows a joke, this would be a good time to tell it so we can all laugh."

"We're under surveillance? I-do-not-like-that!" Annie hissed as she threw more crumbs toward the squirrel, which had emerged to test the waters a second time.

The women spoke softly about nothing as they watched the newcomers out of the corners of their eyes. All three women took note of the man's Brooks Brothers loafers, the woman's heels, and their business attire. There was no blanket being spread. A spur-of-the-moment picnic? A picnic on demand? Whatever was in the paper sack was staying in the paper sack.

"Time to go, ladies!" Maggie said cheerfully. All it took was five seconds to scoop up the food and utensils and jam them into the picnic basket. Myra grabbed the blanket and stuffed it under her arm. Three minutes later, they were in the car.

"Annie, if you drive straight, you can loop around and be on the other side of this lot, and we can see when the picnickers leave, which I'm assuming will be within minutes.

Can this baby burn rubber?"

"Watch, you silly girl!" Annie said, flooring the gas pedal. "And we have liftoff!" Annie squealed as she followed Maggie's directions.

"Mother of God, slow down, Annie. You just gave me whiplash! There it is, see the spot? Pull over and cut this engine. It sounds like it belongs to the Boeing Company."

"Everyone is a critic," Annie grumbled.

"Oh, dear Lord! There they go! Maggie, you were absolutely right! Are we in danger?" Myra dithered. "What should we do now?"

"Let's go to a hotel. At least we'll know it's not bugged. I'm going to call a . . . friend and see about getting my house swept for bugs. The paper and the phones, too. The only problem with that is, with all the high tech that is out there these days, the bugs will be back within hours. And it lets them know, whomever they are, that we are onto them," Maggie said.

"But it's been almost a year and a half since everyone split up. Why wait all that time to do . . . or implement whatever it is they plan on doing?" Myra said stubbornly.

"I don't know, Myra, but I do know this. I am going to e-mail Ted and Espinosa and tell them to hand in their resignations. We need them, and we need them *now.*"

"Will they have to forfeit the monies Global paid them?" Myra asked.

"Probably. At this point I don't think either one of them will care. That's how much they both hate the job," Maggie said. "I don't know why I say this, but I think Ted is key to all of this. I also think he'll be on the next plane out of Rome if I tell him it's okay and that the paper needs them both."

"If he or Joseph needs any added incentives, tell them both I will make up the difference in money. I mean that, Maggie, and won't take no for an answer. You're right, we need Ted and Joseph. Can you text him now?" Annie asked.

"I'm doing it as we speak," Maggie shot back.

"Which hotel do you want me to head for, Maggie? For obvious reasons, I don't know much about Washington hotels. Now Vegas, that's a different story."

"Do you want a five-star hotel?" Maggie asked, her fingers busily texting Ted.

"Absolutely." Annie sniffed, as if she had been insulted by the question.

"Take your pick. There is the Mandarin Oriental, the Hay-Adams, the Ritz-Carlton, or the St. Regis. None of them made five stars this year. All were in the 4.5 range. We could go to the Park Hyatt. It came in at a full five stars. It's just a hop, skip, and a jump from Embassy Row and is in the West End of Georgetown, Twenty-fourth and M, Northwest. We can hang out in the Blue Duck Tavern. Good place to see who comes in who looks like they don't belong. And they have excellent security. Ted did an article on it last year, and Espinosa got some great pictures."

"Then the Park Hyatt it is," Annie said, leaning on the horn to get out from behind a PT Cruiser.

"Tell me, dear, how can you talk and text at the same time?" Myra asked. "What is Ted saying?"

"He's blessing you both up one side and down the other, and packing and texting at the same time. He's so good at multitasking. But to answer your question, Myra, it takes practice. He's telling me Espinosa is telling him the only available seats out of Rome on the next flight are first-class. He wants to know if he should take them, as they are pretty pricey."

"Tell him yes," Annie said as she was forced to slow down to make a right-hand turn. "Tell him to take a car service from the airport when he gets in. The *Post* can afford it."

"Annie, Ted doesn't work for the paper anymore. He and Espinosa resigned. Did you forget that little fact?"

"There is that, but I never accepted his or Joseph's resignation. The two of them are still on the *Post*'s payroll. Their checks are automatically deposited. I thought you knew that, Maggie."

Maggie stopped her furious texting long enough to lean forward. "Annie, that is too kind of you. No, I didn't know, and I'm sure Ted and Espinosa don't know, either."

"I opened separate accounts for them. I guess I forgot to mention it. I appreciate loyalty above all else, and Ted and Joseph have come through for us time and time again. Loyalty should always be rewarded. Look alive, ladies, we're here. Oh, my, all those snappy valet persons are arguing about who gets to park this fine vehicle."

A young man snapped to attention when Annie stepped out of the car. "Do not even breathe when you drive this car to its parking spot. I'll know if you do. Are we clear on that, young man?"

"Yes, ma'am," the young man said as he took a great gulp of air before sliding into the driver's seat. Annie handed over a fifty-dollar bill through the window.

"I'm going to register us. You two head for the Blue Duck Tavern and keep your eyes peeled. Order me a Slamming Sally. Do I have to be cost-conscious on the room rates?" Maggie asked.

"Not if you're booking a room for me. Of course not, Maggie. Just put it on the *Post* account. We have one here, don't we?"

"Actually, we don't, Annie."

"Well, then, open one."

"What do you think a Slamming Sally is, Annie?" Myra asked as they entered the dim Blue Duck Tavern, which even smelled like a tavern.

"Probably something that would knock us on our asses after the first drink. We need to dry out after last night, so we'll drink ginger ale. We'll ask for fancy glasses, and ginger ale looks enough like champagne to pass for it. We got it covered, Myra."

"I wasn't exactly planning on spending the night here, Annie. I have to call Charles and tell him where I am. Don't worry, I won't share any of the details. I wonder if he has any inkling of what Maggie is talking about," Myra whispered.

"Men stick together, you know that, Myra, just the way women stick together. I don't think you should say anything to him until we have something a little more concrete. I'm finding all of this . . . very perplexing. I didn't pick up a thing from Fish during our time together. But now when I think back . . . it explains an awful lot of things. Pillow talk was always uninformative, but I do know this — he thinks the sun rises and sets on Hank Jellicoe."

"Funny you should say that, Annie. Charles thinks the same way. Is this one of those 'birds of a feather stick together' kind of things? Or keep your friends close, your enemies closer?"

"Well, Ted and Joseph Espinosa subscribe to the latter theory. And they were in the trenches, so to speak. I just hate it when I don't know what's going on, Myra."

"I know, dear. I don't like it myself."

Maggie walked into the Blue Duck just as the waitress was setting down their drinks. She slid room keycards across the table. "We're all on the same floor in adjoining rooms."

The minute the waitress walked back to her station, Maggie said, "I made another reservation on my BlackBerry. A friend will be picking up the key any minute now. He'll slip it in an envelope and tell the concierge to hold it for me. No one will be the wiser. Did you see anything? Were all these people here when you got here? What are you drinking?" Maggie asked in a rush as she gulped at her Slamming Sally.

"Champagne," Myra said

"Fibber. That's ginger ale."

Maggie nonchalantly looked around the bar as she sipped at her colorful drink. It was still early in the afternoon, too early for the cocktail crowd; businessmen were still in their meetings while their wives, if they'd been considerate enough to bring them along, were either shopping or sightseeing, while the guests with children were sitting by the pool. "So, no one has come in since you arrived, right?"

"Six customers. The man at the bar looks like he's had one too many. If I were the bartender, I would have cut him off two drinks ago. The couple against the wall had a full-course luncheon and are about finished. The two girls opposite the bar could be hookers. I say could be, I'm no authority. The businesswoman in the blue suit has been on her laptop and hasn't looked up once. I think we're okay so far," Annie said.

"What do we hope to do in here?" Myra asked.

"Not much but drink. I want to see if anyone followed us. I know the two of you think I'm being paranoid, and I want to prove to you that I am not. Paranoid, that is. Unless someone planted a GPS tracker on your car while you were at the *Post* or when it was parked in the lot at the park, we should be in the clear. Now, if someone shows up who we think is questionable, we can be assured there is a GPS on the car," Maggie said, as she kept her eyes fixed on the door leading into the Blue Duck.

"What is our plan if someone does show up?" Annie asked, her eyes sparkling with excitement. "Do we . . . ah . . . take him out? What?"

Maggie sucked the last of her Slamming Sally and held it up so the waitress could see she wanted a refill. "We play it by ear. We should ask for some munchies, peanuts, or some trail mix. I think better when I'm eating." Her drink arrived, and, without missing a beat, she continued to talk and suck through her straw at the same time.

Myra's stubbornness rose to the fore again when she said, "I'm sorry, girls, but I am just not getting any of this. It's been so long since our pardons, and so much time has passed, that I'm having trouble believing any kind of . . . tomfoolery is afoot."

Annie's eyebrows shot upward as her eyes widened. "Did you really say tomfoolery is afoot? My God, Myra, do you realize how that dates you? That sounds like everyone is going to go dancing in the park in their undies. You need to get with the program here and try to look alive and stop fingering those damn pearls. And who might that person be who just entered our domain here?"

Maggie raised her eyes from her drink to look at the man who walked over to the bar and ordered a beer. "Harmless. Not what we are looking for," she said around the straw that was still clutched between her teeth.

"What are we looking for, exactly?" Myra whispered.

"You'll know him or her when you see them. If you don't spot them, then you do not belong in this business," Maggie said, her gaze going to the door, where a tall man was standing. He removed his aviator glasses, rolled his neck like he was a tired businessman in want of something cool to drink.

"Bingo!" Annie chortled. "Mr. Cool himself. He's going to belly up to the bar and order a frosty one. Right, Maggie?"

"I knew that," Myra said, just as Maggie nodded in agreement.

Seven minutes later, a pert redhead in a dove gray pantsuit ambled in, stopped, looked around, then headed for the bar, where she sat down, two stools away from the guy with the aviator glasses.

"Part of the team," Myra said, before anyone could say anything. Maggie nodded again as she slurped the last of her drink. She held her glass aloft for the waitress to see that she needed another refill.

"Start jabbering, ladies. Babies are always a good topic of conversation. I have pictures of Little Jack I don't think you've seen. I think Lizzie has her camera on twenty-four seven, so she doesn't miss a thing. Little Jack is a cutie for sure." Maggie's voice dropped several octaves. "All we need is one more, and my suspicions become fact. The next one will be so ordinary most people wouldn't give him or her a second thought." Maggie's drink arrived as Myra and Annie managed to coo and giggle over the pictures of Little Jack, which wasn't all that hard to do even though they, too, were watching the doorway out of the corners of their eyes.

Seventeen minutes later, Maggie's fourth Slamming Sally arrived just as Myra and Annie finished speculating about Little Jack's bright blue eyes. The room darkened momentarily as a pudgy woman with three rolls of belly fat, wearing a tank top and carrying two shopping bags, huffed and puffed her way to a table near the far end of the bar. The three women smiled as one.

"Tissue paper in the shopping bags. She's just a watcher. She won't interact at all, unlike those two at the bar."

"How do you know this?" Myra asked in a jittery-sounding voice. "What in the world is in those drinks you're guzzling?"

"I'm a reporter. I have instincts. I've seen it all, Myra. It's what I used to do and what I miss most in my life. I've seen this same stakeout scenario, in one form or another, at least a hundred times. We're three for three. They don't know if we're going to split up or not. Whatever, they have us covered. Outside in the lobby, there are three more just like them. You can count on it. Here's something else you can count on. None of them belong to any of the famous alphabet-soup groups here in the District and Virginia. All of them are on Global's payroll. But to answer your question as to the contents of my drink, it's a mixture of passion fruit, pear nectar, acai berry, mango, and orange juice. Guaranteed to give you strength, energy, and stamina. Not a drop of liquor."

"How long are we going to sit here, Maggie?" Annie asked.

"We aren't. We're leaving as soon as I get

the check. "This is the plan. I'm sure by now one of Global Securities' agents hacked into the hotel's computer, and they know exactly what rooms we're in. So, why disappoint them? We'll take the elevator, they'll watch from the lobby to see what floor we get off on. You with me so far?" Both Myra and Annie nodded. "Okay, then we take the stairs to the other room I got for us, which is three floors down. Talk about silly stuff as we leave and while we wait for the elevator."

Maggie signed the check, added a generous tip. Together, the three women left the Blue Duck Tavern without so much as a glance at any of the other patrons. Maggie stopped just long enough to pick up an envelope from the concierge before rejoining the women at the elevator.

"This whole thing is starting to make me nervous," Myra said.

"Maybe you should go back to Charlie and the farm, Myra. Obviously, you aren't cut out for this kind of work. I swear, I do think you've taken the shine right off your pearls with all that fingering you've been doing."

"You need to stop worrying about my pearls, Ms. de Silva. Oh, and you aren't nervous? All I said was, this is making me nervous. If you had a brain, you would be nervous, too, Annie. None of this is computing, and you damn well know it, and no, I do not want to go back to the farm and *Charlie,* and you better not ever call him that to his face. The only person he lets call him Charlie is Hank Jellicoe. Oh, God! No matter what we do or say, that man is involved in some way."

The elevator swished open. The three women stepped in, along with two lanky teenage girls, who got off on the seventh floor. The elevator continued upward and stopped on the seventeenth floor, where they got off. They walked down to the nearest EXIT sign, and walked down three flights to the fourteenth floor. Minutes later they were in a two-bedroom corner suite complete with sitting room, with a view that Annie proclaimed to be crappy. In response to which Myra told her to suck it up and be quiet.

"This is the governor's suite, but I don't know of which state. What all that means, I have no idea. The fridge is stocked with alcohol and soft drinks and snacks. State-of-the-art TV, Internet, and wireless. All the comforts of home for the governor and his posse or, if it is South Carolina or New York, his mistress or high-priced escort. Or perhaps his wife and kiddies," Maggie said with a bite in her tone.

"What do we do now?" Myra asked.

"You guys watch TV while I continue to text Ted. You can order room service if you want. You didn't eat any of the picnic food. And, Annie, you might want to call that dealership to pick up your car. Or, better, have your banker do it. No sense giving our location away by calling from here."

Annie was so outraged that someone had dared to put a GPS tracker on her car she was speechless.

"Get over it, Annie. We have more pressing problems right now," Myra said.

"What was your first clue, Myra?" Annie snapped.

CHAPTER 5

Harry Wong stared down at the pot of steeping tea. He poured it into a fragile cup with no handles just as he heard a knock on the door at the back of the *dojo.* He frowned at the sound as he tried to decide whether he should go to the door or not. He couldn't remember if the door was locked. Yoko had left a half hour earlier to do some grocery shopping. Did she lock the door? He simply didn't know, so he set his cup of tea down on the small counter and walked toward the back door. His jaw dropped when he opened the door to see Maggie, Annie, and Myra smiling at him.

All three women rushed him, hugging him, to his dismay. Annie planted a kiss on his cheek, and gurgled, "Oh, Harry, it is *soooo* good to see you. I've never been here before, and neither has Myra. I hope we aren't interrupting anything."

Harry grinned. It was nice to see some of

his favorite people again after such a long time. His brow furrowed when he saw Maggie put her finger to her lips and motion for Harry to join them outside. He complied because he didn't know what else to do.

The women drew him down the narrow alley, all babbling at the same time. He did his best to make sense out of what they were saying but knew he was missing half of it. What he didn't miss was the worry and fear in the women's eyes. *What the hell is going on,* he wondered. "Whoa, slow down, ladies. One at a time. Should we wait for Yoko to get back from the market so we can both hear what you have to say instead of making you repeat whatever it is you are about to tell me?"

"Seems to me I remember a small picnic table around back. Can we go there?" Maggie asked. "How much longer do you think Yoko will be?"

"I'm surprised that she isn't back by now. She just walked over to the Asian market with her string bag. She buys just for the day. You know, fresh fruits and vegetables. Unless she went to the fish market, which is only two doors away. Even so, she should be back momentarily." Harry pointed to the left of the driveway and said, "It's two blocks away."

Harry bit down on his lip when Maggie said, "I'll walk in that direction to meet her and fill her in while Myra and Annie fill you in."

"What the hell is going on?" Harry asked as he led the way around to the back of the *dojo.*

"To be honest, Harry, we don't know. Maggie seems to think everything is bugged, and there was definitely a GPS on the car I was test-driving. And someone has us under surveillance. We saw that with our own eyes. Ted and Joseph quit Global and are on their way back from Rome as we speak. They're taking on their old positions at the paper," Annie said.

"We're so sorry we missed your wedding, Harry. We so wanted to be there, but no one knew . . . it was such a bad time for . . . oh, I don't know," Myra dithered as she fingered her pearls.

Harry figured it was time to say something, but he didn't know what to say other than to repeat himself by asking again, "What the hell do you *think* is going on?"

"That's a very good question, Harry. We *think* something terrible is going on. Henry Jellicoe has dropped off the face of the earth, as far as we know. We think he's gone to ground but don't know why. Ted and Joseph have not seen him during the course of their employment, according to Maggie. No one can figure out why the two of them were hired by Global Securities in the first place, especially Ted and Joseph. Ted, according to Maggie, has suspected for some time now that things aren't right, but he doesn't know what the problem is, either," Annie said.

"There is also the little matter of Hank becoming engaged to the president of the United States, then disappearing. There has not been a word, a squeak, or a peep about the engagement. We don't know if the engagement is on or off. As far as we know, Jellicoe has not been back at the White House since he walked out the night of the pardons. I know you saw him when you signed your contracts, but Harry, did you ever see him again?"

"No. We all went our separate ways that first month. Then we did our stint at the boot camp, which to me was a joke. Then — I guess the correct term would be 'deployed' — we deployed to the four corners of the globe. Yoko and I went to Israel, where I trained some of their men in martial arts. In the beginning, they had me going in all directions, but Israel was our home base. Every month it was someplace new. Then we ended back up in Israel and were there for the last six months with no other deployments. The Israelis weren't keen on my brand of training, and I had the feeling I was being humored by both the men and their superiors. It was almost, to me, like they were honoring a promise or a debt of some kind by having me there. We were tolerated, barely, and that's it. To be honest, I don't know how Yoko and I lasted as long as we did. She had two miscarriages, and it was her decision to come back to the States, with or without me, was how she put it. As you can see, I'm here, and she sure as hell didn't have to coax me to accompany her. I'm going to have to ask Lizzie to help me negotiate about the payback and canceling the contract. I'm assuming the bonus money has to be paid back and will be prorated. We banked my salary for the year and a half that we were gone. Housing and transportation were free, so our outlay was very little. Yoko is very thrifty, and so am I. We have more than enough money for a down payment on a house with a yard and a fence. That's what Yoko wants. I do, too. In the meantime, we have the *dojo*.

"At this point in time we are no worse off than we were before that out-of-the-blue offer of employment. Definitely better, in the sense that Yoko got her pardon and we got married. I suppose I can now add to my résumé that I helped train Israeli soldiers. I already have a full class signed up for next week, so that means I am here to stay."

"What was it that made you throw in the towel?" Annie asked with an intensity that made Harry's eyebrows shoot upward.

"We both hated the whole deal from day one. I admit, and so does Yoko, that we were dazzled by the money. That didn't last long. Yoko got depressed after her miscarriages and blamed it on being out of the country. I hated seeing her like that. She missed the others terribly. She used to cry every day, and she cursed the day the pardons came through. She went into a real funk when we weren't able to come back for Christmas last year. I did, too, to be honest.

"I think I know what you want me to say here, and yes, it was a job that was created for me that had absolutely no meaning. No one took my brand of training seriously. They're all about guns and 'real' soldiering. Yoko is the one who finally came up with something we both thought made sense. She said Hank Jellicoe wanted to separate us, to scatter us to the four winds. Neither of us could figure out why, but it was the only thing that made any kind of sense. I can't tell you the last time I talked to Jack or Bert. The sat phones always, somehow, mysteriously jammed when I tried to call any of the others. Yoko had the same problem when she tried to call the girls. Neither of us could figure that out, either."

Annie thought she had never heard Harry talk so much. Always a man of few words, he was certainly being more than vocal at the moment, which told her he was more than a little concerned over his present circumstances.

It was Myra's turn to speak. "Harry, I'm going to ask you a question, and I want you to really think before you answer me. Do you think Hank wanted you boys to separate or do you think he wanted the vigilantes to separate? In a way, it is the same thing but not really."

Harry pondered the question, wishing he had his cup of tea to wrap his hands about. "It's strange, Myra, that you should ask me that question. Yoko and I beat it to death so many times I lost count. We both think he wanted to separate the vigilantes. We can't figure out why, though. Is that what you all think?"

"We do, and Maggie agrees," Annie said.

"But like you, we can't figure out the why of it."

Harry rubbed at the bristle on his chin. He wished now that he had shaved earlier. "If you think Charles was into all that covert stuff that goes on all over the world, he's a novice compared to what Jellicoe has going on. That man plows through some really deep shit, or, at least, his people do. Yoko and I are good listeners, and of course, since Jellicoe was our benefactor, we tried to learn as much as we could about Global Securities during our stint away from home, at least back in the beginning. Later on, we didn't want to know any more than we knew at that point. Hank Jellicoe is the eight-hundred-pound gorilla in the espionage and security business. He outshines the CIA by a mile. By the way, do you know that only the CIA and Homeland Security can freeze a person's monies, even a foreign government's monies? A while back I remember reading about that in some article in the paper, probably the *Post.* Well, I'm here to tell you there are *three* organizations that can do it, and number three just happens to be Global Securities."

Myra stared at Harry. "What does that mean, Harry? I mean in regard to us, to you, me, the vigilantes? You must have had a reason for bringing that to our attention."

"Myra, I don't know. I just mentioned it. I guess we have to figure out what it means. Hey, I'm a martial arts kind of guy. I'm not into all that spook stuff. At this point in time, I just feel like I want to burrow in and get on with my life. There are no words to tell you how glad I am to be home. I just wish Jack and Bert were here. The rest of this crap means squat to me personally, but I do care how it affects Yoko. I want to be on record as saying that."

"Duly noted," Annie said.

The world took that moment to move, with Yoko rushing to the back of the *dojo* and throwing herself up against Annie and Myra as tears rolled down her cheeks.

"I think she's happy to see them, don't you, Harry?" Maggie whispered.

Harry laughed — such a strange sound that Maggie grinned. She thought for a moment, and realized she had never actually heard Harry laugh out loud. That had to be a good sign. Of what, she didn't know. She looked down at the BlackBerry in her hand, at the text that was coming through. She felt the fine hairs on the back of her neck start to move. She looked up to see four sets of eyes staring at her.

"Listen, you guys stay here and talk about

old times. I have an errand to run. I shouldn't be more than an hour, and I'll be back." Her voice dropped to a whisper. "Ted wants me to pick up something he says is important."

Sensing an urgency in Maggie, Harry stepped forward. "Do you want me to go with you, Maggie?"

Maggie thought about the offer and shook her head. "No, it's better if you stay here and pretend that everything is normal."

Myra's tone was so anxious, Maggie found herself cringing when she said, "But, dear, where are you going? How can we pretend to be normal when we don't know what passes for normal these days?" Even though it was a question, Myra didn't expect an answer, so she wasn't disappointed when Maggie just shrugged.

"To Neiman Marcus at the Galleria to try on a slinky dress I am going to buy, so I can leave the store with a shopping bag. I shouldn't be more than an hour or so. You can bring each other up to date while I'm gone."

"How wonderful! I so love slinky dresses. Just put it on your expense account, dear," Annie said generously.

"I'm not into slinky, Annie, and thank you for the offer, but I really just need the shopping bag. See ya. But if the dress comes with the deal, who am I to look a gift horse in the mouth."

Jittery small talk followed before Yoko excused herself to take her groceries inside. Everyone looked down at their watches. Yoko was back in less than ten minutes carrying a tray with a teapot, cups, and a plate of honey-rice cakes. The women all started to babble at once as they tried to figure out where and what Maggie was up to other than buying a dress she didn't want.

In the cab she was fortunate to hail almost in front of Harry's *dojo,* Maggie leaned back in the seat to scan the latest text from Ted, who said he would arrive Stateside no later than 8:00 P.M. She scrolled till she found the previous message, the message that had her in this cab at this precise moment. And to think she was going to get a slinky dress out of the deal, compliments of the *Post.* She had no idea where or when she would have an occasion to wear said slinky dress. And at this precise moment, she couldn't care less.

Maggie closed her eyes as she tried to figure out where all of *this* was going. She was almost giddy with the thought that in less than ten hours, give or take a few, she would be talking to Ted and Espinosa. She just wasn't sure if that would be before or after a round of lovemaking. Right now, though, lovemaking was coming in second to the weirdness that was going on in all their lives.

She was back in the game. She could feel it in every bone in her body. She knew in her gut that the others felt the same way. Yoko had come alive inside the fish market the moment she'd voiced her suspicions about what was going on. By the time they reached the alley of the *dojo,* her eyes were sparkling like diamonds.

The only thing throwing her off at the moment was Yoko's question, which she couldn't answer. "Maggie, do you think it's possible something happened to Hank Jellicoe?" Considering his profession, all that the man was involved in, Yoko's question did bear thinking about. And it was a question that she, as a reporter, should have asked herself early on. With all Jellicoe's personal security, his savvy, his knowledge, he wouldn't have been dumb enough to allow himself to be compromised in any way. Then there was his engagement to the president, which was either on or off.

Maggie sighed as the cab slid to the curb. She paid the driver and barreled out. As she stuffed her wallet back into her bag, she also managed to scan the area where the cab had stopped. There were cars everywhere. There were people everywhere. She tried to focus and remember exactly what she was seeing before she headed inside to the escalator that would take her up to Neiman Marcus.

On the ride up the escalator, Maggie did her best to act nonchalant as she looked around as if she didn't have a thing on her mind except shopping. The minute she stepped off the escalator, she headed straight for what she called the Designer Duds Department, where she went through the racks at the speed of light until a matronly woman came up to her with several dresses on her arm.

"I was just about to put these out. They just came in. This one," she said, holding up a slithery black number that Maggie knew had her name on it. Ted would go wild if he ever saw her in anything like that, she thought. She murmured something as the woman led her to a dressing room, where Maggie fiddled and diddled around just long enough for it to appear that she'd tried on the dress and admired herself in it.

Back outside at the cashier's station, the woman made a production of asking if she wanted a garment bag or a shopping bag.

Maggie opted for the shopping bag since the dress was so soft and crushable. "Just wrap it in tissue paper." She whipped out her credit card, watched it being scanned, and gulped at the amount the dress cost.

Five minutes later, she was tripping her way back toward the escalator, carrying her gaily colored shopping bag, which seemed suspiciously heavy. She wondered if anyone would notice. She fixed a happy-go-lucky smile on her face as she swung the bag back and forth like she didn't have a care in the world. She just knew she had outfoxed all those unseen eyes that were watching her.

Thirty-five minutes later, Maggie was back at the *dojo* and sitting at the picnic table with the others. "What we have here, ladies and gentleman, are burn phones. We each get one. I guess Ted knows someone who got these, had them programmed, and they are untraceable. So he says. Now, let's test them out by calling Bert, Kathryn, Nikki, and Jack and see what, if anything, comes out of the calls. While you all do that, I am going to call Lizzie on mine and ask her to find a reason to go to the White House. I want the skinny on that damn engagement. Who better to worm it out of the president than Lizzie?"

"Good thinking, dear. I think once we

know what that particular situation is, we might be able to figure things out, or at least get a lead on which direction we should go," Myra said. Maggie did not fail to see the glint in Myra's eyes. Myra was her old self, and Annie . . . Annie was about to go up in smoke any moment with all the excitement going on around her.

Life was suddenly taking a turn upward. Yessireee.

Chapter 6

"I don't know about you, Myra, but I think this table looks particularly festive," Annie said as she placed gardenia-scented candles around the table. "But you know what I think is best?" Not waiting for a reply, she continued, "Little Lady and her pups getting underfoot and wanting us to play with them. It's like this old farmhouse has come alive again. A family, Myra. I can't wait for the gang to get here. I did so hope Lizzie would be able to make it, but she said Little Jack has an upper respiratory infection. Baby comes first, so we will just have to settle for the video conference after dinner."

Myra's eyes started to mist as she bent down to pick up one of the pups, which was clawing at her shoe. "There is nothing sweeter in this whole wide world than a new baby and a new pup. Absolutely nothing."

"I couldn't agree more," Annie said as she, too, picked up a pup to cuddle. "We're going to have to name these little guys pretty soon. We can't keep calling them One, Two, Three, and Four. Don't say A, B, C, and D."

Myra laughed. "Maybe our guests will have some ideas for names. I'm so excited that they're all coming for dinner. It's almost like old times, isn't it, Annie?"

"Almost. It's been three days since we came back from town. There is still no word from the others. Joseph called to say that Alexis was on her way home with Grady last night, so she'll be here for dinner. Did you notice I set the extra place?"

"Annie, I was there. I heard the conversation on the speakerphone. It's all so wonderful. I hope Little Lady and Grady get along together."

"I'm sure they will, and I do think I hear a car. In fact, I think Little Lady hears it, too. The hair on the scruff of her neck is on end. I'm so glad you got this dog, Myra. I just love this hustle and bustle and the fact that we're all going to be together again. Well, five of our crew are missing, six if you count Stu Franklin, seven if we count Fish, which I am not inclined to do, but for the most part, we're all here. I'm excited, aren't you, Myra?"

"I am, more than you will ever know."

Within minutes it was like old times as all of Charles's chicks bounded into the kitchen. On cue, they ooohed and aaahed over the delicious aromas wafting about. They hugged Charles, smooched him on the cheek, then they all settled down to watch the interaction between Grady, Little Lady, and the four pups wobbling about the kitchen on their rubbery legs.

"This is so good for Grady. Even though he flew with me first class, thanks to Annie, he's been cooped up way too long. He can run here to his heart's content. He missed Murphy so much back in the beginning. He wouldn't eat and he got sick, and we were in a foreign country. It was just awful. When I told him we were *going home,* he was a new dog. They like each other," she said, pointing to the two dogs, who were nuzzling each other. "And now he has four additional playmates. Win! Win! Oh, God, Myra, I am so very happy to be here again. I am never, ever going to leave these shores again. Write that down, everybody, because I mean it."

"There is no need to write it down, darling girl. We will not allow any of you to separate from us again. We had our fill of being alone, and none of us liked it. Family is family, and we're sticking close this time around," Myra said happily.

Yoko smiled through her tears as she cuddled one of the pups close to her chest. No one missed the concern in Harry's eyes.

Small talk continued as Charles poured wine. The toast was simple. "To family and togetherness."

The gathering trooped into the dining room as the dogs headed to Little Lady's lair and the pen where the pups slept.

"Voilà!" Charles said, throwing open the door to the dining room.

"It's like Thanksgiving!" Ted said. "I want a drumstick!"

"Everything, just like Thanksgiving," Yoko said. "We do have so much to be thankful for today."

"I wish the others were here," Maggie said.

"They are, dear, in spirit. See, Charles set places for them. Joseph is going to take some pictures and send them on to Bert and Jack," Annie said. "We're hoping when they see us all here at the farmhouse, they will put it together and get in touch somehow. That is, if the pictures make it through cyberspace."

Espinosa stood up behind his chair as Charles poured yet a second toast. He captured forever on film the sparkling glasses being held aloft, the smiles, the beautiful table setting, the succulent turkey, and the pups — who, fortuitously, had just escaped their pen.

Myra said she thought that on this day, and during this particular dinner, she was the happiest she'd been since being granted her pardon. Her declaration was received with whoops of agreement from all those at the table. Underneath, the pups whined, demanding to be picked up. Little Lady and Grady picked them up, one by one, by the scruffs of the necks and returned them to their pen.

The "Thanksgiving" meal progressed until the men loosened their belts and the women sighed with contentment, all professing they couldn't eat another bite. Well, they finally conceded an hour later that maybe they could eat the pumpkin pie with homemade whipped cream. Hazelnut coffee was served, and the meal was truly over.

"I hope we can all be alert and not fall asleep when we do the video conference with Lizzie," Maggie said.

The dining room and kitchen were a beehive of activity as everyone fell into their old routine — *I cook, you all clean up.* One of many rules Charles had initiated early on.

"You have no idea how I missed all of

this," Yoko said, motioning to everyone scurrying about. "We worked so well together. It was as if we could read each other's minds."

"Don't you dare start boohooing, Yoko," Alexis said fiercely, a catch in her voice.

Yoko sucked in her breath and smiled. "Is it time yet?"

"It is now," Charles said as he turned the dial on the dishwasher. "Follow me."

Their steps were light, their murmurings hushed as they followed Charles to the secret war room they'd utilized beneath the old farmhouse in the early days when they had all come together for the first time.

"It seems like forever since we've been here," Alexis said as she took her old seat at the huge, round table. "This," she said, pointing to the chair on her left, "used to be Julia's chair. It's Annie's chair now. Nikki sat there, Isabelle over there. Myra was the head chair, and Yoko is sitting where she always sat," she said for the benefit of the others, even though they were all aware of the previous seating arrangements. She was babbling, and she knew it but was unable to stop herself. "It's like we've come full circle somehow. And yet . . . I don't know how to explain it. It's a feeling not unlike what I felt the first time I stepped into this room.

Back then, I knew that my life as I knew it was going to change and never be the same again. I feel that way right now. This might sound trite to all of you, but I feel like I, personally, am at a crossroads this very moment. Do . . . do any of you feel like that?"

Every hand in the room shot in the air. Alexis sighed in relief.

"Has *anyone* heard from Isabelle?" Maggie asked. Every head wagged back and forth.

Myra stood up and cleared her throat. Her hands were steady on the table and not at the pearls at her throat. That fact alone told the others something serious was about to be discussed, and this meeting was not just about a video conference with Lizzie.

"Charles, I want you to sit at the table with all of us. We have some things we need to share with you before we do the video conference. I suppose it's possible you already know of our concerns and have not voiced them to us, and it is also possible we're going to tell you things you don't know, things that have just come to light that concern . . . our little family that really isn't all that little anymore. I'm going to turn the floor over to Maggie now."

Maggie stood up the moment Myra sat down and started to talk. Only Charles appeared shocked, or as Annie later put it, stunned. Maggie wound down her report and motioned to the others at the table. "They've all tendered their resignations to Global, Charles. We're having no luck reaching Bert, Jack, or Isabelle. If you know anything you haven't shared, this might be a good time to speak up."

Charles's arms flapped in the air. He looked genuinely shocked. "I think I would have . . . no, correct that to, I would have *known* something was going on if you're right in your thinking. Snowden has always been on top of things, along with all my other people."

"With all due respect, Charles," Ted said, "Jellicoe is so far up the food chain, *your people* are novices compared to him. That guy and *his people* seem to have a lock on the covert-security world. I'm talking worldwide, not just here in Alphabet City. Look at us! We're the proof. And you didn't know we quit until now. Admit it, and let's move on here." There was such a bite to Ted's tone that, to everyone's dismay, Charles flinched.

Myra reached over and patted Charles's hand. "It's all right, dear. We just found out ourselves thanks to Annie's return and Maggie's keen instincts. We have to figure out what is going on, and more important, why it's going on."

To everyone's surprise, Espinosa, who usually observed rather than being vocal, spoke up. "Like Ted said, with all due respect, Charles, do you mind telling us what you've been doing for the past year and a half that you aren't up on what's going on? Or should we just assume that once the girls' pardons came through, the world stopped on a dime."

Alexis scooted her chair a little closer to Espinosa's. The move told the others that she was on his side and she, too, wanted an answer.

"It's a fair question, Joseph. And to a certain extent, you're right. I did let the world stop in a way once the pardons came through. My personal life, which had been pretty much on hold, suddenly became active. I've been attempting to write my memoirs and taking care of . . . of my late son's affairs. And, of course, seeing to the daily affairs here at the farm. I suppose that's no excuse, but it's the best I can offer at the moment. If any of you think that's inadequate as an explanation, tell me."

"I see no reason to place blame anywhere. None of us became aware of this situation, and, in all honesty, we really didn't even know for certain we had a situation, until a few days ago. It is entirely possible we're all overreacting. Unlikely as it seems, I am trying to be the voice of reason here," Annie said.

Harry leaned forward. Like Espinosa, Harry was a man of few words, and when he did decide to speak, everyone paid attention. "If I'm not mistaken, aren't you a personal friend of Hank Jellicoe's?" Not waiting for a response, he said, "Can you get in touch with him? That would certainly take the edge off things."

"There are friends, Harry, then there are friends. I do know Hank, have known him for years and years. I know him well enough to visit unannounced, which I did a while back. Since that visit, I have not heard from him, but that in itself does not mean anything. Years go by sometimes, and we are not in touch with the exception of the proverbial Christmas card. The Hank Jellicoe I know and respect would never do anything wrong. The man is all about God and country and family. He reveres all three. He's that rare man you want at your side in a crisis. I don't know what else to say."

"Call him, Charles," Yoko said.

Charles excused himself from the table and walked up the two steps to his workstation. He returned with his sat phone. All eyes were on him as he punched in Hank Jellicoe's number. Those same eyes watched as he nibbled on his lower lip, and as one they knew he had reached Jellicoe's voice mail. "Charlie, Hank. I need you to call me as soon as you get this message."

Charles frowned. "That doesn't have to mean anything. He could be indisposed. He could be out of range, although I think that's unlikely. He could be on a plane and the phone is off. It could be anything. In the past he has always, and I want to stress *always,* returned my call within hours. I can call the farmhouse and see what his people tell me."

"I think you should do that, dear," Myra said. Charles nodded, went back to his workstation, and returned with a number on a pad. He punched in the number and waited. "Charles Martin here, Mr. Wylie. I'm trying to locate Hank. I've left a message on his phone, but this is a bit of an emergency. I was wondering if you could reach him and have him return my call if that's possible."

The call ended. "Mr. Wylie, Hank's foreman and head of security at his farm, said that when he heard from Jellicoe, he would relay my message. That's it. There is no one or anywhere else to call unless we try Avery Snowden to see what, if anything, he comes up with. I understand how all of you are feeling right now, but since you are all so edgy, I don't see that we have anything to lose and possibly something to gain. A show of hands would be nice." Every hand in the room shot upward. "Consider it done."

The conversation was curt and terse. "It might take a while, possibly a few hours. So, unless there is nothing else on our agenda, I think we should move on with our video conference with Lizzie."

"I think we should try Jack and Bert again. I've been texting Isabelle with no results. I don't think any of us know how to reach Stu Franklin." Maggie turned to Annie, and said, "What about Fish? Do you think he knows anything?"

Annie's voice was grim when she said, "If he does, he didn't share it with me. Actually, I haven't heard from him since I got here." Her voice turned defensive when she said, "We don't as a rule live in each other's pockets — he has his life, and I have mine. We don't . . . explain ourselves to each other."

"That's not a bad thing, Annie," Myra said comfortingly. "It's how you remain an individual." The others agreed.

"So where is this all leading, or where does it leave us?" Alexis asked.

"Right where we were when we entered this room," Yoko said.

Harry reared up and bellowed at the top of his lungs. Everyone froze. "I want to know where Jack and Bert are, and I goddamn well want to know *NOW!*"

"Yeah, well, as much as you want to know where they are, that's how much I want to know where Isabelle is!" Maggie bellowed in return.

"Shouting and getting angry isn't going to help us. We need cool heads right now, and we need a plan, a strategy, a map to help us out. Charles has taken the first step by calling Mr. Snowden. I'm confident nothing is going to come of Charles's calls to Mr. Jellicoe's home and to his private phone number. I believe it is safe to assume the man is not going to return Charles's call. I think we are all in agreement on that. We're on our own. And if it was Mr. Jellicoe's intention back in the beginning to separate us, it didn't work, now, did it? Four of us are here along with Maggie and the boys, and we all know something is wrong. Now, let's try and figure out what it is. But let's do the videoconference with Lizzie first. We need her input, and we need her to get in touch with the president. After that, I think we'll have a clearer picture of what we're up against," Myra said in her take-charge voice.

"I'll set things up," Charles said.

The room went silent while they waited for the huge screen in the room to come alive. All it took was eight minutes, and Lizzie's beautiful face appeared on the screen. Five minutes of small talk ensued before Myra once again took charge. Lizzie listened attentively, and said, "I can make the call to the president's private number. That doesn't mean she will take the call. When she wants to talk to me, she calls in the middle of the night East Coast time. Even though we're close personal friends, that is no guarantee she's going to share details of her love life with me. I'll do my best, but I cannot guarantee a return call."

"Have you heard from Jack, Bert, or Isabelle?" Maggie asked.

"No. I've tried. I wanted to send pictures of Little Jack to Jack, but everything bounced back. When I call Bert, it goes to voice mail, and Isabelle is the same. I finally just gave up. Now that I think about it, it's been since Thanksgiving last year. Are you telling me none of you have heard from them, either?"

"None of us have heard a thing. As you

can see, Ted, Espinosa, and Alexis are here. They resigned and are back at the paper. Yoko and Harry came back last week. Harry resigned, too. The boys need you to help them with their contracts and to make arrangements to return their sign-on bonuses, prorated of course," Maggie said.

"Where is Hank?" Lizzie asked.

"That's what we'd all like to know. As far as we can figure out, when he walked out of his offices the day the boys signed their contracts, he disappeared. That's as much as we know, Lizzie," Annie said.

"You can call us anytime, dear. We're all at the farm. How is Little Jack?" Myra asked.

"Kind of fussy, he had an upper respiratory infection, but it's almost cleared up. Now he just has gas."

The talk turned to babies and formulas until Charles held up his hand to indicate the conference was over. Good-byes rang loud and clear.

"I have an idea," Maggie said. "Let's call the architectural board to see if Isabelle renewed her license and if they have a new address on file for her. Maybe we could get some snail mail to her since she doesn't answer her phone. I wish I understood how they can jam all the phones like that. You'd think by now Bert and Jack would have realized what's going on. The fact that none of us have heard from them is starting to worry me big-time."

"I've been worried for a long time," Harry said so quietly, the others had to strain to hear his words. "Jack's like my brother, Bert, too. Some way, somehow, they would have found a way to get in touch with me if something was wrong."

"What if that *something* is wrong on *their* end?" Annie said ominously.

"Chamomile tea, dear," Annie and Myra said at the same time. "Works every time."

Chapter 7

Half a world away, Jack Emery, a murderous look on his face, walked into his designer office and kicked the chair from behind the desk. He felt mentally sore and bruised from fight number 986 with Nikki. He sat down and bellowed for his secretary to fetch him some coffee. When there was no response, he got up and walked out to her office. The door was closed and locked, which meant she hadn't arrived yet, which in itself was a puzzle. Possibly even a cause for concern. Sari had never been late, never missed a day since he'd taken over the office. He checked the phone to be sure there was no message, but Sari had not called in. The back of his neck started to itch as he made his way to the designer kitchen that matched his office. Well, he knew how to make coffee, not that he'd done it in a while. There were a lot of things he hadn't done in a while.

While he waited for the coffee to drip, Jack made his way to the main computer room, where faxes and computers lined one whole wall. Here in this foreign land, Global Securities did not rely on the postal system. Everything was electronic, 24/7. Normally, Sari had everything precisely aligned on his desk by the time he got in in the morning.

Jack looked down at his watch. Sari was thirty minutes late. The part-time help wasn't due for another hour. With nothing else to do but wait for the coffee and think about his latest go-round with Nikki, he picked up the faxes and turned on the computer to check the e-mails. He scanned the e-mails briefly and printed them out, then added them to the stack of faxes. He carried them back to his desk, then made his way back to the kitchen for his coffee. He grew even more annoyed that there were no donuts or muffins. He'd been in such a huff when he left the house earlier, he hadn't even thought to take along a piece of fruit. Christ, how he hated this place and everything in it.

Jack stomped his way back to his office, spilling half the coffee on the way. He looked down at the small puddles and muttered, "Like I give a good rat's ass!"

And thus began what Jack later described

as his day of personal divine intervention, the day the good Lord saw fit to waken him to reality.

As he sipped his less-than-perfect coffee, he scanned the faxes in front of him. At first he thought he was hallucinating. He rubbed his eyes, sucked in his breath, and looked down at what he was seeing. The words exploded out of his mouth like gunshots. "Son of a fucking bitch!"

Jack spread the three sheets of paper across his desk. Resignations tendered by Ted Robinson, Joe Espinosa, and Harry Wong. He looked at the dates. Harry's was more than a week old, which meant good old Harry was probably back in the States already. Ted's and Espinosa's were four days old, which meant they, too, were probably back in the States.

Jack's eyes narrowed to slits as he let his mind race. He wondered if he would ever have seen the resignations if Sari hadn't been late that morning. Would she have filed them and not bothered to tell him? Probably, since the no-fraternization rules within Global Securities were strictly enforced. Early on in one of many briefings, he'd been told that no one ever left Global, because it was the perfect job. As one veteran put it, "You hired on, you signed your life away, you got paid five times what you were worth, and you died in the job." When he'd told all of that to Nikki, she'd gone ballistic. She'd looked him square in the eye and said, "Jack, this is just temporary. If it's long-term for you, I'm leaving now!" He'd been quick to agree to short-term. That was when all the trouble started. Newly married and starting out with that kind of baggage was pretty hard to handle. For both of them.

Nikki's parting words that morning before he'd slammed out of the opulent house were, "I can't take this anymore. I want out of here!" He wanted to scream the same words back to her, but he couldn't for some reason. He was committed to this goddamn job for another three and a half years.

Suddenly, Jack felt like he couldn't breathe. He pushed his chair back from the desk. Owing three and a half years to Global didn't seem to be an issue with Ted, Espinosa, and Harry. They'd packed it in. And all at the same time. Something was going on. Ted? Ted had gut instincts. Reporter instincts. Espinosa was good, too, but Ted was the leader. Harry, now, Harry was a horse of a whole other kind. Harry honored contracts. Harry always did the right thing. Unless he was doing something wrong at his, Jack's, behest. Harry would never quit such a lucrative job without a reason. Ted and Espinosa had ethics, too. So what happened to make the three of them up and quit and head for American shores? Home and hearth? All at the same time. What?

Without thinking, Jack picked up the strange phone from the console that all Global offices had and pressed the number two, which would connect him with Bert Navarro. He didn't even want to think about the damn crazy phone that was so programmed, so futuristic, it made him nuts. Nikki said it was Global's way of cutting him off from the outside world so he could concentrate on the world of Global Securities. The only thing that counted in this godforsaken place. They'd had so many fights over that, he'd lost track.

"Navarro."

"Emery," Jack said through clenched teeth. He hated this stupid repartee. "I have here on my desk three resignations. The only reason I think I have them is because my secretary didn't come in this morning, and I personally checked the fax machine and the e-mails. Harry, Ted, and Espinosa quit. I can't be sure, but I think they're all Stateside. Do you know anything about this?"

The silence lasted almost a full minute

before Bert replied. "No, Jack, I didn't know. Hell, you were at that same briefing I attended. No one quits or leaves Global unless he's dead, because it's a perfect place to work. What was their reason for leaving?"

"There's nothing on here. And, buddy, just for the record, I hate this fucking job. All Nikki and I do is fight. She slammed me this morning and said she couldn't take it anymore. To be honest, I don't know whether she'll be there when I get home."

"That's pretty funny, Jack, because Kathryn and I had the same fight last night. She actually packed her bags. She wouldn't look at me this morning. You know what else? I'm with you, I hate this fucking job. I think we were all nuts to sign on to begin with. Are you trying to tell me something here?"

"I was just going to ask you the same question. Look, I love Nikki. If push comes to shove, and we're definitely at the shoving stage right now, I'm going with her. Jellicoe can shove this job with all his rules and regs right up his ass for all I care. By the way, have you seen the great man lately?"

"Not since we walked out of the office after we signed those contracts. I have come to the conclusion, with Kathryn's help, that I am simply not dedicated enough to work for this organization."

Jack snorted. "I want to know why I have been cut off from all my old friends. Since we all work for the same company, why is that? Every goddamn phone either is jammed or isn't programmed for making calls other than internal ones. I tried going to Internet cafés to get hold of Harry and the others, but the calls won't connect. Nikki said we're Hank Jellicoe's prisoners, and we're just too stupid to know it."

"That's the same thing Kathryn said," Bert muttered.

"Like I said, Bert, if my secretary had arrived on time, I seriously doubt I'd even know about Ted, Espinosa, and Harry. But I do know now. You know what else? I'm going home, but I'm going to stop at that swanky hotel on the hill and see if I can get a call through to the States. I think my best bet will be Maggie. You're four hours from me, Bert, what are you going to do?"

"Wait for you to call me back."

"I might not be coming back. The only way I can reach you is through this dumbass phone I'm talking on now."

"I know you, Jack. You already made up your mind. You aren't coming back. So what's the plan?"

"Jesus, Bert, what do you want from me? I'm actually dizzy with the thought that maybe I can get out of here. Okay, okay, I'm going home to talk to Nikki. Unless she agrees to leave right away, today, I'll come back and call you in, let's say, two hours. That will give you time to go home and talk to Kathryn. You're right. I want out. I wish I'd had the guts to do it earlier."

"You're seriously thinking of throwing in the towel because . . ."

"Harry had a reason, so did Ted and Espinosa. Leaving wasn't something they did on a whim; they thought it through. You know them, Bert. They're all thinkers. I don't know what those reasons are, but whatever they turn out to be, that's good enough for me. So, yeah, I'm not just thinking about it, I'm going to do it. I just hope I'm not too late where Nikki is concerned. Listen, I only know this because Nikki said there is a flight out of Heathrow in London at two-thirty in the afternoon. Every afternoon, I assume. Obviously, she has or had a plan in place to leave on her own at some point. If we can get a flight out of here in time, and if all goes well and Nikki hasn't left on her own, we'll be on that flight. If you don't hear from me and are planning to leave, meet us at Heathrow. We'll wait for you until the day after tomorrow. But if you're not there, we'll take the two-thirty that day to the States. Right now, the only thing that matters to me is Nikki and saving my marriage. You do what you have to do, Bert. I'm going to do what I have to do. See ya, buddy."

Jack felt like he was walking on air as he galloped out of the office and down the two flights of stairs of the impressive building that belonged to Global Securities. He zipped through the door and jogged to the nearest Internet café, where he paid for Internet service and fired off an e-mail to Maggie Spritzer at the *Post* in Washington, D.C. The message was short and sweet. *Watch the skies, we're coming home.* He hit the SEND button and wanted to cry when the message wouldn't go through. He deleted the message and left the café. "Screw you, Jellicoe!" *Please let her be there when I get home,* he said silently over and over as he walked the short distance to the house he shared with Nikki, the house owned by Global. Not for the first time, he wondered if the house was bugged. Nikki said it was, but she couldn't find the bugs.

Jack blasted through the front door, shouting Nikki's name as he made his way through the thirteen-thousand-square-foot house, which was twelve thousand square feet too big for him and Nikki.

Nikki appeared at a set of French doors. Jack never came home in the middle of the morning. "What's wrong?" she said, alarm ringing in her voice.

"I don't know what's wrong, but something is going on that is giving me the heebie-jeebies. What I do know is we're going home. And we're going *NOW.* Do you want to pack, or are you ready to go as you are? There's not one damn thing I want to take with me. There's a flight out of here in ninety minutes. We might get lucky and snag seats."

"Oh, Jack, are you sure? I thought this day would never come. I hate it here, Jack. I hate Global. I hate this house. I hate this country. But I do love you. I'm ready. There's nothing I want to take from here, either," she said breathlessly as she reached for her purse, which was hanging on a hook by the front door. She checked to make sure her passport was inside. It was. "Where's your passport, Jack?"

Jack held the door for his wife as he patted the inside of his jacket. "I say we drive and leave the car at the airport. I'll lock it and mail the keys back to this office."

"Oh, my God! Are you sure we're going to be able to leave? What if we can't get a flight?" Nikki fretted.

Jack settled himself behind the wheel of a top-of-the-line Mercedes Benz and turned the key. Without missing a beat as he backed up the car, he said, "We are taking the next flight out of here, and I don't give a shit where it's going. You okay with that, Nik?"

"Better than okay," Nikki said, squeezing her husband's arm. "Do you want to tell me what's going on?"

Jack took his eyes off the road, mouthed the word "bug," and said, "We'll have all the time in the world to talk on the plane. It's a long flight."

That was good enough for Nikki. She squeezed his arm again and tried to inch closer, but the console in the middle kept her at bay. "Oh, Jack, I am so happy. Every day since we got here and all those other stopover places, I have prayed that we could go home. I know we're going to have to pay back the money. I don't care about that. I'll waitress, I'll clean people's houses, I'll work three jobs, I don't care."

"It's not going to come to that, Nik. I can still practice law, and for all you know, your license was reinstated in the time we've been gone. Our lives from here on in will be whatever we make of them. I hope Bert makes his flight. I told him we'd meet up in London at Heathrow. Whoever gets there first waits for the other one."

"Is . . . is this mutiny, Jack?" Nikki whispered. Jack nodded, his face grim.

Jack concentrated on the road and the dust clouds that were everywhere. God, how he hated this place. He shook his head to clear his thoughts. Never in his life had he made such a rash, wildly impetuous move as this one. He'd always considered himself a stable, think-it-through kind of guy. And here he was, throwing in the towel, tossing money down the tubes, and heading back to safe, familiar shores with a relief so profound that no words could describe it.

As the powerful Mercedes bounced along the rutted road, Nikki's hold on Jack's arm grew tighter. By the time they were two miles from the airport her hold on Jack's arm was leaving bruises, but he didn't care. His own grip on the steering wheel was vise-like.

"Promise me, Jack, that you will never, ever take me to a zoo where they have camels. Promise me you will never, ever show me a picture of this country. Because if you do, I will have to kill you. Do you hear me, Jack?"

"Yes, Nikki, I hear you, and I promise. I'm thinking this is kind of like those pumpkins from way back. I hate all things pumpkin."

In spite of herself, Nikki laughed. "Can't you speed it up, Jack?"

"And break an axle and have to hoof the last mile? I-don't-think-so. I can see the airport. We're almost there. No luggage might pose a problem."

"I don't see why," Nikki said. "Well, I do see why, but I'm sure we can talk our way through it. After all, you're Global's top dog here in this hellhole. All you have to do is throw your weight around. You can do that, can't you, Jack?"

Jack correctly interpreted the anxiety level in his wife's voice and just nodded. The truth was, he had no idea what to expect when he got to the airport. He knew for a fact there was a contingent of Global's field agents on duty because he had personally deployed them. All of the agents worked under him. But as everyone in the Global Securities network knew, there was only one real boss, and that was Hank Jellicoe, who had all the power centers of this country under lock and key. He nodded again, more to reassure himself than Nikki.

"You know what, I'm just going to leave the car out front and have one of the guys take it back to the house. That way I won't have to worry about the keys."

"Sounds good. We're here, Jack."
"Yeah, we're here! We have thirty-three minutes till the flight boards. Let's just hope we can get out of *here.*"

CHAPTER 8

Isabelle Flanders bolted upright, her body flushing, her head pounding. Her eyes were wild as she looked around the room she had been sleeping in for the past year and a half. It was ostentatious, but she hadn't decorated it, and it wasn't to her taste. Too much furniture — costly furniture — too many statues and knickknacks. The architect in her liked clean, straight lines, no clutter. It was obvious to her trained eye that whoever had decorated the entire house did not have a budget, and money had been no object. At least that's what Stu had told her. The bottom line was that she hated the place and everything in it.

Her head continued to pound as Isabelle swung her legs over the side of the bed and made her way to the shower. Maybe, just maybe, she could head off what she knew was coming. It had been years since she'd had one of what she called her *spells*. Back when her life had been turned upside down by an employee who'd blamed her for a deadly car accident and went on to steal her business, her fiancé, her money, and her life. She'd lost her architect's license and been one step away from killing herself when Nikki Quinn came into her life and somehow, with her help and that of the other vigilantes, she became whole again, and the awful spells or *visions,* as the others called them, stopped. And now the visions were with her again, and there was nothing she could do to stop them. Stress, one doctor had said. Another said it was a gift and to enjoy the experience. There were more doctors who said the same thing, only using different words. She knew they thought she was crazy, and sometimes she thought she was, too. Until something happened that proved she really did see what she saw in her visions.

Isabelle looked into the vanity mirror and wondered who the person staring at her was. Panic rivered through her. She stepped back and turned on the shower. If she didn't turn on the exhaust fan, the mirror would steam up, and she wouldn't *see* anything.

She knew she was in the shower because she could feel the water from the thirty-seven jets pummeling her head and body, but she was somewhere else, fully clothed, watching Jack Emery looking at a stack of papers on his desk. Sand was blowing from all directions, almost blinding her. She desperately wanted to talk to Jack, but there was sand in her mouth. Ted, Harry, and Joe Espinosa's names were on the papers. She blinked and blinked again because she was now in Harry's *dojo.* No, that was wrong, she was outside Harry's *dojo* and everyone was talking at once — Myra, Maggie, and Annie — but she couldn't hear what they were saying because it was raining, and the rain was getting inside her ears. Yoko, sweet Yoko, was holding out rice cakes no one wanted, and she had tears in her eyes. She looked down at the newspaper on the picnic table. It was the *Post,* Maggie's paper, the very paper Annie owned. She squinted and saw the date. Today's date. She tried to make her tongue work, but no words came out. She flapped her arms and hands, but no one seemed to notice. She tried screaming. At the top of her lungs. She heard no sound.

Isabelle sucked in her breath when she saw herself seated on an airplane. She was safe; she was going home. The picture in her mind raced forward as she watched Jack and Nikki clutch at one another. Nikki was crying, and Jack was trying to comfort her. All she could hear were the words *we're going home* over and over again. Home.

Isabelle moved then because the water had turned cool. She reached up to adjust the hot water faucet, then sat down on the marble bench inside the massive shower, which could hold a dozen people. The terrible, pounding headache was gone, but she was shaking and shivering, the warm water cascading over her naked body, doing nothing to warm her. She was cold to the bone.

Somehow, she managed to get out of the shower into the fog of steam that had engulfed the bathroom. She reached for where she thought the bath sheet was, found it, and wrapped it around her. Then she ran out the French doors to the terrace, where the sun was scorching hot. She took a deep breath before she curled up on a gaily colored chaise. More deep breaths. Still more deep breaths. And then she was okay. She felt the blazing heat but didn't move. She needed to think. Think *hard.* If only she had someone to talk to, to confide in. If only.

God, how she missed the others. She'd give anything, anything, to be back on the mountain with Annie, Myra, and the others. She wished now that President Connor had never pardoned any of them. At least she'd been happy back then. It wasn't that she was exactly unhappy here in Paraguay. She still couldn't believe she was here, living under Hank Jellicoe's roof and obeying his rules. She'd been a fool to follow Stu. But it had seemed like the thing to do at the time. How wrong she'd been. At least she had the good sense not to get married. That alone left her a free agent. But she wasn't really free, and she knew it full well. The eyes and ears of Hank Jellicoe's people were all around her. When she complained about the spying, the reports on everything she said or did, Stu just said, "That's the way it is. Accept it because it's for your own safety."

Stu had been away more these last months than he was home. In truth, she was always relieved when she saw him packing for a trip to God only knew where. In the beginning she had cried when Stu said she couldn't leave to go home to visit. Then she'd started to scheme and plot behind the scenes. Once she got the lay of the land and learned how the household worked, she'd gone to work behind closed doors. She was an architect, for God's sake. How hard could it be to doctor up a passport? It had taken her three months to fine-tune everything. She was good to go if she had the guts to attempt the move. If she wanted any confirmation, today's vision was all she needed to spur her on. With Stu on the move, all she had to contend with were her handlers and the household help. The truth was, her handlers of late had become rather lax in their watchfulness, something she hoped would work to her advantage. Why she needed handlers or watchers was something she still hadn't figured out after all this time. Stu telling her it was for her own safety was a crock, and he knew she knew it. She didn't believe for a minute when she hounded him unmercifully saying *they* were just being careful since she was in a foreign country and was an American citizen.

Yeah, well, this place and Stu, too, came with an expiration date and, as far as she was concerned, that date had arrived. The thought left her light-headed.

Isabelle got up and left the terrace. Inside, she drew the sheer curtains covering the French doors and headed to a walk-in closet that was as big as a two-bedroom apartment in the Watergate. She walked among the racks of clothing she rarely wore and finally selected a white dress that would show off her tan, high-heeled sandals, and a perky little hat with a brim of the kind all the ladies in town wore as they shopped. Today, she would be the lady in white. When she boarded the flight to wherever it was going, she would be a lady in lime green, an outfit she'd never worn. She quickly ripped off the tags, ran to the bathroom, and flushed them. She folded the clothing neatly and tightly to fit into the white straw bag that she always carried. A small green-and-white clutch on a slender chain and no bigger than an oversize wallet went into the bottom of the straw bag, along with matching sandals. A strawberry blond wig followed. She was glad now that she'd had her hair cut short just a week ago; less hair to stuff under the wig, which was long and straight. She was sure Alexis would approve.

Back in her bathroom, Isabelle opened an ornate container of body powder and ran her fingers through it until she found the small package of latex she'd hidden there months earlier. Just enough of it to her nose, chin, and cheeks, and she would no longer look like Isabelle Flanders. The new name on her passport said she was Consuela Cardoza from Brazil. She was so glad now that she had paid attention to Alexis when she disguised them back on the mountain. She remembered Alexis's words, "Less is more, so be careful or it will look obvious. You just want a subtle change."

Back inside the walk-in closet, Isabelle dropped the latex into the straw bag.

She ran back and forth, adding, taking out, making sure the straw bag didn't appear heavier than normal. She took one last jittery look at the passport that she had labored over for months. If there was a flaw anywhere, she couldn't see it. She carefully folded enough local currency, the equivalent of a thousand American dollars, and slipped the passport back into the clutch along with enough cash for bribes and to get her stateside. She stuffed another wad in her bra.

According to the locals, cash was king in this country, enough to make the recipient look the other way. She felt like a spy and decided she rather liked the feeling. If only the Sisters could see her now. She felt her eyes starting to fill up. Soon.

As she dressed, Isabelle wondered whom she would draw today to follow her. She hoped it would be Marta, the small dumpy woman with the bad feet who tended to sleep standing up while Isabelle shopped. More often than not, Isabelle had to wake Marta from her siesta to tell her she was ready to go home. She pulled the cord beside the bed, and, within seconds, a young girl of sixteen or so poked her head in the door. "I'm going shopping. Have someone fetch the car and bring it to the front. Who is going with me today?"

"Marta is the only one here today. She said you went shopping yesterday, and today is to rest. That is why no one else is here but me, and I cannot leave the house unattended. She said today is to rest," she repeated stubbornly.

"I changed my mind," Isabelle snapped. "Tell her to get in the car or stay home. I really don't care. Tell cook I would like roast chicken for dinner and to serve at eight o'clock. I plan to shop until I drop. I will bring you something pretty for being so helpful."

The girl's eyes sparkled. "Yes, ma'am. Thank you for being so kind to me."

The last thing Isabelle did, before leaving the bedroom she hoped she would never have to see again, was to take two bottles of ice-cold water out of the minibar. She cracked one open and dropped in two twenty-milligram Valium tablets. By the time they reached the shopping district, Marta would have consumed the entire bottle of water and hopefully would sleep for six or seven hours in the backseat while Isabelle made her getaway.

Isabelle, her insides quaking, strode

through the house like the mistress she was. Outside, a gleaming silver Mercedes sat in the hot sun, the engine running, Marta in the backseat. In the beginning, when she had first arrived, she'd been assigned a chauffeur. That lasted all of two days before she put her foot down and said she would drive herself. In the end, she had to agree to bring Marta or someone like her. Following that incident, it had only taken her one week to realize she was being watched 24/7.

She'd had a rousing fight with Stu, and things went steadily downhill after that. But she'd stayed on because she couldn't see any other available options. It wasn't until months later, after a horrible fight when she threatened to leave, that Stu told her she was there for the length of the contract. She'd cried for hours, days, weeks. When she couldn't cry anymore, she spent endless hours wondering what the other Sisters would do in her place. The scenarios ran from the sublime to the ridiculous. That was when she finally, finally, realized she was going to have to go it alone and figure out a way to get back to the States. Life was a bitch sometimes.

Behind the wheel, Isabelle found herself watching the rearview mirror every few seconds to see if anyone was following her, and listening to Marta grumble and whine. There were times, and this was one of those times, when she wondered if Marta was as stupid as she seemed. "I told you I saw a dress I liked in a magazine, and I want to see if I can find it. I don't care if it takes me all day, and it probably will, to find it. I plan on going to every single store in the shopping district. You can walk along with me, or you can stay in the car and eat ice cream from the vendors. I'll be sure to park in the shade. You did say you like talking to all of the sidewalk vendors. I'll leave the keys with you so you can keep the air-conditioning on. That means stop whining right now, or I will stop this car and push you out. Well?"

"Today was to rest," the dumpy woman said stubbornly.

Isabelle clenched her teeth. The water bottle was half-full. Marta should be getting drowsy by now. "Yes, for you, not me. You need to get more exercise. I see you are putting on too much weight. That is why your feet hurt you all the time. Is there anything you would like me to buy you today? Some chocolates, some sticky cakes? Or maybe some of my perfume that you like to *borrow* from time to time."

"Hmmm," Marta said as she struggled to keep her eyes open. "Yes, some chocolates would be nice."

Ten minutes later, Isabelle brought the high-powered Mercedes to a stop on a shady, tree-lined street in the elegant shopping district. All she wanted to do was get out of the car and gallop to the nearest store. But she had to play the game and observe a certain protocol in case Marta wasn't the only one watching her.

Isabelle got out of the car, her bag secure on her shoulder. She opened the back door to poke at Marta. "We're here, Marta. Do you want to come with me or are you going to stay in the car? Here are the keys."

Marta roused herself enough to mumble that she would stay in the car for a little while. Isabelle handed over the second bottle of water.

Isabelle looked around. Everything looked the way it did when she shopped on other days. To her left was the ice-cream vendor, a friend of sorts to Marta. She walked over to him and motioned to the car and Marta in the backseat. She handed over some local currency and said, "Watch over her. I am going to be late. If she gets hungry, buy her some food." The vendor nodded and pocketed the money.

Isabelle's legs felt like rubber as she made her way down the fragrant street. As always, she marveled at the lush plants and flowers outside each store. It really was a pretty street. Right now she had more important things on her mind than plants and flowers.

As Isabelle meandered down the shop-lined sidewalk, she stopped to peer into windows. The bright sun reflecting off the shiny glass let her see if anyone was following a little too close for comfort. She hoped she was pulling off a nonchalance she was far from feeling. Finally, she chose a store that was so cluttered with racks and bins of clothing it was hard to find walking space. She'd been in it many times and knew exactly where the dressing rooms were. And there was a huge EXIT sign over a door in the back hallway that she knew led to a minuscule parking lot for the store employees that, in turn, led to a small side street that would, if she turned left, take her out to the main thoroughfare, where she could flag a rickety taxi. The only problem with taking a taxi was that taxi drivers talked. Even when they took money not to.

An elegant, charming saleswoman approached Isabelle. "Madame Flanders, how nice to see you again. Come, we have some nice things in the back." What that meant to Isabelle was, the couture items for the well-heeled matrons were kept safely away from the riffraff, as well as the blatant thieves, who snatched and ran.

"Oh, Elena, that sounds decadent. I can hardly wait to see what you have."

"Straight off the runways. Only someone like you can do them justice, Madame Flanders. Wait one little minute, and I will bring these treasures for you. There are six of them, and all in your size. No alterations will be necessary. I know this."

"Wonderful! Elena," Isabelle whispered, "I wonder if you might help me. I'll take all six dresses. Just put them on my account. Right now I don't have time to try them on. I find myself in a rather ticklish position. I need to . . . ah . . . go somewhere" — she winked roguishly — "and I have no way to get there. Would it be possible for you to . . . ah . . . loan me your car?"

"Ah, love, but of course. It is the Renault in the back. Wait, one little minute and I will fetch the key. All six, you say?"

"All six, yes, Elena. Just put them on my credit card and send them to the house. Tomorrow will do nicely."

"And what do I say to that sour old woman who follows you like a nanny if she shows up looking for you?"

"Tell her I ran off with the plumber. Just be haughty. Now, where shall I leave the car? I do not want to come back here till very late. You understand, do you not?"

"Most assuredly. Do not worry. I'll report it stolen, but not until tomorrow, when you are safely home awaiting the delivery of your six new dresses. Ah, I wish I was young again with a lover waiting for me." She leaned in closer. "Are people watching you?" she whispered.

Isabelle nodded and pointed to her bag as she started to strip off her white linen outfit. Feverishly, she pulled out the lime green ensemble, one she'd purchased from Elena months ago.

Elena nodded her approval. She watched, fascinated as Isabelle worked deftly with the latex. Her eyes popped wide when Isabelle whirled and twirled for her benefit. "This man who waits for you, he is worthy of all this . . ."

"He is my soul mate, Elena. Our hearts beat as one. He is kind, generous, witty, he lives and breathes only to make me happy, and . . . and he is *RICH!*"

"Say no more." The older woman smiled. "I see how happy you are. Rich is always good," she twittered.

Isabelle handed over her discarded clothing. "You can take care of these for me?"

"But of course."

Isabelle reached into her green-and-white clutch and withdrew a wad of banknotes. She pressed them into Elena's hand. "Keep my secret, and there will be more when I come again to shop. My lover showers me with banknotes. It will be my pleasure to share some with you for your help. Oh, I love him so much!"

"Your secret is safe with me, Madame Flanders. No words shall escape these lips. Oh, dear, I see I was wrong. There are eight new outfits." She raised her eyebrows in question.

"I'll take the others, too. I must go now. Thank you, Elena. Listen to me — if anyone comes looking for me, do not believe what they tell you. Unless they tell you I ran off with my lover." The woman nodded, happy with the commission she was making for the day plus her little windfall, with more to come. She watched as Isabelle literally ran out of the dressing room to the little hall that would take her outside to the gray Renault. She did love a good story and a conspiracy.

Elena looked at the banknotes in her hand. Three American hundred-dollar bills. Mother of God! For certain she would never give up any information on such a fine lady, no matter who came asking questions. Not even the *patrón,* Hank Jellicoe himself.

The lady in green, as Isabelle thought of herself, made good time to the Asuncion Silvio Pettirossi International Airport, where she would board a plane that would take her somewhere, anywhere, out of Paraguay and out of the reach of Stu Franklin, Hank Jellicoe, and Global Securities. She got out of the car and locked it. She didn't know what to do with the key, so she dropped it into her handbag. She received many admiring looks from business travelers as she made her way inside the modern, air-conditioned airport. She looked up at the monitors, trying to decide which flight was scheduled to leave within the next forty minutes. If she hurried, she could get her ticket; breeze through security, because she had no bags; slither through the Customs line; and be on the tarmac with the other passengers, all in time to board. It was all doable, she told herself over and over as she waited to see if her passport would pass muster. She almost fainted when the man waved her through as he pocketed the local *guaraní* currency he removed from her passport.

Isabelle knew she wasn't out of the woods yet. Only when she was thirty thousand feet in the air would she relax. Until then she would think about Fortaleza, Brazil, which was where her ticket said she was going. From there she would board a flight to Miami, and from Miami, a flight to Washington. Travel time with layovers, almost twenty-four hours.

With ten minutes till boarding, Isabelle hit the restroom, where a gaggle of young girls were giggling and laughing. Those who weren't giggling and laughing were chattering on their phones. If only she could get one of those phones. Well, she wouldn't know if she didn't ask. She approached one of the giggling girls with a few folded bills in her hand. At best, her Spanish left a lot to be desired, so she simply pointed to the girl's phone and held out the money. She made a motion to indicate she'd dropped her own on the marble floor, and it had ceased to work and was now in the trash can that she pointed to. The girl smiled, handed over the phone, and the charger from her bag, and graciously accepted the money Isabelle held in her hand.

"There is a God," Isabelle whispered as she entered the stall and immediately tried to call Myra Rutledge.

CHAPTER 9

Bert Navarro knew he was strung tighter than a guitar string. He also knew he'd never felt this way before, not even when he was in the line of fire. He turned his head slightly to look out the plane window from his window seat. They were on the ground. On the ground. In England. Son of a bitch, they had actually made it. That it was too easy made his heart pound. They'd been sitting for ninety minutes waiting to roll up to the plane's designated jetway so they could disembark. By craning his neck, he could see that nothing was blocking the plane's progress, so why the hell were they just sitting here?

Bert closed his eyes. The tension and hostility emanating from Kathryn, who was sitting next to him, was so intense he thought he was going to jump right out of his skin. Over the course of his life he'd heard the expression "ticking time bomb," but he'd never actually been able to apply it to a person or a situation until now. If they didn't get off this damn plane soon, she was going to explode. Aside from the tension and energy, he could feel her anger.

Kathryn took that moment to turn and look at him. Her eyes were colder than ice, her words harder than steel. "This is a Jellicoe Global Securities Gulfstream. Either you get me off this plane like *NOW* or I won't be responsible for what happens next. Do you hear me, Bert?"

Bert nodded because he didn't trust himself to speak. Even though they were just sitting on the runway, he hadn't unbuckled his seat belt. He did so immediately.

"Another thing," Kathryn hissed. "This was just way too easy, Mr. Navarro. For a year and a half you and Global wouldn't let me leave that hellhole, and now here we are sitting on a runway in Merry Old England, and we can't get off the damn plane. What's wrong with this picture, *Bert?*"

Like he had the answer. "I don't know, honey." He moved past her to head toward the cockpit.

"Don't you 'honey' me! Don't you ever 'honey' me again, Bert Navarro," Kathryn said through clenched teeth.

Kathryn watched through narrowed eyes

as Bert walked forward and spoke quietly to the frazzled hostess, who was trying to talk to him and knock on the cockpit door at the same time. She was here, on friendly soil, just a heartbeat away from seeing Nikki and Jack, and she couldn't get off the plane. In the whole of her life, she'd never been as angry as she was at that minute. *I'm being punished,* she told herself. *For my wild and wicked ways.* Meaning, of course, running off with Bert to what she called never-never land when she'd promised Alan, her dead husband, she would never get married to or love anyone else. Well, she hadn't married Bert, so that was a good thing. Or not. These days she didn't seem to know anything.

She'd never been a crier. The last time she'd cried was at Alan's funeral. And that seemed like a lifetime ago. A lone tear rolled down her cheek. She brushed at it with a trembling hand at the same moment she felt the plane start to glide forward. "Thank you, God. Thank you, God. Thank you, God," she whispered to herself.

Bert was back in his seat and whispering, "Just a computer glitch that . . ."

"Computer glitch, my ass," Kathryn seethed. "All they had to do was open the door, roll up the stairway, and we could have been off this goddamn plane eighty minutes ago."

"It doesn't work that way, hon . . . Kathryn."

"Yeah, Bert, it does work that way. Right now, I hate you. Don't talk to me, don't touch me. I just want off this plane. Where is Murphy?"

"You know damn well where the dog is. He's with the pilot. He'll get out at the same time you do. I thought you didn't want me to talk to you. And just for the record, Kathryn, I broke a hundred rules to smuggle that dog on board."

"Cry me a river, okay?" Kathryn snarled, just as the plane came to a smooth stop. A nanosecond later, Kathryn was out of her seat and rushing forward. She let loose with an ear-piercing whistle and was rewarded with a thunderous bark. The cockpit door opened, and Murphy, the 120-pound German shepherd, had both paws on Kathryn's shoulders. Kathryn squeezed him so tight the big dog yelped, then quieted down.

Kathryn did her best to settle her jangling nerves. Murphy, sensing things weren't quite right, hugged her side, his huge body quivering with anxiety. She knew in her heart, her mind, her gut, that if there was anyone standing outside the plane door barring her run to freedom, she would, with the aid of Murphy, kill them on the spot.

The door opened, and the only person standing to the side on the gangway was a man in a lime green vest, one of the airline employees.

God in heaven, she was really here! She was. For just a moment, she felt dizzy with the knowledge. Then she was moving forward, Murphy at her side, up the jetway and out to the area where she had to go through Customs.

With nothing to declare except her purse and Murphy's papers, she hopped from one foot to the other while another man in a bright orange vest checked her through. He squinted at the huge dog at Kathryn's side, at his papers, used the Micromax Scanner Kathryn handed him and checked Murphy's ISO microchip, then nodded that she could be on her way. She knew Bert was somewhere behind her but she didn't care. Off she went, following the signs. She'd memorized the details Bert had given her on where they were to meet up with Nikki and Jack. Her eyes were like ricocheting bullets as she raked the various signs that would take her and Murphy to where the couple was waiting.

Suddenly, Murphy stopped short, his head

went up, and a long sigh escaped his lips. He let out with a monster bark but didn't move. He barked again. People turned to stare, smile, frown, and moved on.

Kathryn heard her name being shouted, and she started to run, Murphy galloping along at her side.

"Kathryn!"

"Nikki!"

Then they were holding on to each other for dear life, hugging, squeezing, and crying all at the same time. Murphy whined and growled playfully until Nikki dropped to her knees in the middle of the concourse to hug him. The big dog nuzzled and pawed her.

"I have to take him out to pee. Can we get back in? Do we have time?"

"Yes and yes. Myra chartered a plane for us. We aren't flying commercial, so we have all the time in the world. We just have to go through security again, that's all. Oh, God, Kathryn, it is so good to see you. We *need* to talk. Where's Bert?"

"Ask someone who cares. Which way, Nikki?"

"Follow me. I've been up and down and around this airport so many times I lost count. We've been waiting four hours for you to get here. I assume your relationship is about the same as mine is with Jack. We were such fools, Kathryn. How could we have been so stupid?"

"We were in love. And the guys were greedy. I think that sums it up, at least for me," Kathryn said.

"Past tense?"

"Yeah, for now. This is how I look at it, Nikki: I was robbed of a year and a half of my life. That bullshit about not being able to leave, the phones that didn't work, all of it made me sick. Look how easy it was all of a sudden. We're in England! We're almost home. I had so many nightmares, I thought I would go out of my mind. I think I was out of my mind. What about you?"

Nikki linked her arm with Kathryn's as they headed to the door that would lead them outside. "You know what, Kathryn, I was packing to leave when Jack roared into the house and said we were going home. I was leaving him. I was going to go to the embassy and ask them to get me home. I'm still not sure what's going on."

Murphy strained at his leash as he headed to a trash can and lifted his leg.

Then they were back inside and headed toward the gate, where Nikki said a private charter waited for them. "It's burning fuel as we speak. Myra said not to worry — the only thing that was important was getting aboard and heading back across the pond. We'll be back in the States in six hours, and an hour from that time, we'll be at the farm, where the others are waiting for us. Annie said we are going to *partieeeee* big-time. By the way, Isabelle is winging her way north from Miami. She skedaddled, too. Must be something in the air." Nikki giggled nervously.

"Nikki, what the hell is going on?"

"I don't know. I don't think Jack knows, either. What about Bert?"

"Bert is like a clam. All those years at the FBI. Everything with him is NTK. I guess he thought I didn't need to know when I *did* need to know. I didn't marry him, Nikki. I kept remembering that promise I made to Alan. I just couldn't do it. I'm not sorry, either. How do you like being Mrs. Jack Emery?"

"It had its moments. There they are. Let's save anything else we want to share until we get *home.* I wish we'd never gotten those damn pardons," Nikki blurted.

"Yeah. I've had nightmares over that, too."

The two women came to a stop in front of Jack and Bert. Both of their expressions were full of anger and hostility. Murphy, picking up on their mood, growled.

"Why are you looking at us like we're the enemy?" Jack said.

"Because you are!" Kathryn said.

"We can discuss all of this later. We have a plane waiting for us. I know the way, so let's just get out of here." There was no lilt in Nikki's voice, but there was grim determination as she whirled around to head toward the plane waiting on the tarmac.

Nikki and Kathryn, Murphy between them, set off, Jack and Bert directly behind them as they literally sprinted down the concourse to an EXIT sign that led them out a jetway and down a set of movable stairs to where a Gulfstream waited. They bounded up a second set of movable stairs, Murphy in the lead. He sniffed the captain, the co-captain, and the two hostesses who were waiting to welcome them. Then he turned, the hair on the back of his neck standing on end. He let loose with a mind-bending howl that brought the foursome on the stairway to a stop.

"Something's not right." Kathryn leaned in closer to Nikki so she could hear better over the roar of the jet's whining engine. "I knew it was too good to be true. Thank God for Murphy."

Still growling, the fur on the back of his neck staying on end, Murphy tried to force his mistress back down the stairs. It wasn't a hard sell on the dog's part or Kathryn's.

"Change of plans, boys," Kathryn said as she took the steps downward, two at a time, Nikki behind her. They raced to the door they'd just exited.

Jack and Bert looked up at the confused expressions on the pilot's and hostesses' faces. "The lady called it, change of plans." Without another word, they, too, galloped down the stairway and raced to the door Nikki and Kathryn had just entered.

Inside, breathless, Jack demanded to know what was going on. "What? Ten minutes ago we were the enemy, you couldn't wait to get on that plane, then when you're almost there, you chicken out. What the hell is it with you two?"

Not to be left out, Bert weighed in. "Yeah, what the hell is it with you two?"

Kathryn turned, snarling as only Kathryn could snarl, and said, "I'll tell you what, Mr. Ex–FBI Director, Mr. Ex–Global Securities Slave, you and your buddy Jack get on that damn plane. Nikki, Murphy, and I will find our own way home, thank you very much."

"That means put up or shut up. I goddamn well dare the two of you to get on that plane!" Nikki shouted as she headed down the concourse. Where she was going, she had no idea. Kathryn and Murphy hugged her sides.

Jack looked at Bert, and Bert looked at Jack. Both of them said, "What the hell!" in unison.

"We going or staying?" Bert demanded. "I can't believe we're staying behind because that damn dog pitched a fit."

Jack bristled. "That damn dog, as you put it, has saved our asses on more than one occasion, and I'd put my money on him any day of the week. Something isn't right on that plane. For a charter flight no one but us and the flight crew should be aboard, and the crew were right there to be seen at the top of the stairway. With the way the light was shining on the window, I saw four more forms in the back of the plane. I saw them, but Murphy *smelled* them. Now are you getting it? It means, in case you're interested, those two women are smarter than we are on our best day, and this sure as hell isn't our best day. I wish Harry were here."

"What? I'm chopped liver? Why the hell didn't you say something, Jack?"

"As you constantly remind me, you're the brains of this outfit. Jellicoe went to you first. How come I'm the one that spotted the figures in the back and not you?"

"Well, you were still going to get on, Mr. Know-It-All. And you're taller than I am and blocked my view," Bert said defensively.

"Bullshit!" Jack said as he picked up his feet and sprinted after the two women. He almost laughed when Murphy turned around, saw him, and barked, a joyous sound to Jack's ears. He felt stupid when he offered the dog a thumbs-up, but he didn't care. Murphy barked again when Bert came abreast of him.

Murphy's world was right side up, at least for the moment.

Outside in the dismal gray weather, the foursome gathered under an overhang. "We can talk about this later. Right now we have to make a plan. In order to do that, we need a new phone so we can call home. I feel like E.T. right now. I don't trust any of the phones we have," Nikki said. "I think we need to find someone who is willing to part with their phone or at least let us use theirs to make some calls. How much cash do we have among us?"

"Two thousand," Jack said as he tallied up the money being shown him. Kathryn snatched the money in the blink of an eye. The others watched her as she approached an elderly lady huddled under a bright pink umbrella. She returned five minutes later minus a thousand dollars but plus one phone. "She said the pound is worth more than the dollar. I wasn't about to argue," Kathryn said, as she scanned the cell phone in her hand. "Okay, I think I know how this one works." She started pressing numbers.

"Who are you calling?" Bert asked.

Kathryn shot him a withering look. "I'm calling the only person who has the contacts and the chutzpah to get us out of whatever mess we're standing in."

"Oh, Charles," Jack said, relief ringing in his voice.

"Not likely! I'm calling Maggie Spritzer!" Murphy barked to show his approval. Nikki was grinning from ear to ear as Jack and Bert slunk off to the side, where both men lit up cigarettes.

Kathryn snapped the phone shut and said, "She's on it. She said this is right up Abner Tookus's alley, but it's going to cost. You heard me, I told her I didn't care how much it cost, just to get us home. You're okay with that, right, Nikki?"

"Absolutely. Did she give you a time frame?"

"She just said to sit tight and she'd get back to us as soon as possible. When I pressed her, she went out on a limb and said we should be airborne within three hours. What the hell are we going to do for three whole hours?"

An evil grin splashed across Nikki's face as she let her gaze wander to Jack and Bert. "How about we make their lives a little more miserable than they are already."

"I like that. Murphy likes it, too. See, he's grinning."

"You ever gonna marry Bert?"

"Nope."

"But you still love him?"

"Yep."

Nikki laughed. "Understood."

"God, I missed you and the others," Kathryn said, her eyes filling up.

"Not half as much as I missed you," Nikki said as she brushed at her eyes. "I can't believe we're actually going home."

"You know what I wish, Nikki? I wish we were headed back to the mountain. I know, I know. All we did was moan and groan when we were there, but we all had something back then. I was happy. So were you and the others. This . . . this . . ." Kathryn said, waving her arms about, "is not what it's cracked up to be. Can we get yesterday back, Nikki?"

Nikki draped her arm around Kathryn's shoulders. "I don't know, but we sure as hell can try, can't we?"

"Yeah, let's try," Kathryn said so quietly that Nikki had to strain to hear the words.

Chapter 10

A dazed expression on her face, Maggie left her office at the *Post* building at a fast run the minute she clicked off her cell phone. She stopped just long enough to snatch her secretary's cell phone, which was sitting on top of her desk. She put her finger to her lips to mean silence. All manner of thoughts were scurrying around inside her brain as she made her way to the busy twenty-four-hour corner deli that was always jammed to the rafters. Once inside she made her way to the kitchen and then out the door to a Dumpster-packed area. She looked upward, knowing but not really understanding the stuff about cell phone towers, satellite imagery, bouncing signals, and all that went with tracking calls and numbers. Call her a Neanderthal, but she still preferred her little tape recorder and her notebook and pencil. She absolutely detested cell phones and texting because it meant she could never hide out. With all the new technology, she always had to be available, and, in her opinion, that sucked big-time. She pressed in a number and waited to be connected. Knowing she didn't have time to finesse her friend, Maggie got right to the point. "I need you to do something for me, and I need it ten minutes ago. We can negotiate later; now is not the time. If you don't do what I want, I'm turning you in to the FBI, the CIA, and every other crazy-ass initials organization in this fine city. Are we on the same page, Abner?" Abner Tookus was Maggie's one-of-a-kind hacker, bar none.

"Whatever you say, Maggie," the man responded meekly.

The hairs on the back of Maggie's neck stirred. She looked upward. Surely, they, whoever *they* were, hadn't gotten to Abner. "Why are you being so nice and agreeable all of a sudden?"

Maggie heard Abner's sigh. "Because you are by far my best customer, you pay on time, and I know I can't win, so I'm agreeing right off the bat. Whatcha want, friend?"

Still suspicious, Maggie sought just the right words. When none were forthcoming, she blurted out what she needed.

"Well, that takes the cake! I'm a hacker, Maggie. I do not exactly travel in the Gulfstream circles of the rich and famous. What? You think I carry a list of owners in my pocket?"

Maggie ignored him. "So, how long is it going to take you?"

Maggie heard the sigh again. "Twenty minutes if I'm lucky."

"Twenty minutes!" Maggie screeched.

"Okay, maybe seventeen. I'm hitting the keys as we speak."

"Fifteen and you get a bonus. Don't ask me what the bonus is. I have to confer with the owner of the paper. I have to hang up — I don't want anyone tracking this call. I'm calling you back in fifteen minutes, so be prepared to rattle off my instructions. You got that, Abner?"

"I do. I really do. Hang up, or you're dead meat."

Maggie snapped the cell shut and looked down at her watch. A second later she had pen and notepad in hand as she watched the digital mechanism on her watch count down the minutes.

She tapped her foot, finger-combed her unruly curls, checked the contents of her bag, kicked away some debris from where she was standing, and was dismayed to see only two minutes had gone by. A family of scrawny cats circled the Dumpster in search of food. She whipped through the door leading to the kitchen, where she demanded a mountain of food to be loaded into a cardboard container. She plopped down three ten-dollar bills and whipped back through the door. She set the food down and watched as the cats did their best to devour it all. A glance at her watch told her she'd used up six minutes. "Crap!" she said succinctly. When the last contented feline waddled off, Maggie picked up the containers and threw them into the Dumpster. She'd used up another minute and a half.

Maggie paced up and down the small enclosed area a dozen or more times as she waited for the time to pass. With nothing better to do, she did some stretches and knee bends. God, how she hated exercising. Her watch told her she had seven minutes to go. Screw the seven minutes. She yanked at the cell phone and punched in the numbers. "I want it *now!*"

"Ask and you shall receive," Abner said sweetly. "You got a pen?"

"Of course I have a pen, you nitwit!" Maggie scribbled furiously in her and Ted's shorthand. "Got it!"

"I want a bonus on top of the bonus for coming in seven minutes earlier than the time I quoted you."

"And you think I care what you want? Stop by the paper later, and I'll pay up. Hey, Abby, thanks."

"You got it, sweet cheeks. Remember now, a bonus on top of the bonus."

"Yeah, yeah," Maggie mumbled as she powered down. She raced back through the kitchen and out of the deli. She waited a full minute, then powered up again. In seconds, she had Kathryn on the line. She rattled off the information from her notes and again powered down, at which point she dropped her secretary's phone on the sidewalk and stomped on it. No one paid the slightest bit of attention to what she was doing. As she raced back to the *Post,* she dropped bits and pieces of the mangled phone into various trash cans along the way. She knew her secretary was going to pitch a fit, but hopefully a top-of-the-line, new whatever was on the market would appease her. Hopefully.

With the speed at which she was sprinting, Maggie ran right past the place she was looking for. She turned around and ran into the small Internet café, paid for time, and settled herself at the computer, then she e-mailed Charles using the special encrypted code he'd given her previously. She took a second to wonder if the code was uncrackable, for want of a better term. That done, she leaned back in the chair and let her breath out in a long sigh. Well, she'd done her best. From here on in, the others had to fend for themselves. Finally, she logged off, left the café, and walked sedately back to the *Post.*

It was pouring rain when Kathryn walked back into the terminal with Murphy, who was busily shaking the water from his coat. She marched up to the others, who were waiting, and said, "We're good to go. Maggie's friend got us a ride all the way to Washington. But there is a hitch. Maggie said our ride is a luxurious Gulfstream, privately owned by a small group of businessmen who travel this way once or twice a week. There will be three or four other passengers on board, possibly more, presumably the owners, but they are willing to accommodate us for a sizable remuneration. She said she took care of that, compliments of the *Post.* For all intents and purposes, should the other passengers ask, we're foreign correspondents. The plane is boarding as we speak. Yes or no?"

"Let's go!" Nikki said as she beelined around milling passengers to the gate that would take them outdoors in the rain to board the plane.

Drenched to the skin, the foursome and Murphy bounded up the steps of the plane, where three hostesses handed out fluffy white towels as they personally apologized for the downpour.

"You're to sit in the front; the owners are in conference at the back, and they asked that you do not disturb them," a pert redhead said as she showed them to their seats. More fresh towels were handed out as a second hostess poured champagne.

"It's luxurious, but Annie's Gulfstream is nicer," Nikki sniffed as she sat down in a comfortable chair and buckled up.

"I could get used to this real quick," Kathryn said as she toweled her wet hair. "Ah, someone turned on some heat. This is heavenly."

Bert and Jack just sat looking like old-fashioned cigar store Indians. The women continued to jabber to each other, ignoring both men. Murphy was already asleep at Kathryn's feet.

The third hostess approached and said in a musical voice, "We'll be serving dinner when we reach a cruising altitude. Take a moment to look over the menu and check off what you would like."

"Yep, I could get used to this real quick,"

Kathryn said a second time.

"Did Maggie happen to mention the name of the company that owns this plane?" Bert asked.

"She just said a small group of businessmen. Why, is it important?" Kathryn asked.

"It could be."

"Pretty damn convenient the way this worked out, if you want my opinion," Jack said. Three blank faces stared at him. "I'm just saying."

"What does that mean, Jack?" Nikki said, twirling around in her chair. Her voice was neither friendly nor unfriendly.

"What it means is, we passed on the other plane because people were on board and yet here we are on this plane, commandeered by Maggie, with people on board. I just find it a little strange, considering our current circumstances, the way this is working out."

"We didn't get on the other plane because Murphy was letting us know something was wrong. If you noticed, he did not alert us on this one and is now sleeping peacefully here at Kathryn's feet." Nikki's voice was decidedly unfriendly.

The pert redhead approached to take their wineglasses. "Buckle up," she said.

Bert wagged a finger. "Miss, who does this

plane belong to? Do you know?"

The hostess in turn wagged a finger at Bert and offered up a gamine grin just as the plane started to taxi down the runway. "But of course I know. I work for the company. The owners are sitting in the back."

"And that would be . . . ?" Bert asked, smiling. The smile didn't reach his eyes.

The redhead giggled. "HLJ Enterprises. We're based here in London."

They were in the air and climbing when Bert opened his briefcase and yanked out what looked like a small business directory. "Son of a bitch!"

"I knew it!" Jack growled.

"Knew what?" Kathryn and Nikki asked as one.

"HLJ stands for Henry Lawrence Jellicoe. HLJ Enterprises is a subsidiary of Global Securities." There was a bite to Bert's tone that none of them had ever heard before.

Kathryn's eyes were wild as she stared at Bert. Nikki reached out to clutch at Kathryn's arm. "What exactly does that mean, Bert? You know how I feel about coincidence. There is no such thing."

Her eyes blazing, Nikki unbuckled her seat belt and moved forward. She braced herself against a chair, leaned down just as all three hostesses warned her to get back in her seat until the pilot announced they were at cruising altitude. "Yes, yes, but where exactly is this plane going?"

The three women offered up blank stares. "Don't you know where you're going?" the pert redhead asked.

"Let's put it this way, I know where I'm *supposed* to be going, but I'd like some confirmation that I'm right. Where is this plane headed?"

"Your nation's capital. Washington, D.C. Dulles Airport, to be exact. We have some good tailwinds, so we might even arrive twenty to thirty minutes early. Please, go back to your seat and fasten your seat belt." The hostess's voice was so firm that there was nothing for Nikki to do but retreat.

Buckled up, she leaned forward. "At least we're going to Washington — Dulles, to be precise. Unless she was lying. She said we might get in early because of good tailwinds." Three glum faces stared at her. Nikki shrugged. "There is nothing we can do until we land, so we might as well settle in."

Jack and Bert twirled their comfortable chairs around until they were facing each other. They leaned forward, talking softly. Nikki and Kathryn did the same thing.

"So, Kathryn, just out of curiosity, how *fit* are you these days?"

"Top form, my friend. All I did for the past year and a half was exercise, swim, and exercise even more. And, of course, I ate right. I found a book on martial arts at one of the bazaars. I taught myself a little and perfected what Yoko and Harry taught us." Kathryn's eyes narrowed when she said, "Are you asking me what I think you're asking me? How about you?"

"I think it's safe to say I can hold my own . . . against . . . let us say, three hostesses, and if appearances are correct, those aging, balding, fat-around-the-middle men in the back. But to answer your question, I'm fit. I think Harry and Yoko both would walk away huffing and puffing if they took me on. I know they'd win, but I'd give them a fight they'd never forget. They've been practicing practically from the day they were born, and you and I had to learn the art of self-defense. You know, Kathryn, even though my nerves are twanging, Murphy is sleeping peacefully. He's not sensing any trouble, for whatever that's worth."

"Let me tell you exactly what *that's* worth. I had to tranquilize Murphy. He's going to sleep all the way across the Atlantic. It was one of the conditions to get him the okay to fly out of the country. I have a ream of paperwork with his name on it."

"Damn," Nikki said.

Thirty silent minutes went by before the hostesses prepared to serve dinner, a delectable concoction of crab, shrimp, lobster, and filet mignon. One of the hostesses poured wine, another poured coffee, and the third served the actual dinner on fine china.

"It looks good, smells good, but suddenly I seem to have lost my appetite," Jack said as he played with his sat phone, a holdover from back in the day when he was in contact with Charles Martin on a daily basis. He had refused to give it up and had charged it during the wait at Heathrow. Nikki had done the same thing as she looked guiltily at him. Then she had turned defensive, and said, "I'm charging this phone because once it's working, I will truly know I am headed home. Why are you doing it, Jack?" His own tone had been just as defensive when he said, "For the same damn reason you are." And that had been the end of that. In the blink of an eye, the sat phone was shoved under his thigh. No sense advertising anything until the current situation became a little more clear.

The moment the hostesses moved to the

rear of the plane with their linen-covered serving cart, Nikki whispered, "I don't think we should eat this food, and don't drink the coffee, either. I watched the blonde uncork the wine, so I think that's safe to drink. Or water, anything that's been sealed." The others nodded to show they understood. Murphy continued to sleep peacefully at Kathryn's feet.

A quarter of the way into their flight time, the hostesses prepared to clear away the dishes and the uneaten food. None of them made a comment about the untouched dinners. Minutes later, they returned with a platter of cheese, crackers, and a mound of grapes of all colors.

"We have several new movies. Are you interested?" one of the hostesses asked. The foursome shook their heads. The hostess shrugged and moved back to her station behind the dark blue curtain, leaving the foursome to their own devices.

They were facing each other now, Murphy between them. Jack ground his thigh into the sat phone to reassure himself that it was still there. His head was buzzing like a beehive. He looked over at Bert, who looked as if he was in a trance. Nikki and Kathryn sat stiffly in their chairs, but Jack just knew that every nerve in their bodies was twanging like an out-of-control banjo at a country and western sing-along. "If anything is going to happen, it's going to happen real soon."

"This might be a good time to share your thoughts, Jack," Kathryn hissed. "Tell us how you arrived at this prescient conclusion."

"How's this for starters?" Bert said. "The redhead carried six dinners back there. I counted them. But there are only five guys sitting at the table. So, unless one has been in the lavatory all this time —"

"Or someone wanted two dinners," Nikki interrupted. When Jack offered her a withering look, Nikki bit down on her lip. She was angry at herself that Bert had picked up on something she'd missed. Kathryn looked angrier than a hornet. Obviously, she had missed the sixth plate, too.

Jack squirmed in his seat, his hand reaching for the sat phone under his thigh when he felt the air stir and circle the chair where he was sitting. He swiveled around, and said, "I do believe our hosts . . . are they still our hosts if the *Post* paid for us . . . are headed our way." He swiveled back around and surreptitiously snapped open the phone. He pressed number one for Harry Wong. "C'mon, c'mon, you dumb shit, answer the phone," he murmured to himself. He listened as the phone continued to ring. Finally, on the seventh ring, Jack heard Harry identify himself. "Harry," he hissed, "listen up, we're being *hijacked!*"

"Huh? Jesus, Jack, is that you?"

"Harry, listen to me, this is not shits and giggles. We're being fucking hijacked. You gotta do something, buddy."

Back in Washington, Harry's eyes did their best to widen. "Jack! Where the hell are you?"

Harry strained to hear whatever Jack was going to say next. But all he heard was a strange voice with a strong accent say, "I'll take that phone now, Mr. Emery."

Chapter 11

Maggie and Ted Robinson exited one of Washington's popular watering holes just as Maggie's phone chirped in her pocket. She pulled it out and said, "What's up, Harry? You never call me." She listened, her face turning white. Ted reached out a long arm to catch her as she stumbled. "Slow down, Harry, I can't understand a thing you're saying. Okay, okay. Stop jabbering in whatever language that is." She listened, then said, "Oh, *shITTT!* Are you sure Jack wasn't playing a joke on you?"

Ted started dancing around, waving his arms and mouthing, "What? What?" Maggie just waved her arms the same way. She ignored him, but her color was coming back, which was a good thing.

"We're on our way, Harry. Sit tight."

Before Ted could ask again, Maggie was hitting her speed dial. "Just listen, and I won't have to repeat this. . . . Listen to me,

Abner Tookus, I am personally going to hunt you down and castrate you. I might kill you first or not, I haven't decided. And I'm canceling that check I gave you. Do you hear me, you . . . you . . . *hacker?* What do you mean, what am I talking about? I'm talking about that airplane you got my friends a ride on. It's being hijacked as we speak. You better say something now, Abner. I paid out good money from the *Post* for that ride home for my friends. The owner is not going to like this, Abner. What do you mean, why am I blaming you? I'm damn well blaming you because you're the one who got the plane. It belongs to HLJ Enterprises, that's why. It's a subsidiary of Global Securities and belongs to Hank Jellicoe!"

"And that's supposed to mean something to me?" Abner screeched.

"Well, yeah, you dumb cluck. . . . No, I am not going to the FBI; hell, they can't find their way in the dark even with a Maglite. You better find out where that damn plane is, get hold of the pilot or someone else aboard, or your ass is grass. I will hunt you down and skin you alive. Now hang up and call me when you have news, and it better be soon. I hate you, Abner Tookus."

Ted stopped his furious dancing and

threw his hands up in the air. "Shit!"

Maggie was already at the curb, trying to flag down a taxi. Ted had to run to catch up with her and literally fell into the cab as it was moving away from the curb. Maggie gave the address of Harry's *dojo,* then said, "Burn rubber!" Like the Pakistani driver really knew what it meant to burn rubber. The stars were definitely not aligned right today.

"Jesus, this is unbelievable, Maggie. What can we do?"

"I don't know, Ted. I've never been involved in a hijacking. I don't think you or I ever covered anything like that, either. I have never heard Harry so agitated, and I know full well that I barely got a quarter of what he was saying because he was jabbering away in several different languages. I can't believe this, Ted; they were on their way home. Home!"

"Shouldn't we be calling Charles?"

"Probably, but Harry called me first, so there has to be a reason why he didn't call Charles. Maybe it has something to do with Charles being friends with Hank Jellicoe. I don't know, Ted, I'm just talking to hear myself. Where are Espinosa and Alexis?"

"Probably in the sack, where they spend most of their time. All they think about is sex," Ted said pointedly.

"That's more than I needed to know, Ted. How can you think about sex at a time like this, anyway? Tell them to get on the stick and meet us at Harry's. I'm going to call Lizzie right now."

"I think we need to alert Charles," Ted said stubbornly.

"Well, I don't, and I'm the boss. Where's Isabelle? Did she get in yet?"

"How the hell am I supposed to know that, Maggie?" Ted said, his fingers flying over the keys as he fired off a terse text message to Espinosa and one to Alexis.

"I don't understand why they would hijack Bert, Jack, and the girls," Ted grumbled. "Why?"

"How about maybe because whoever the hijackers are, they want to sweat Bert and Jack to get information? Like I said, I don't know, Ted, I'm just guessing."

"These things never end well," Ted mumbled.

"No, they don't. Shut up now, I have to talk to Lizzie."

Maggie quickly outlined the situation to Lizzie the moment she heard the lawyer's voice. "I don't know what to do, Lizzie. We're on our way to Harry's *dojo* now. No, we didn't call the farm. Why? I guess because if Jack could make only one call, he chose to call Harry instead of Charles. To me, that has to mean something. What it means, though, I have no idea. Now that you're in the loop, see if you can come up with anything. I vaguely recall your saying you could always get in touch with Jellicoe if need be. This might be a good time to put that statement to the test. I'll get back to you. When we go out to the farm, which I'm sure we will at some point, I'll call Elias, since he used to be the director of the FBI, and see what he has to say. Isabelle is back! Good. I wasn't sure. She's at the farm! Even better. Stay in touch. Yeah, I'm just sick over this, too, Lizzie."

Maggie powered down and glared at Ted. "Well?"

"They're on their way to Harry's." Ted pointed to the taxi driver, his eyes questioning.

"He's listening to some kind of Pakistani music, can't you see his earbuds? Okay, we're here. Pay the driver, Ted."

Ted shoved some bills under the Plexiglas and bailed out of the cab, with Maggie on his heels. They ran around the corner of the building to the back door of the *dojo.* Maggie didn't know what to expect but what she saw certainly wasn't anything near what she could have thought about. Yoko was on her knees next to Harry, her arms around his shoulders, tears rolling down her cheeks. Harry was sitting on one of the practice mats hugging his knees and wailing, a high-pitched sound that sent shivers up Maggie's arms and down Ted's spine.

"Enough histrionics already! They aren't going to get us anywhere. Up and at 'em, Harry. We need to talk," Maggie bellowed at the top of her lungs.

Yoko leaped to her feet. With Ted's help, Harry was upright a second later. His eyes were glazed, but they slowly started to focus. Ted snapped his fingers a few times until Harry had had enough and knocked his hand out of the way. Espinosa and Alexis took that moment to arrive, along with six students from the police academy. Ted made short work of them and said they should call to find out when their class was rescheduled. He locked the door and made his way back to the workout room.

Maggie took the floor. "This is where we pool our knowledge. This is what we know for certain. The flight the gang was supposed to take didn't sit well with Kathryn's dog. He balked at getting on the plane, and through the window Bert saw people at the back of the plane. It was a private Gulfstream, and no passengers were supposed to be on the flight other than our guys. They bailed, went back inside the terminal, and called me. Jack seemed to think it was a setup of some kind. I thought he was being overly paranoid, but I called a friend who managed to get another private Gulfstream, but we had to pay to get the guys on board, which we did. The flight originated at Heathrow and was . . . is supposed to land at Dulles. If my calculations are correct, they're halfway into the flight. Which means we have another two to two and a half hours till they land. *If* they land. The plane is registered and owned by HLJ Enterprises, which is a subsidiary of Global Securities. In other words, your previous employer, Hank Jellicoe. Lizzie told me Isabelle is out at the farm, so we're all present and accounted for except for Bert, Kathryn, Nikki, and Jack. It's your turn, Harry."

Harry shrugged. "The phone rang, I picked it up, and it was Jack. I could tell he was talking softly, almost whispering. He said, 'Harry, listen up, we're being hijacked.' I was so happy to hear his voice. I thought he was playing a joke. Then he said, 'Harry, listen to me, this is not shits and giggles. We're being hijacked. You gotta do something, buddy.' I said, 'Jack! Where the hell are you?' He didn't answer me. The next thing I heard was a voice saying, 'I'll take that phone now, Mr. Emery.' The voice had an accent. I'm not sure what it was or from where, but it was definitely not an English-sounding voice. That's it."

"Was that verbatim?" Ted asked.

"Word for word. The words are seared into my brain. Why the hell would anyone want to hijack Bert and Jack? That whole damn episode with Global was nothing more than . . . I don't know what it was, but it sure as hell wasn't legitimate. So we quit, so what? So Jack and Bert quit. So what? People take jobs and quit all the time. Why them?"

"Do any of you care to hear my opinion?" Yoko asked quietly.

"Well, good God, yes, Yoko," Alexis said. "I think I know what you're going to say before you say it, but go ahead."

"They didn't hijack Bert and Jack. Well, they did, but they were really hijacking Nikki and Kathryn. There, I said it. Go ahead and laugh at me if you want to."

"You don't see any of us laughing, do you, Yoko? That's exactly what I was going to say, which just goes to prove my point. When Jellicoe offered up all those fabulous jobs to the boys, then split them all up, it was to get rid of the vigilantes. I don't know the why of it, but I think all of us pretty much think the same thing."

"Then we have to figure out the *why* of it," Maggie said. "If you give me a few minutes to call the paper and make some arrangements, we can all head out to Myra's. I think this is one of those times when we all need to be present when we discuss it. Besides, I want to observe Charles when we break the news. Everyone in agreement?" They all raised their hands.

"Why do I feel like I'm in the seventh grade again?" Ted grumbled.

"Because you're stupid, that's why," Harry said. Ted didn't bother to stand up for himself. He was just glad Harry was back to being the old Harry.

Maggie finished making her calls and looked around. "Transportation?"

"You and Ted go with me and Alexis. Harry and Yoko on the Ducati. Problem solved," Espinosa said.

Mother-hen Maggie said, "Anyone have to go to the bathroom? It's a fifty-minute ride out to the farm." Five pairs of disgusted eyes clearly stated that bathroom necessities were not paramount and urged Maggie to hurry along, which she did.

Harry locked up, picked up his and Yoko's

helmets, and they were on the way.

Seventy miles away as the crow flies, Annie was carrying a bag of trash out to the huge can near the electronic gate. She heard the roar of Harry's Ducati before she saw him blaze down the driveway. Directly behind him, she saw a flashy red car hot on his trail. Company. She did love company.

Yoko slid off the rear end of the cycle and ran to Annie. She was breathless when she said, "Nikki, Kathryn, Bert, and Jack have been hijacked! In a plane! At thirty thousand feet! Jack got a call off to Harry. That's why we're all here. We have to do something!"

Annie's eyes sparked. A hostage situation! God in heaven! Her adrenaline kicked in as she gathered her little group and shooed them all indoors.

Isabelle leaped up from the table and ran to the group to hug and kiss everyone. While they all billed and cooed, Annie shared Yoko's news with Myra and Charles.

"That can't be!" Myra wailed. "Why would someone hijack our people?"

"You need to get with the program, Myra. Whatever this is all about, I am certain that it has something to do with that Jellicoe person who did his best to make all our lives so miserable for the past year and a half."

Her tone turned sour when she said, "And remember, he obviously thought that you and I were no threat to him and whatever he was doing. You do remember that, don't you, Myra dear?"

"What do you think, Charles?" Annie asked as she looked at Charles, her gaze filled with shooting daggers.

Charles held Annie's gaze, but he didn't fail to notice how the others moved back a step. "To be honest, Annie, I don't know what to think. I'd like to get on this immediately if you are all in agreement. If not, say so. Has it occurred to any of you that we should be calling the authorities?"

"Well, yeah, Charles," Maggie drawled. "My question to you is, has it occurred to you that Jack called Harry? I have to assume if Jack got a call off, Bert could just as easily have called the FBI. Or you. Jack called Harry for a reason. That's why we're all here. I think I speak for the others when I say we'd like you to find out all you can about Hank Jellicoe, where he is, how that plane came to be at the right place at just the right moment, etc., etc., etc."

"Then I will get right on it."

"Whose side are you on, Charles? Hank Jellicoe's or the vigilantes?" Isabelle suddenly demanded.

"I'm going to ignore that question and believe that you are tired and cranky due to your long trip. I would also like to say if you have to ask me that question, one of us doesn't belong here."

"I just wanted to be sure. There's something I haven't told all of you," Isabelle said as she massaged her temples, trying to ward off the headache she knew would surface in just moments.

"What's wrong, dear?" Myra said, reaching out to Isabelle. "Tell us so we can help you. You're so pale. Annie, get some brandy."

"The headaches, the visions, are back. Remember how they started after I had that horrible accident and how I had them when we all first met? They started back up several days ago. They scared me. That was why I packed up and left as soon as Stu went off to do whatever it is he does. I knew something was going to happen. I saw Nikki and Jack on the plane. I saw other things, too. Oh, God, I'm getting another one!"

The others watched, their startled faces full of questions as Isabelle pressed at her temples, moaning softly as she slumped in the kitchen chair.

CHAPTER 12

Charles Martin skirted the dining room and made his way to the formal living room and the one-of-a-kind ageless bookshelves that a master craftsman had built long before Charles was even a twinkle in his mother's eye. He stood still for a few seconds to admire the carved roses that ran down the side of the cases. He counted down and pressed the center of the correct rose. He waited patiently for the humongous shelf to silently glide inward. He still marveled, even to this day, that the authorities had never found the catacombs and his and the vigilantes' war room, from which they had conducted business for so long.

Charles descended the long flight of stone steps, whose risers were covered with moss. In the beginning, they had made concerted efforts to get rid of the moss, all to no avail. Myra finally said to leave it; it belonged to this place and the long-ago time when her ancestors had participated in the Underground Railroad.

Eons ago, his and Myra's daughter Barbara and Nikki Quinn, their adopted daughter, had played down here. He and Myra had strung bells every few feet to make sure the girls never got lost. Somehow or other, they never did. He smiled at the memory. He touched one of the clusters now and was rewarded with a sound so pure, so melodious, it was hard to fathom how that could still be after all these years. Another one of those little mysteries in life that would probably go unanswered until the end of time.

Charles opened the door to the huge climate-controlled room and switched on every light. There were so many memories here. He swallowed hard as he looked at the round oak table and the chairs so neatly placed. He blinked as he recalled the seating arrangement. Julia was gone now, their only casualty. He closed his eyes and offered up a prayer for the repose of her soul. He knew for a fact that the girls did the same thing whenever they entered the room. He knew this because Myra had told him.

What had started out as a small group — the Sisterhood or the vigilantes, depending on who was describing them — had been small. Now their numbers, out of necessity, had increased, all to the better, in their fight to right injustice and save those they could. They'd operated in this fortress for longer than he cared to remember. There were good days, bad days, good times, and some not so good times, but the Sisterhood had prevailed.

Charles pulled out Myra's chair and sat down. His legs were wobbly, his eyes burning. For the first time in his life, he didn't know what to do. He raised his eyes to the ceiling. The girls were expecting him to perform a miracle. He knew his limitations, and the problem now facing him and the Sisters was so far above his pay grade that he wanted to bellow to the gods to help him. After all, he was just a mortal. Yes, he was skilled in covert espionage, yes, he had people at his disposal, and yes, he had unlimited financial reserves to draw on, but what he didn't have was the ability to stop a midair hijacking.

Charles's thoughts were scattered, but he always came back to the same spot, which was that the hijacking was a hoax. Why had Jack Emery called Harry Wong instead of him? In his dark thoughts, it didn't compute. Unless . . . Harry was number one on Jack's speed dial. Or he'd misdialed. Then again, maybe it was a clue of some sort, and he wasn't getting it. Obviously, Harry hadn't gotten it, either.

Who would want to hijack Bert, Jack, Nikki, and Kathryn? Who? And why would they be hijacked in the first place? Who and why? Well, he was never going to figure it out if he kept sitting here with his dark thoughts. When he felt certain that his legs would hold him upright, Charles got to his feet, settled Myra's chair back in place, then climbed the three steps that would take him to the wall covered with computers. He flipped a switch, and bells and whistles sounded. It was comforting. *This* he understood. *This* he could deal with. Because it was his world, a world he understood. He closed his eyes, shifted mental gears, and went to work, his fingers tapping coded messages at what seemed like the speed of light.

Almost instantly, encrypted messages were returned. There were more bells and whistles, more buzzing and papers flying out of the fax machine. When his sat phone chirped, Charles reached for it like a lifeline. "Snowden here, Sir Malcolm."

"Let's dispense with the formalities, Avery. I'm Charles Martin. Sir Malcolm belongs to that long-ago world we all left behind us. Now, tell me your thoughts."

"It's only been minutes, Charles. I have the lads on it. I'm going to need at least an hour before I can report anything concrete or nebulous, as the case may be. The only thing I can tell you with any certainty is that the plane does belong to HLJ Enterprises and it is headed to Dulles Airport in Washington, D.C. I have the best air-trackers in the world on it. They still have two hours of flight time to go. That's not to say they can't change course and land somewhere else, pleading mechanical problems. It takes time, Charles. The lads won't let us down, you know that."

"It's not making any sense, Avery."

"Of course it makes sense, Charles, you just don't want to accept the fact that your old buddy could suddenly be on the wrong end of things. That whole retirement thing and Jellicoe turning his global business over to people he barely knew never made sense to either one of us. I don't want to hear that old ditty that money is the most powerful motivator in the world, either. Hank Jellicoe isn't interested in money. He probably has almost as much money as Anna de Silva. No, I think it's safe to say it is something else entirely."

"Hank went dark over a year and a half ago," Charles said, using a covert term to indicate that Hank Jellicoe had disappeared. "When you go off the grid like that, it has to be something *BIG*. Especially for someone like Jellicoe."

Snowden's voice turned testy when he said, "Well, Charles, nothing earth-shattering has happened in the last year and a half, so what you're saying isn't quite holding up in my eyes. If Jellicoe suddenly became an active player and went to ground, why hasn't there been any chatter that we've picked up on? I grant you the guy is good, but he isn't *that* good. We have people placed all over; someone would have kicked something to us by now. Have you given any thought to maybe this is all *personal* on his part? Maybe the man is sick. Have you given that a thought?"

"I know the man. In my opinion, it's not personal. He's not sick, either. Actually, he's probably in better health than both of us put together. He did admit to high cholesterol that's under control, along with fifty percent of the world's population, but that's it. He also told me he bought a million shares of Pfizer when Lipitor first came out, and he still owns every single share. Hank is all about God, country, and the American way. He'd give up his life if he thought it would help the country."

"Okayyy," Snowden drawled. "How do you explain his very public engagement to the president of the United States on the night she handed out the pardons to your ladies? He gets engaged to the most visible, important person in the world, gives her a diamond ring big enough to be a headlight, then he goes off the grid? Not another word. Is he still engaged? Is he in contact with his fiancée? No one knows. Maybe the guy finally cracked. It happens, Charles. We've both seen it."

"I can't explain it, but I have someone on it. What about the passenger list — how soon before you can get the names of the people on board?"

"Momentarily. A fiver will get you a ten spot that they're all John Smiths or Bill Joneses or something similar."

"That's a sucker bet. No, thanks." There was no point in saying it, but he said it anyway. "Get back to me the minute you know something."

Charles looked across the room at the bank of clocks that gave the time all over the world. He tapped a few times on the computer and saw that the Gulfstream owned by HLJ Enterprises still had an hour and forty minutes of airtime until it landed at Dulles. *If* it landed there.

Charles let his mind wander as he contemplated how Jack and Bert would handle a hijacking. He knew Nikki and Kathryn were more than capable of taking on their hijackers given the chance. If he was a betting man, he'd put his money on the girls, but then Bert and Jack had gone to what Hank called his *boot camp,* where such things were taught around the clock, and either you washed out or you passed the course with flying colors, because Hank Jellicoe would accept nothing less. Which brought still another thought to mind. He tapped quickly and asked the question, Where do private Gulfstream owners get their hostesses? Are they private employees, or do they hire them from a central booking agency? He had his two-word answer within minutes: private employees. That had to mean they were on Jellicoe's payroll. A package deal of some kind. Men and women who were on call whenever the Gulfstream took to the air. They were probably well compensated to sit idly by waiting for the owner to decide that the plane needed to fly somewhere.

Now who would have a list of Jellicoe's employees? In a heartbeat, he had Ted Robinson on the line. "Do you have Jellicoe's roster of employees, Ted?"

"I do. Why do you ask?" Ted's voice

sharpened as he waited for Charles's response.

"Under Global Securities, did you happen to come across the names of the airline hostesses he uses? Also the pilots. How many Gulfstreams does the mother company own? Can you get back to me as soon as possible on this?"

"How about right now? There are ten hostesses on the payroll. He has ten pilots and ten copilots. They have five Gulfstreams, three Blackhawk helicopters, and four regulation whirlybirds. They rotate on a weekly basis. I did a whole section on that for the news magazine Jellicoe wanted done. Twenty-four pages of glossy, good-looking men and women all duded up in spiffy uniforms. There was even a section devoted to the five-star gourmet meals served to clients."

"I need names, Ted."

" 'Thank you, Ted,' " Ted sniped. "They're on the way to you. Look at your computer. Anything else you want to pick my brain about?"

"Sorry, Ted," Charles said contritely. "It's just that —"

"I know, I know. Good luck. Hey, I have the addresses and phone numbers of all those guys if you want them. I can download them, and you'll have them in minutes," Ted volunteered.

"Yes, yes, of course. Thank you."

"Don't mention it," Ted said.

Ted was as good as his word. Like magic, the names, addresses, and cell phone numbers appeared on Charles's computer screen. In the blink of an eye, they were on their way to Avery Snowden. Like any of Jellicoe's employees would willingly give up information on their savior. Still, Avery Snowden and his people had a way with reluctant people who clammed up.

Charles spent the next forty minutes perusing the incoming faxes and printed e-mails, his gaze going to the bank of clocks every few seconds. He was hyperaware of the fact Avery Snowden had not returned his call.

The thick bundle of papers in hand, Charles headed for the exit into the catacombs just as his sat phone rang. He listened carefully to what Snowden was telling him.

"Aside from your four people, there are six passengers aboard the Gulfstream, not five. The sixth passenger has no name. Pierre Laroux, Ambrose Fallon, Mitchell Blakely, Fergus Duffy, and Ari Gold."

Charles sucked in his breath and let it out

with a loud swoosh. He had to struggle to make his tongue work. "The Sûreté, MI5, Interpol, Scotland Yard, and Mossad. It's not a hijacking, Avery, it's an intervention. They don't want Jack and Bert, they want Nikki and Kathryn. That plane will land on time at Dulles, those men will disappear, and I'll wager that our sixth man is Henry Lawrence Jellicoe himself. I want . . ."

"I have people on the way. You want to know where the five go, how they get spirited out, then you want your people taken to the farm. How am I doing so far, Charles?"

"Splendidly."

"Guess that's why you pay me the big bucks, eh?"

When Charles closed his sat phone, he was back to being wobbly in the legs, and he was definitely having trouble breathing. He sat down on the stone steps as relief flooded through his body. So much to think about. Now that he knew the *who,* all he had to do was figure out the *why* of it all. He reached out and gave the string of bells at the foot of the stone steps a gentle tap. He closed his eyes at the clear purity of the sound before he got up and made his way to the main part of the old farmhouse. At least now he wouldn't be reporting dire things to the people waiting to hear what he'd come up with.

CHAPTER 13

"Who were you calling, Mr. Emery?" a squat fire hydrant of a balding man asked cheerfully. "Never mind, I can figure it out myself."

Jack watched as the fire hydrant peered down at the device in his hand, then frowned as he pressed button after button with no readout forthcoming.

"Knock yourself out," Jack snarled.

"Trust me, I will. By the way, just for the record, this plane is not being hijacked, as you so erroneously reported to your mystery caller. Actually, my colleagues here and I have gone out of our way to accommodate you and see that you arrive safely back in your homeland. Reporting a hijacking that is not taking place could earn you some serious prison time, Mr. Emery. It's a federal offense in your country, I understand, to report a hijacking if there is no hijacking going on. That's assuming you care." The fire hydrant waved his arms expansively. "As I said, we accommodated you in the short window of time for a tenth of what it would have cost you to fly even privately on another charter or commercially. We served you a fine gourmet meal, champagne, and excellent coffee along with quality after-dinner mints. We have the latest movies on board, the latest newspapers and magazines to make your trip as enjoyable as possible. Why, we even allowed Ms. Lucas's dog on board. I call that hospitality at its finest.

"I came forward to invite Miss Quinn, oh, excuse me, Mrs. Emery, and Ms. Lucas to join me and the others in the back for a . . . little chat."

"Why?" Bert demanded.

"NTK, Mr. Navarro. So, ladies, are you agreeable to joining me and my companions for a little chat? Our hostess has prepared fresh coffee, and we have some excellent hundred-year-old brandy to give it a little kick."

Nikki looked at Kathryn, who simply shrugged.

"Wait a minute. Why aren't Bert and I included in your *little chat?*" Jack demanded.

"Because it isn't necessary, and we do not require your input. At this time. Let me stress again, you are not being hijacked. In a little less than two hours, this plane will set down at Dulles Airport, you will disembark, go through Customs, and be on your way. Hopefully, you will consider this just a fond memory and thank us for getting you safely to your homeland. If not . . . oh, well. Oh, one other thing. Don't do something stupid like trying to insist on joining us."

The fire hydrant stepped back as Nikki and Kathryn rose to their feet. He waved them forward.

"Is that guy who I think he is?" Jack hissed to Bert.

"If you mean Ari Gold, second-in-command to the Israeli prime minister, then, yeah, you're right," Bert said. "You want to make a little bet here, Jack, that we can figure out who those other guys are in the next few minutes?"

"I'm not really up on all that high-profile stuff, and I've never met any of those guys the way you have when you were the director of the FBI, but I think the tall, suave, good-looking guy is Pierre something or other from France."

"Laroux," Bert said.

"Laroux," Jack repeated. "The one who looks like he has a broom up his butt is Ambrose Fallon, the stuffy-looking, bookish guy is Mitch Blakely, and the redheaded guy is Fergus Duffy. How am I doing, Bert?"

Bert sucked in his breath. "You got it nailed, Jack. The Sûreté, MI5, Interpol, Scotland Yard, and Mossad. All on the same plane. Now that had to take some doing." His voice was so full of awe, Jack blinked, but he had to agree. Something *BIG* was going on here that he and Bert weren't going to be privy to. He felt insulted.

"A hell of a lot of doing, my friend. Then there is the guy behind the screen, the sixth guy. It's got to be Hank Jellicoe. I'd bet my life on it," Jack said.

"But why?" Bert demanded.

"Obviously, it's not about you and me, that's for sure. It's about them," Jack said, jerking his head in the direction of the round table in the back. "This is just a guess on my part, but I don't think it's just about Kathryn and Nikki, either. I think it's about the *vigilantes.*"

"Now that we know who our hosts are, why are we whispering? It's a given this plane is bugged from top to bottom. We're the dumb-asses here, Jack."

"Nikki said from the git-go it was about the vigilantes, scattering them to the four corners of the globe. She was right, I see it now, but I have to admit, I was blinded back in the beginning. How naive we were to think it was about us and what we considered our capabilities."

Bert chewed on his lower lip. "Jack, in the back of this plane are five, six if we're right, and it is Jellicoe, of the most powerful men in the world. The only person missing is the head of the CIA. Ask yourself why that is. It can't be because she's a woman, can it? What in the damn hell is going on? Why isn't the good old U. S. of A. represented here?"

"Beats the shit out of me, unless the four of us are the good old U. S. of A.'s contingent, and I find that hard to believe. I have a headache, Bert. This headache is going to turn into a nightmare any second now. I can feel it, smell it, taste it. Since the head of the CIA isn't on this plane, maybe it concerns her. Did you give that a thought?"

"Oh, yeah. It's just another *why.* But according to Gold, who seems to be the spokesperson for that posse back there, this was a spur-of-the-moment endeavor. These guys can apparently just pick up and go wherever they want, without any opposition. But so can the director of the CIA, I would guess. So, yeah, I think in some way the CIA is involved in this somehow, some way. What the hell are they talking about, anyway?" Bert said, craning his neck in the direction of the round table surrounded by people in the back of the plane. "Looks pretty intense to me, whatever it is."

"Guess that sixth man is still hiding behind the screen. No movement there? I wish Harry were here. Between us, we could have taken those guys and been drinking champagne while we watched them struggle with whatever we would have tied them up with," Jack said morosely.

"What? I'm chopped liver? Are you saying the two of us, with the girls' help, couldn't take out those guys?"

There was such outrage in Bert's voice, Jack winced. "Yeah, that's what I'm saying. We're good, Bert, don't get me wrong, but Harry . . . Harry is a horse of a whole other color."

"You're probably right." Bert's outrage was gone, replaced with acceptance of his abilities, which was that he was not a one-man army the way Harry Wong was.

"Whatever it is they're trying to sell to the girls, it seems to be a hard sell," Jack said.

Bert snorted. "Kathryn will not bend an inch if she thinks she's right. I learned that the hard way."

"Yeah, Nikki is like that, too. Hell, all the girls are like that, even Myra and Annie.

Charles told me once he learned never to go up against Myra for the very same reason. I guess that's why the girls are like sisters. That's not a bad thing, Bert. At least I don't think it is.

"Listen, there's something else," Jack said, lowering his voice to a whisper and speaking directly into Bert's ear. "Nikki has a hate on for Hank Jellicoe that has no equal. Before this is all over and done with, whatever the hell *this* is, the girls are going to pound that guy's ass so far into the ground, he will never see the light of day again." Now that he was wound up, Jack continued, "Think about every ugly, hateful, vicious punishment those women have doled out over the years in their time as the vigilantes, then multiply that by about ten, and that's what that asshole Hank Jellicoe is looking at once they get their collective mitts on him. The best part is, the guy doesn't even know it's coming his way."

He started to laugh and couldn't stop. When Bert finally digested all that Jack had said, he slapped his knees and doubled over, guffawing out loud.

In the back of the plane, the men seated at the table looked toward the front of the plane, startled expressions on their faces as Bert and Jack continued to laugh and pound each other on the back.

Nikki and Kathryn smiled expansively. The men's startled expressions turned decidedly uneasy as Scotland Yard's Fergus Duffy pressed a small button on his watch that would allow Jack's and Bert's words, before they were consumed with laughter, to play into their earbuds.

The expansive smile stayed on Nikki's face because she was almost certain she knew what Jack and Bert were discussing. "Tell us, gentlemen, what can my friend Kathryn and I do for you? I'd thank you for the accommodations, but we paid for them, so the point is moot. This appears to be your party, so let's get on with it."

Kathryn leaned forward. "Not so fast, Nikki. Don't we want *all* our hosts seated here at the table for the party? A party isn't a party unless everyone is seated at the table. Anything less is rude, don't you think?"

Nikki feigned embarrassment. "You're right, Kathryn, silly me. Of course we want everyone present so there can be no 'he said, she said,' later on." She eyeballed the man who had introduced himself as Mitchell Blakely. Nikki's voice turned arctic. "Get him out here *now,* gentlemen, or this party just fizzled out."

When nothing happened, Kathryn turned her chair around and stood up. She yawned elaborately, then said, "Party's over, Nikki."

The elaborate, decorative screen Annie would have called tacky moved slightly, and a man stepped forward and took his seat close to the table. The others moved slightly to accommodate him.

"And you would be . . . ?" Nikki said pleasantly.

The voice was gruff, a mixture of molasses and hard whiskey. "Whoever you want me to be. Names aren't important at thirty thousand feet."

"As a disguise," Kathryn said, "yours, Mr. Jellicoe, sucks. You look like a bad white imitation of Bob Marley. Those dreadlocks are not becoming. And I see you've put on a little weight since we last met. What did you use to stain your skin?" Not bothering to wait for a response, she continued. "Probably walnut juice. I want it known right here and now that my partner and I, and of course the other . . . ah . . . vigilantes, hate your guts. Now would be a good time to say something before we rejoin our mates up front.

"You look surprised, Mr. Jellicoe, that we recognized you. We're experts on disguises, even with plastic surgery, or did you forget that? Latex is something else, isn't it? In the blink of an eye, latex can transform a person to someone totally different. Add in a bushel of deep, dark hatred, and what we have right here, in front of our very own eyes, is . . . *you,*" Kathryn said. "I think I can smell your chagrin from where I'm seated. Right now, Mr. Jellicoe, you look like a man who lost his mojo, and that is not a good thing. Oh, and none of us care if you can do the *New York Times* crossword puzzle *in ink* or not."

Nikki watched the others seated at the table out of the corner of her eye. They, too, appeared stunned at Kathryn's denunciation of Hank Jellicoe. She knew exactly what the men were thinking — these women are as good as their reputation. She felt pleased with the thought. She glanced over at Kathryn, who was smiling from ear to ear. She felt a grin coming on that she couldn't stifle.

"Is something amusing, ladies?" Ambrose Fallon asked. Kathryn's smile grew wider at the jittery sound of the man's question. She almost out and out laughed when she saw a nervous tic in Hank Jellicoe's left eye.

"Well, yes, now that you ask, but you must allow us ladies our little secrets." Kathryn's smile disappeared as did Nikki's ear-to-ear grin. Her voice returned to steel. "Let's get on with it. Why are you here, and what do you want from us? The short version will do."

"We need your help. All of us here have tried for the past year and a half to get to the bottom of a very serious problem, and as much as we hate to admit it, we have . . . failed. Not only have we failed, we failed miserably," Ari Gold said. Honesty and humiliation rang in his tortured voice. "In addition, by way of explaining our failure, we listened to Mr. Jellicoe because he said he could control you. By you, I mean the vigilantes. We know now that has not been the case."

Kathryn and Nikki allowed themselves to chuckle over the man's humiliating admission.

"Let me get this straight, just so there is no confusion on our part. The Sûreté, MI5, Interpol, Scotland Yard, and Mossad have collectively failed in a united effort of some sort. Ooops, I forgot to mention the most prestigious organization of all, Global Securities, the premier security operation in the entire world, if you believe the man himself." Nikki sniffed. "Personally, I never believed the man's press; he's too damn arrogant for my taste. That makes you all a bunch of fools. Don't you agree, Kathryn?"

"I absolutely do, Nikki. But then, what do

I know? I'm just some dumb woman he wanted to get rid of. How do you feel about that, Nikki?"

"I don't like it one little bit. Okay, you're up, Jellicoe. Why are you here, and what is it you want from us? You had better make it good, because you only get one shot at an explanation." Nikki looked at her watch. "If the pilot is right, we have about one hour of flight time left, so it behooves you to make this quick. If you want to confer among yourselves, Kathryn and I will rejoin our companions and return when you've come to a decision."

CHAPTER 14

"That won't be necessary, Mrs. Emery. As you so accurately pointed out, time is of the essence," Ambrose Fallon said in a clipped British accent.

Nikki took pleasure in seeing the sheen of perspiration on the head of MI5's forehead as the air-conditioning was so cold she was shivering. She watched, as did Kathryn, as the man's gaze went around the table, finally settling on Fergus Duffy, the head of Scotland Yard. The group's spokesperson, she decided. She risked a glance at Hank Jellicoe and was more than pleased to see the war going on in his eyes. For all intents and purposes, it appeared that one Hank Jellicoe had been relegated to the number six position on the totem pole.

"We're listening," Kathryn said coldly.

Fergus Duffy, who looked like he could be the world's grandfather, cleared his throat. "A while back — eighteen months ago, to be exact — we picked up on some chatter that did not bode well for your current president and her administration. When we as a group, and I am including Mr. Jellicoe in the group, went to your CIA, they professed not to have heard the chatter. As a group, we found that a little hard to believe. To our credit, again as a group, we didn't sweep it under the rug. We pursued the matter. Mr. Jellicoe, to *his* credit, agreed to put his life on hold and to go *deep,* as the saying goes. But I'm getting ahead of myself here. We, the group, met in secret, and it was Mr. Jellicoe who feared that you . . . *ladies* . . . would somehow find out and take matters into your own hands. He said we couldn't risk that happening."

"Find out what?" Nikki said.

"Before I answer that question, I want to refresh your memory on a few matters. You do recall that the current administration back in the beginning was plagued with problems. First, it was the vice president, then it was key positions occupied by people who had their own agendas. Every day there was a resignation, a new appointee, until we, as a group, started to get nervous. When we get nervous, the world gets nervous. It got to the point where your own president didn't know whom she could trust. That's when she implored your friend Elizabeth Fox to help her, which Ms. Fox did.

"President Connor granted your pardons against all advice, and in doing so made quite a few enemies in her own administration. As you both know, the lady is a woman of her word. So she held out, and today you are free women. I don't think there's any need for us to go into the president's personal relationship with Mr. Jellicoe. It is what it is."

"Fine, fine, we know all this, so what is your point here?" Kathryn asked irritably.

"The point is . . . your CIA is denying that there is a problem, which is why the director of that organization is not among those briefing you here, when in actuality there is a very *big* problem facing your president. Someone is planning to kill her. I can't be any more explicit than that. Your Department of Homeland Security is following the lead of your CIA, which is remarkable on the face of it, leading us to believe there is a mole in either the CIA or DHS, possibly both. All your alphabet agencies in Washington like to act independently and not tell each other what is going on. Our countries have a good relationship with your new president, and we'd like to keep it that way. Our organizations, on the other hand, do not have a similar regard for your CIA. If your people continue to ignore what is going on, great harm can and will befall President Connor."

Nikki grimaced. "Eighteen months have gone by, Mr. Duffy. Nothing has happened to our president. Have you considered the fact that maybe the chatter you heard was just that, someone expounding out of frustration or more likely stirring the pot so you all got your knickers in a knot?"

"Actually, we did consider it, but we all, as individual agencies, came to the same conclusion. The chatter, the source, was legitimate. Mr. Jellicoe went to President Connor and apprised her of what we all thought was going to happen. She in turn raised all kinds of merry hell with the CIA and DHS. All that did was alert them to the fact that we were onto something. Hence the delay or lack of activity. Which translated means they're lying low. As I said, Mr. Jellicoe, with our approval, decided to take action because we *knew* President Connor's next move would be to contact you via Elizabeth Fox.

"None of us had any doubt that you vigilantes would ferret out the mole and take care of him or her, as the case might be, but taking out the mole wasn't important enough by itself to allow you to do so. We need to neutralize the cell, the organization, and you ladies, according to Mr. Jellicoe, are not equipped to take on a mission of that sort. It goes without saying that we no longer agree with him."

Nikki looked at Kathryn and burst out laughing.

"Really!" was all Kathryn said. Fergus Duffy and the others had the good grace to look embarrassed, which only made Nikki and Kathryn laugh even more.

When Nikki was finally able to catch her breath, she said, "So here we are, eighteen months later, and you're right back at your starting point." She fixed her icy stare on Hank Jellicoe and said, "You decided to play God with our lives. You separated us all, you made it impossible for us to be in touch, you paid outrageous sums of money when all you had to do was talk to us. You robbed us all of eighteen months of our lives, and I, for one, am never, ever going to forget that, Mr. Jellicoe. You are now on my radar screen, and I feel confident enough to speak for my fellow Sisters when I say you are now officially a target for the vigilantes. Normally, we do not issue a warning. We simply act. I want to be clear on that in case any of you have a problem with what I just said."

Five hands waved in dismissal, which meant that none of the group originally at the table had any problem with Nikki's words. Jellicoe simply glared at both women.

"I couldn't take the chance you'd screw it up. Women don't belong in this business; it's too dangerous. I was actually trying to protect you. Why can't you see that?" he said coldly.

"Because we don't think with a dick like you do," Kathryn snarled. "You really need to get over yourself, Mr. Jellicoe. I feel confident enough right this minute when I say I think we could have settled the matter eighteen months ago. Instead, here we are, cruising at however many feet, and you are sitting there with your tail between your legs. Do you mind telling us what went wrong? And then I think it's time for *someone* to tell us what it is you want from us. Like *NOW!*"

Ari Gold took the floor. "Mr. Jellicoe, with all his connections, decided to infiltrate an organization he thought was the source. He arranged to get all of you as far away from Washington as was humanly possible, and it's obvious he succeeded. He had some plastic surgery, dyed his skin, as you so aptly pointed out, and went to ground in the hopes of ferreting out our mole. All of us created a dossier of this bad boy with millions on his head, meaning Mr. Jellicoe. We had him covered eight ways to Sunday. It didn't work. Eighteen months later, he's come up with dry hole after dry hole. If all of you hadn't chosen to mutiny when you did, we'd still be chasing our tails. None of us are proud of our current situation. I also want to make it clear right now, this very second, that Mr. Jellicoe implored us to prevent your escapes from happening. He wanted you detained at various airports, but we refused. We are now taking matters back into our own hands, where they should have been from the beginning. Which then brings me to your question at hand. What do we want from you?"

"I can't wait to hear," Kathryn said sourly. Nikki nodded.

"We want to hire you. All of us," Ari said sternly. "Oh, one other thing — you can all forget about repaying Global Securities the monies Jellicoe paid out to you. You owe him nothing. You keep your bonuses, because we all contributed to them. None of us want you to think he was that generous. Name your price, and it's yours. We are not prepared to quibble."

Nikki leaned closer to the table. "You want

to hire the vigilantes to . . . I assume, ferret out the mole who is either at the CIA or Homeland Security. We're free agents today, thanks to our pardons. Why would you even think we'd give that up to help you?"

"Because we will guarantee no harm will come to you in that respect. You will be bona fide secret agents working for us to help your president."

The Frenchman from the Sûreté spoke. "If you so much as get a traffic ticket, all you have to do is make one phone call, and it never happened. As you Americans like to say, we have your back, your front, and everything in between covered. Are you interested?"

Nikki was so interested she wanted to leap across the table and hug the man with the lovely accent. She sensed the excitement in Kathryn and decided to play it cool. "We might be. 'Might' is the operative word here. If, and I want to stress the *if,* we decide to help you, we would of course want proper paperwork drawn up by Elizabeth Fox. We will need to confer among ourselves as to remuneration. I have to warn you, the fee will be so far outside the box and over the top you might want to reconsider your offer."

Five of the six dismissed the comment as

though Nikki were discussing the price of lettuce.

"Where does that *schmuck* fit into all of this?" Kathryn asked.

"I am not familiar with the term, Miss Lucas," the man from Interpol said.

"Jellicoe, the son of a bitch sitting right there, the idiot who is responsible for all of this, that *schmuck.*"

"Ah, I see. An advisor, nothing more. He had his chance, and he failed. You should consider him as someone you used to know."

Kathryn laughed. Nikki thought it was the most evil sound she'd ever heard in her life. She grinned from ear to ear. To make her point, she got up from the table, walked around to where Hank Jellicoe was sitting, and leaned down. "First rule, Mr. Jellicoe, never let someone tower over you, especially a woman. From this moment on, you are number one on the vigilante hit list. The time and place has yet to be determined. You can run, you can hide, but we *will* find you."

Nikki turned to look at the others. "Will your blanket immunity cover such a thing, gentlemen? Think carefully before you answer."

There was not a moment's hesitation.

"Absolutely," came the reply.

Kathryn allowed herself a small giggle. She looked up at Nikki and laughed out loud. "See how easy that was? We'll need at least thirty-six hours before we give you our answer. How do we get in touch with you?"

Ari Gold tossed Kathryn a burn phone and said, "Power up and hit the number one and I'll be on the other end, no matter the time of day or night."

"The payment would have to be in advance. No one trusts the Swiss anymore," Nikki said.

"Understood. If you agree to sign on, it will take at least forty-eight hours to transfer the fee to wherever you want it."

"You do understand that if we agree to sign on, as you put it, we will need time for Ms. Fox to handle matters for us. I would think, if we agree to help you, five days from today you will hear from us one way or the other. Do you find that acceptable?"

Five heads nodded affirmatively.

Kathryn stood up. "The red light is on. That means we're getting ready to make our descent." It was all Kathryn could do not to burst out laughing when she saw Nikki wag her finger under Hank Jellicoe's nose and whisper loudly enough for everyone to hear but still low enough to be menacing. "Remember, Mr. Jellicoe, you're *ours!*"

On the way back to their seats in the front of the plane, Kathryn whispered, "Those guys hate his guts, did you notice?"

"Oh, yeah, I noticed. But no one can hate that man as much as I do. Having said that, I think we're in business again, Kathryn."

"What was your first clue?"

Nikki grinned. "Damn, I feel good!"

"Not half as good as I do," Kathryn said.

The moment Jack, Bert, Nikki, and Kathryn stepped onto the tarmac, a groggy Murphy next to them, the portable stairs were wheeled away and the door to the plane closed. Wind from the powerful jets made conversation impossible, but each of them knew what the other was screaming as they ran toward the barricade that would allow them access to the Dulles terminal. *They aren't getting off; they're heading right back. No one can prove they were ever here.*

Inside, the women smoothed down their hair, shrugged their clothing into place, and looked at one another. With no one about at this hour except maintenance crews and a few airline personnel, Nikki leaned against the wall and started to cry. "I cannot believe I'm here. I'm home. I think this is the happiest day of my life."

Kathryn rushed to Nikki and clung to her. "I thought this day would never come." She leaned closer and whispered in Nikki's ear, "I'm going to find a way to kill that son of a bitch with or without your help. Just so you know."

"Not if I get to him first," Nikki whispered in return.

Jack felt the fine hairs on the back of his neck stand to attention when he saw the expressions on the two women's faces. He mentally thanked God he wasn't going to be the recipient of whatever they'd be planning. He sneaked a glance at Bert, who appeared to be on his wavelength. "Let's get this show on the road," he said gruffly. "The sooner we get through Customs, the sooner we can be on our way to the farm. It should be quick and easy, with no baggage and nothing to declare."

Thirty minutes later, Jack found himself airborne. And then, in a heartbeat, he was being smothered by one Harry Wong.

"I'm feeling the love, Harry. You can stop hugging me. Ahhh, you aren't going to kiss me, are you? Shit, Harry, now for sure people will talk. Christ alone knows how I missed you, buddy. Ahhh, Harry, I didn't know you knew how to cry," Jack said, wiping his own eyes with the sleeve of his shirt.

"You ever make a call like that to me again and you'll be with your ancestors wherever they are. Good to see you, Jack," Harry said formally as he bowed, to the others' amusement. Jack bowed back, and the two hugged again, this time with a few manly slaps to the back and one more bone-crushing hug. The others smiled at this blatant show of affection between the two old friends.

"What's new, Harry?" Bert chirped.

Harry rolled his eyes, which was no easy feat. "There's got to be a hundred people around who were just waiting to see if the plane really was going to land. The odds weren't good until thirty minutes ago. What the hell is going on?"

"You know what, Harry, we're here safe and sound. I'd kind of like to wait till we get to the farm so I don't have to explain it all again. Thanks for being here." Jack's eyes misted over again. He had never felt so loved, so cared about by anyone, not even by Nikki, than he did right this minute, with Harry's arm around his shoulder. This, he decided, was what having a brother was all about. Obviously, Harry was of the same mind-set because he gave Jack's shoulder a hard squeeze.

Yessireee, there was no place like home with friends who cared enough about you to go to the mat for you, no questions asked and no thanks expected.

Outside the terminal, the foursome looked around, huge smiles on their faces as people, strangers, high-fived them, smiled, some said "welcome home," others offered a quick clap on the back. Charles's people. It was beyond comforting to know that his back, along with those of his companions, was being covered.

"Your ride!" Harry said, his arms waving every which way as a stretch limousine slid gracefully to the curb. "I'll see you at the farm, Jack." He pecked the girls on their cheeks and shook Bert's hand before he ran in the direction of the parking lot, where he'd left his Ducati. There was no doubt in Jack's mind that Harry would arrive way ahead of the limo. Still, there was a possibility Harry would feel duty-bound to escort the limo out to the farm. Jack negated that thought the moment it surfaced in his brain. He grinned when he saw his best friend in the whole world do a hop, skip, and a fast two-step before he danced out of sight.

Squeals, laughter, and tears were the order of the day when Jack finally settled himself next to Nikki in the limousine. He reached for her hand, and she squeezed it.

"I know I said this a dozen times, but I

don't care. I am sooo happy to be home. God, there is nothing in my life that has ever felt as good as this moment," Nikki said.

"Hear! Hear!" Kathryn said as she uncorked a bottle of champagne that all limousines seemed to come equipped with. A ripe discussion ensued as Kathryn poured the bubbly.

"*What* should we toast?"

"*Who* should we toast? Or, is that *whom* should we toast?"

"The world, Mom and Dad, apple pie, hot dogs, the Redskins?"

"Nikki held her glass aloft. "This toast has to mean something. Really mean something."

Instead of deferring to her husband, Nikki looked over at Kathryn.

Kathryn raised her glass and said, "To Hank Jellicoe and our impossible dream that is now possible. Is that profound or what?"

Nikki smiled. "It is definitely profound, Kathryn." Murphy took that moment to let loose with a sharp bark of approval before he lay back down and went to sleep.

"That's all I need by way of approval," Kathryn said as she sipped from her glass of bubbly.

Jack and Bert looked nonplussed but had the good sense not to ask questions as Nikki continued to smile.

CHAPTER 15

"What do you mean, ladies only?" Jack demanded irritably. "I'm your husband, Nikki. Harry is Yoko's husband. We should be able to sit in on the conference. And what about Bert, Ted, and Espinosa? What are we, chopped liver? For years you all said we were members of this elite group. What's wrong with this picture?"

"Well, *dear,* that was back in the day when we were an elite little group before you guys screwed it up, and now you have to take responsibility for your actions. Furthermore, we are no longer the vigilantes. That ended with our pardons and your screwup. Need I say more?" Nikki asked.

"Hell, yes, you need to say more. What about us?" Jack demanded, waving his arm about to indicate the scowling faces of Bert, Harry, Ted, and Espinosa.

"We voted, and it was seven to one to exclude you from this meeting," Kathryn said coldly.

Ted swallowed hard and voiced an opinion with a nudge from Bert. "Yeah, well, what about Maggie? She isn't a bona fide vigilante. She's the EIC of the paper. How come she gets to sit in?"

Maggie waved her hand, the left hand with her engagement ring. "Do not go there, Ted."

Another nudge, this one harder by Jack, caused Ted to sputter, his face turning red. He started to wave his hands around like a maniac. "Yeah, yeah, but who do you call when you need something taken care of? Us, that's who. If we aren't good enough to sit in, then we aren't good enough to follow your orders! Right, guys?"

A lot of mumbling started to take place.

"Like I said, we voted, and for now you are excluded from this meeting. Now toddle off so we can get down to business," Kathryn ordered.

It was a dismissal, pure and simple. Blustering and growling, the men slammed their way through the kitchen door to an elevated terrace, where cool drinks, compliments of Charles, waited for them.

Charles offered up a pitying look, shrugging before he turned on his heel to follow the women to the underground war room.

His parting shot caused all four men to cringe. "They're right, you know. This is all your fault. Personally, I'm surprised that all of you haven't been dismembered and found floating in the Potomac."

"Well, that damn well sucks," Jack said.

Harry kicked out at one of the iron chairs resting under a huge umbrella. The heavy chair flew across the terrace. "Charles is right. It is your fault, Jack. Yours, too, Bert. You convinced the three of us to . . . how shall I put it . . . sign on for a dream of a lifetime. My ass, Jack. This has been a nightmare. And those women down below are going to make us pay and pay, then pay some more for those eighteen months. When they're done making us pay is when they're going to kill us. You listening to me, Jack?"

"Of course I'm listening. So is half the world. Let's be clear on something. Neither Bert nor I twisted your arm. We did not conk you on the head to follow us. We presented an opportunity that at the time seemed to be unequaled. Look, he conned us all. We went into it with our eyes wide open, so don't go blaming me and Bert for your own greed. I'm willing to take a fifth of the blame, but that's all. Kathryn was right, we're each responsible for our own actions. Let me be the first to say this out loud. I do not know how to make this right with the girls. As you know, they are not the most forgiving of women."

"You had to say that, didn't you, Jack?" Harry said, kicking out at another chair.

Espinosa, who rarely voiced an opinion, voiced one now. "I say we lie low and fall back and regroup. Sooner or later, the girls will come around. They need us," he finished up lamely.

Four sets of eyes zeroed in on Espinosa. "No, Espinosa, they don't need us. We convinced ourselves that we're needed, but we're all delusional. What the hell planet are you living on?" Jack demanded.

Espinosa stood firm, which was also unusual.

"Do you know something we don't know?" Ted asked craftily.

"No, but I know women. I have a lot of sisters. I know how their minds work. They will need us at some point. That's when we all have to decide if we want to join up again or go back to our less-than-exciting lives. I, for one, plan on joining up. You want to kill me, go for it."

"Crap!" Bert said succinctly.

"So we just sit here and twiddle our thumbs?" Ted muttered.

"Unless you have a better idea," Jack muttered in return.

"What do you think they're going to do?" Harry asked, his voice sounding anxious. "Damn, they're free now, they can do whatever they want, go wherever they want. If they revert to vigilante status, it's all over."

"Not if they have blanket immunity," Bert said. "Five bucks says that is exactly what they're going to do. Jesus, did you see Annie's face? She couldn't wait to go down to that war room to stir things up. Hell, all of them were so excited, I almost blacked out. We are toast, gentlemen."

"You're an asshole, Bert. I don't see that happening," Jack said, but there was no conviction in his voice.

"I hate lemonade," Harry said. "I'm going to make some tea. Anyone want some?"

"I don't think Myra keeps that shitty green stuff you drink, Harry," Jack said.

Harry rummaged in his pocket and brought out a little string bag that he carried with him for situations such as this. A moment later they heard the screen door bang shut. Ten minutes later, Harry was back with a cup of steaming hot tea. "Did you talk about me while I was gone?"

"You aren't worth talking about, Harry, so get over yourself," Ted said.

"What should we talk about?" Espinosa said as he propped his feet up on the terrace railing.

"Lizzie Fox is flying in today. I think that means something. As in the girls are actually considering the offer from those intelligence and law-enforcement agencies. When someone offers unlimited compensation, as in name your own price with no quibbling, then offers blanket immunity on top of that, then yes, I think they have just about made up their minds to go back into business," Jack said. "By the way, did I tell you my old boss offered me my job back when I called him to say I was back in town? I told him I had to think about it."

"I talked to Elias Cummings early this morning, and he told me that the guy who replaced me as director of the FBI is not loved and adored and said it was another mistake Martine Connor made. Elias said this new guy is just like Elias's predecessor, Mitch Riley, the guy the girls took down way back when. Elias said this new twit, that's what he called him, a twit, has his own agenda, and it's called, 'Hey, look at me, I'm the director of the FBI.' His people do not like him."

"And that means what?" Jack asked.

"Probably nothing," Bert said morosely.

"I'm not used to sitting around doing nothing. I need a job. Women do not like men who sit around on their asses doing nothing while they, those women, are going full bore. You guys have any suggestions?" When there was no response, Bert said, "Yeah, that's what I thought. Maybe I'll look into setting up in private practice. You want to partner up, Jack?"

Jack eyed a fat squirrel perched on the far railing of the terrace. Since Charles hadn't seen fit to leave a plate of biscuits or cookies, there were no crumbs to scatter for the squirrel. Jack thought that was a sad state of affairs. He looked over at Bert and said, "If it comes to that, I'll consider it. I have to warn you, I'd make a piss-poor defense attorney. I like the prosecutor's office.

"You know, I've been thinking. If the girls don't want to include us, why don't we all pack up and go west to my cabin? We could do some fishing, hang out, lie to each other, and cook hot dogs over a campfire. Our bonding has been torn asunder. We need to get back our old camaraderie. What do you say?"

" 'Torn asunder'? What the fuck does that mean? I hate you, Jack," Harry said.

"What the hell are they doing down there?" Ted demanded. When his question was met with silence, Ted slouched lower in his chair and closed his eyes.

In point of fact, what was going on *down there* was an argument that was about to rise to an incendiary level thanks to Kathryn and her take-no-prisoners attitude. Charles was doing his best to hold his temper in check, but it was a losing battle as his chicks, as he referred to the Sisters, lambasted him up one side and down the other.

"You can't possibly be serious, ladies!" Even to his own ears, his words came across as weak and ineffectual. One look at Myra's face told him all he needed to know. His chicks were deadly serious, and Myra was just as much so.

Charles tried another tack. "Give me one good reason, just one, that would make you throw away your lives when you were given a second chance. It can't be the money; there's enough here to last us all through several lifetimes. We all know not to fight for principle, because fighting for principle is a losing battle, and you never win. I don't care how many contracts those guys offer you or who signs them, when the devil wants his due, he wants it on his terms, and no contract is going to stand in the way even if Lizzie Fox is the one who draws up the contracts.

"Having said that, if the best of the best couldn't nail down the chatter, the cell, the organization, what makes you think *you* can do what he couldn't do? Name me one thing, one reason, just one." Charles's voice rose to a level just short of shrillness, a sound the Sisters had never heard from him.

A smug smile tugged at the corners of Isabelle's mouth. "Well, Charles," she drawled, "you seem to be the only person in this room who thinks and believes that Henry, *call me Hank,* Jellicoe is the best of the best. The man is addicted to himself. He really believes he can walk on water. He wants monuments built to his ego. That ain't gonna happen, Charles. We decided we want to eliminate him. We voted, and the vote was unanimous."

Charles looked around the table and had a hard time believing these were the same women who had chatted him up over the lunch that he'd prepared for them. Who were these hateful, angry women? "You can't possibly be serious. Hank Jellicoe is the most patriotic man in the world. He would donate his entire wealth, his life, if necessary, for the country he loves, and you're talking about *taking him out!* I cannot be a party to this. I simply cannot."

The Sisters looked at one another. Nikki picked up where Isabelle left off. "Hank Jellicoe is not the person you think he is. Oh, he might be an old friend, a drinking buddy, someone to shoot the breeze with every so often, but if he was all the things he professes to be, then he would have gotten whatever he claimed to be going after. He lost the respect of the men on the plane. When he stepped off the reservation, so to speak, he had a reason. At that time he also had the respect and the approval of the other intelligence and law-enforcement chiefs. As far back as then, he had to have known and was afraid of us as a group. That's why he separated us. The burning question is why?"

"I think you are flattering yourselves if you believe that," Charles said coolly.

"Is that what you think, Charles?" Kathryn shot back. "Well, aren't you going to be surprised when we take matters into our own hands and prove to you that Jellicoe isn't who he claims to be!"

"And just who do you think he is?" Charles demanded.

"An egomaniac who went off the rails," Annie said. "Don't forget for one minute that he, your patriotic friend, Hank Jellicoe, decided Myra and I were no threat to him. Yet he managed to screw up Myra's life so that she was virtually a prisoner here at the farm. And you along with her. I think he was more than a little concerned with you, Charles. I also think, and this is just a guess on my part, but I think Fish is just a little too close to Jellicoe, and he thought Fish was keeping me in line until I bolted. Which doesn't say much for Fish. I never did like his allegiance to Jellicoe, because I thought it was obsessive to the point he'd compromised himself."

"That's exactly what I thought about Stu, Annie," Isabelle said, excitement ringing in her voice. "By the time I managed to escape that hellhole in Paraguay, Stu and I weren't even speaking to one another. I seriously doubt we'll ever speak to one another again."

"Charles, ask yourself why your old friend wanted to separate us. What was he afraid we'd do? We didn't know about that supposed chatter he and the others were talking about. We were just going to go back to our normal lives until he stepped in and ruined them. Meaning our lives. What was he afraid of, Charles?" Alexis asked for the second time.

"You're blowing this all out of proportion," Charles said.

"No, Charles, *we* are not blowing this out of proportion. Perhaps you have forgotten about how miserable we were for the past eighteen months, but I haven't. If you want to bury your head in the sand, do so, but you will be there all by yourself. We are more than capable of making a decision as to what to do and then acting on it. If you'd like a show of hands to reinforce what I just said, say so now," Myra demanded with a bite in her voice that was strong enough to tear through bone.

Charles looked around at the grim faces staring at him. "Is that why you didn't want the boys down here for this meeting?"

"Well, yes, Charles, that is one of the reasons. Men are far too emotional in matters such as this," Yoko said quietly, so quietly that Charles had to strain to hear the words. "We need cool heads and a hundred percent agreement among ourselves. Ourselves, Charles, no one else."

Charles leaned back in his chair and crossed his arms over his chest. "Is that your way of saying if I don't agree to what all of you want, I'm to walk away? I want to make sure I understand what exactly is going on here."

"Bingo!" Kathryn snarled.

"Even if we manage to sway you to our way of thinking, I doubt we could trust you, Charles," Nikki said. "I never thought I would live to see the day when I would say something like that to you of all people." She looked pointedly at Myra to gauge her reaction to what she'd just said.

Myra didn't miss a beat. "Nikki is right. We won't be able to trust you."

Charles threw his hands in the air. "Why are you all being so bloody foolish? I understand your being angry for losing eighteen months of your lives. But to set out to ruin a man and his life's work because you all got your knickers in a knot is so far beneath the lot of you, I cannot fathom it."

"Well, fathom this, Charles. We have to start somewhere, and since it all started with Hank Jellicoe, that's our jumping-off point. We can't possibly help the men who want to engage our services with Jellicoe running around like some deranged maniac. We have to rein him in and take care of the problem. Once we do that, we can concentrate on the matter at hand and sign on to become . . . free agents," Kathryn said.

"And you're going to do this . . . how? No one was able to find Hank, not even me or our people. What makes you think *you* can find him?" Charles asked irritably, not liking where this conversation was going.

"Do ya think that maybe because we're women we can do it, dear?" Myra asked sweetly.

Charles bristled at his wife's tone. He knew he was dead in the water. "All right! All right! I can see there is nothing I can say to make any of you change your mind. I want to assure you that you *can* trust me. I swear on my Queen that I will not betray you. I swear on my Queen that I will do everything in my power to help and not hinder you in whatever you decide to do. I will be with you every step of the way."

"Is that the same Queen who gave you the boot and told you not to set foot on British soil ever again?" Kathryn shrilled.

"One and the same, dear girl. My allegiance to my Queen is forever, even with the boot. It is the same as it is to you and the others. I give you my word and my undying support."

It was Myra and Annie who looked skeptical at Charles's words.

"So, if you take me at my word and believe in me, let's put our heads together and make a plan."

There was no mad scramble among the women to do what Charles suggested. Instead, they slid their chairs back from the table and moved to the far end of the war room, where they hissed at each other like a pitful of vipers. In the end, it was Yoko who said, "We have the power, if it isn't working out with Charles, and he proves untrustworthy, to do what we have to do. I do believe we can trust him, but that is my opinion. Everyone deserves a chance. Don't you agree?"

"You have a point," Isabelle said. "Eight sets of eyes, if we count Maggie, on a person twenty-four seven might just tend to keep that person on our side. I also believe if Charles had to make a choice between Hank Jellicoe and us, he'd choose us. Having said that, are we in agreement that we're going to sign up for the job to be done, or do we have more to discuss?"

"You can count on Myra and me," Annie said.

The others grinned and counted themselves in, too.

"Then let's set the wheels in motion so when Lizzie gets here, she doesn't have to deal with any indecision on our part. So it's a go then?" Nikki asked.

"It's a go, dear," Myra said, her thumb shooting in the air.

"Way to go, Myra!" Annie said, clapping Myra on the back. "From this moment on, you are our team leader as always. Charles is second-in-command. We'll deal with the boys later."

Until then, Maggie had remained voiceless. "I have an idea," she said.

CHAPTER 16

"And that idea would be . . . ?" Nikki asked.

Maggie's eyes sparkled. "I know you probably haven't kept up with the *Post* while you were away, but Myra and Annie have. A few months back, actually after the holidays, I started two new columns in the Lifestyle section of the paper, and they have proved to be wildly successful. One is called Sight and Sound, and it was the first. The other one is a local advice column called Ask Amy. We have a blog now, and we're on Facebook. There are times when we can't handle all the entries. Our personal Web site has crashed so many times, I've lost count. I've had to hire extra people to keep up to date."

"Who is Amy?" Alexis asked.

Maggie grinned. "That would be me. We created a person named Amy Abrams. Mostly Amy deals with female political questions. We do get male queries, but usually they're on the stupid side. The bottom line is it's just another gossip forum, but the stuff that comes through from time to time will make your hair stand on end. We could send in some ringers, you know, questions to which we want to feed just the right responses. Sight and Sound is where readers write or call in and tell us what they've heard and seen. You have to sift through the garbage and pull out what looks legit and work it. Then there is the blog, which we feed daily."

"And what do you see us feeding all these beasts with teeth, dear?" Annie asked. Not waiting for a response she asked, "Is this going to be something like the Drudge Report?"

"It's going to be whatever we want it to be since it is already in place. No one can say we at the *Post* just came up with the idea and are gunning for someone in particular. See, that's the beauty of the whole thing. We could start with Hank Jellicoe, and it won't look staged, because Sight and Sound has been around a while. We can start asking questions about his life from the moment he was nothing more than, as Charles says, a twinkle in his mother's eye, and go forward to the present. We can make the person asking the questions obsessive.

There will always be someone out there who knows something and can't wait to spit it out."

Maggie motioned for the others to move in closer. "When I first got this idea, I had an office put in the basement. I had a friend of mine set it all up. We have everything in that room, and it is soundproof. You have to be eye-scanned to gain entry. My . . . ah . . . friend got me the people I need. You know, they bounce things off satellites and bury things so deep no one can trace or track the originating point." She looked at Annie, and continued, "It cost a lot to set up, Annie, but I think now is when we're going to get our money's worth out of it. Hey, we're good to go." Annie waved her hand to dismiss Maggie's concern over the cost.

"We could start off Ask Amy by asking if there was some kind of world summit aboard a private Gulfstream at thirty thousand feet. That would certainly shake up a lot of people. What do you all think?"

"Maggie, I think this is fabulous beyond words," Myra whispered. The others crowded closer and congratulated her on a job well done. Maggie beamed with pleasure, as Annie and the others headed back toward the table, where Charles sat, waiting to get down to business.

The chatter ceased; gazes were expectant as the Sisters stared at Charles to see if they could discern any changes in his attitude toward them. There were none. It was business as usual, Charles's style. "Ladies, I do have a question, and I want honest answers. I understand your feelings, your motivation where Hank Jellicoe is concerned. You want to . . . get him first before you either sign on or not with the intelligence and law-enforcement head honchos. Convince me that this is the way to go rather than starting work on the real job. And if you won't do the work, then the point is moot. Tell me why you want to go after Hank Jellicoe first."

The women looked at one another. Kathryn took the floor. "We told you, Charles; it started with Jellicoe, so that has to be our starting point. We need to find out why he failed. I, for one, want to know if maybe this was something he made up. Those men on the plane told us our very own CIA and DHS claim they didn't pick up on any chatter concerning the president or her administration. If Jellicoe is as important in the world as he says he is, why are the CIA and DHS denying what he said, and why did he lone wolf it?"

"I'm not really clear in my own mind if Jellicoe convinced the other nations' intelligence and law-enforcement services' leaders about what his people heard by way of an uptick in chatter concerning the administration or whether those services' own people heard the same thing. I think they danced around that a little bit," Nikki said, her brow furrowed in thought.

"Who's to say Jellicoe didn't stir all this up for personal reasons, whatever they might be. Personally, the man would have to be nuts to do something like that, but from all I am hearing about him and what I read about him, it is possible. Maybe he crossed the line and is demented," Isabelle said.

"Hank Jellicoe may be many things, but demented he is not. The man never does anything without a reason. Do not start sniping at me, ladies. What I just said is what I know and for you to know. The more knowledge you have at hand, the better you can deal with the problem. In a global organization such as Jellicoe's, there are safeguards in place and people who would know if he stepped off the rails. Those safeguards would be acted upon at the first sign of trouble," Charles said.

"Point taken, dear," Myra said soothingly. Charles flushed a bright pink, to the Sisters' delight.

"The bastard is clever," Alexis said.

"Why? We do not know the why of anything where he is concerned. And right now, we do not know where he is. He has been in hiding . . . gone . . . for over eighteen months, and no one could find him," Yoko said. "I repeat, why?"

"What you mean is that people Hank Jellicoe didn't want to find him couldn't find him. You can rest assured his people knew where he was every minute of the day," Charles said. "Remember, the man didn't get where he is today by giving away his secrets."

Kathryn pounced. "So you admit the man has secrets!"

"Everyone has secrets, Kathryn." Charles sighed. "I suspect Hank Jellicoe has more than most."

"And yet after eighteen long months of whatever he was doing, he failed. Nothing happened, Charles! He failed in the eyes of the other world intelligence and law-enforcement leaders. Since you are such a staunch supporter of Hank Jellicoe, tell us how that happened, Charles?" Annie said.

"I wish I could, but I can't, Annie. Since you're all so gung ho, I'm sure you will ferret it out one way or the other. I would like to remind you that in the covert world, setting up a kill, as we call it, or a mission, sometimes takes years before it is acted on."

"Martine Connor does not have years unless she runs for a second term. We need an inside source at the CIA," Maggie said. "How about we have the *Post* do an exposé of the CIA. We wouldn't necessarily have to do it; just the hint that it was forthcoming might stir things up. Those people get away with murder, and I've heard they answer to no one, not even the president. Well, they do, but they thumb their nose at the administration and go about their business. No one wants a major worldwide newspaper sniffing into their secrets and how they conduct business. We did it with the FBI, you may remember, and they were crawling out of the woodwork to show the world how warm and fuzzy they were."

Annie's voice was gleeful. "That's a wonderful idea. Do any of you think Elias Cummings might know someone high enough up on the food chain at the CIA? I know, I know, the FBI and the CIA hate each other, but Elias is retired now, and possibly someone he knew at the CIA is retired now, too. Maybe, just maybe, they could get together and sort of have a talk. You know, two old cronies talking about their glory days, that kind of thing. They do that all the time in spy novels."

"We can run it up the flagpole," Nikki said. "If anyone salutes, we act on it. Myra, make a note to call Nellie and run this by her so she can run it by Elias. And, let's not forget Bert. He might know a few higher-ups who would be willing to talk. It's worth a shot."

Maggie started to text Ted, outlining a course of action.

Charles Martin looked around the table. It was all getting away from him, and he was powerless to help his old friend. He slumped in his chair and waited for the next volley of give-and-take.

Outside on the terrace, the lemonade pitcher was empty, as was Harry's teacup. Espinosa got up and lowered the retractable awning. "It sure is taking the girls a long time to do whatever it is they're doing," he said sourly.

"Why don't you just say it like it is: They're plotting to take down Hank Jellicoe, and I can't say I blame them. The guy is a real son of a bitch. I hope they fry his ass in hell," Bert said.

"We need to get real here, guys. We went into it with our eyes wide open. Good old Hank played to our greed, so we can't fault him for that. The guy's smart. But the bastard could have gotten the same results from us if he'd just leveled with us from the beginning. The one thing that guy didn't count on was the bond the girls have among themselves. He totally discounted that, and now he's going to pay, and I don't feel one bit sorry for him," Jack said.

"That was all personal. We need to look at the whole picture here and get to the bottom of why Jellicoe did what he did. I'm just not buying that chatter business and a threat to the president, yada yada yada," Bert said.

"So what is it?" Ted asked.

"Let's try dissecting it and see what we come up with. First, he offers us jobs for outrageous sums of money. We agree. The girls are pardoned just hours before he makes the offer. We quit our jobs, take him up on his offer, the girls agree to go where he stations us. We all agreed on this so far?" Four heads bobbed up and down. "We go to a stupid boot camp, then we split up. Our jobs are just window dressing. There was no meat to them. We reviewed reports, did a payroll, monitored the complaint box with no complaints. We had the best of everything, and the money just kept rolling in. The perks were outstanding. But . . . we were cut off from each other. There was no way for us to communicate. The girls figured it out before we did, and that doesn't say much for us," Jack observed.

"We had access to world news via the Internet, and nothing was going down anywhere in the world that involved Global Securities or us. Correct me if I'm wrong and I missed something." The others simply shrugged.

"Our relationships soured. Jack is right, the girls figured it out before we did. Harry was the first to revolt. Then Ted and Espinosa. You, Jack, because of the luck of the draw, found out and set the wheels in motion to leave and you clued me in and here we are. We were almost hijacked. And let me tell you something else. Those figures you saw on that first private plane were the same guys who were on the one we took. If Murphy hadn't balked, we would have gotten on that plane. We backed away, and they had to scurry to make arrangements for the second plane. We thought our side was doing all the arranging, but I bet my life savings our side played into their side, and it worked out perfectly for them. Who the hell is going to say no to people like them? They make their offer, the girls say they'll think about it, and we get off the plane. We get off, they don't. Which brings us to where we are right now, sitting here on this terrace with an empty lemonade pitcher. It was the girls all along. That's who they wanted to separate. Not us dumb clucks — them, the girls," Bert said as he paced up and down the terrace, smacking one fist into the other in frustration.

"Why? What did Jellicoe think the girls could or would do? It's not like they were best buds with the president. They didn't have in-and-out access to the White House," Ted said.

"No, they didn't, but Lizzie did and probably still does. Jellicoe knows about the bond the girls have with Lizzie. This is all about female bonding, something none of us sitting here can or will ever understand. See, Jellicoe is just like us; he didn't understand it, either. His downfall," Jack said.

"You said when you saw Jellicoe on the plane it looked like he'd disguised himself. You said maybe plastic surgery or some latex on his face. Nikki said he admitted to staining his skin with walnut juice and that he had dreadlocks," Espinosa said.

"Yeah, so?" Jack said.

"So why did he have to go to those lengths to disguise himself? Where was he, and was he alone? Why didn't he send his people, who are trained in all this crap, to do whatever he did. The guy is no youngster. He's got to be in his midsixties, maybe older. I thought someone said he was the same age or around the same age as Charles," Espinosa said, refusing to give up without an answer. "My point is, men that age do not go around infiltrating nefarious cells or organizations like a rookie would. I read espionage novels, and those guys are always retired out around forty because of the stress and their cover getting blown. It's a young guy's game, not for some old geezer like Jellicoe."

Bert rubbed at the bristles on his chin. "You know something, Espinosa, sometimes you make a lot of sense, and this is one of those times. What you didn't mention is that Jellicoe would have to have invented what we call in the business a background to fit the identity he's assuming, and you're right, we send our best agents out to pasture after forty. Mainly because they're burned out. They get desk jobs, try to salvage their family life, which went on without him or her, as the case may be. The agents tend to end up drinking too much and leave the Bureau and work as security guards or for someone like Jellicoe because it's in their blood. Which now brings us back to the question

Espinosa asked: Why?"

"Well, according to the girls, it has to do with an attempt on the president's life, which would cripple her administration. Do not forget that Jellicoe handed over a rather large sparkler to the president the night she gave out the pardons. Maggie said that has been off-limits to the press and not one word has ever been mentioned about the president's romantic life after that night. We don't even know if she still has the ring. With Lizzie coming in later today, I am sure her first assignment will be a trip to the White House to find out what she can," Jack said.

"What's bothering me the most is why the CIA and DHS would deny to the others that they had picked up on the chatter, unless they are telling the truth and the others are lying. That's more and more what I'm beginning to think," Ted said. "I want to work on that angle."

"You have my permission," Bert said. "I hate those guys at Langley. They're all full of themselves, and pricks in the bargain. They wouldn't admit to a rainstorm if they were standing in water up to their necks."

"I agree with Bert," Jack said. "What about you, Harry?"

"I train some of their top agents twice a

year. They're okay guys, full of themselves, and their eyes are empty," Harry said. "The refresher course is coming up soon. All of my scheduling got screwed up while I was away."

As a group, they swooped in on Harry as they pelted him with questions. "Harry, I absolutely, truly, unequivocally love you with all my heart. We want names. Can you call those agents in and say something like you're going away and you need to up their time or something? I bet you even have some weeds or herbs you could put in that shitty tea you make them drink to cleanse their digestive tract. You know, stuff that will make them spill their guts and not remember we grilled them. You can do that, right, Harry?"

"Eat shit, Jack. That's against the law. The answer is no."

"Okay, then Bert and I will do it. We'll take the refresher course with them. I'm feeling the love here, Harry. I mean, I'm really feeling it. I knew you'd come through for us, buddy. Harry Wong, you are my knight in shining armor," Jack gushed.

Jack saw the squirrel on the terrace eyeing him as he sailed through the air and landed in a bush full of brilliant purple flowers. He picked up his bruised and battered body and hobbled his way back up to the terrace, where he made sure to stay as far away from Harry as he could. Though, to Harry's dismay, he made kissing cooing noises.

"I know you're always short on words, Harry, and going physical is your way of showing affection. I *soooo* love you, Harry," Jack said.

In spite of himself Harry burst out laughing.

CHAPTER 17

Lizzie Fox arrived at Pinewood to a robust greeting just as dusk was settling. In the mad scramble to get to the kitchen from the terrace, silver and crystal flew in all directions. Charles, hoping for a little approval from his guests, had outdone himself with dinner, which he served on the terrace. He stood up with the boys and trailed into the kitchen. His heart felt warm and yet sad at the same time as he listened to the excitement Lizzie's visit generated. He squeezed his eyes shut when they started to burn. How could Hank have so misjudged these wonderful women and the bond they had? How? Even the boys, who admitted they knew nothing about the female mystique, understood what the women had missed in what the Sisters now referred to as their eighteen months of captivity.

And then they were all in the kitchen, the excitement still high as Lizzie whipped out picture after picture of Little Jack and described him and all his accomplishments right down to, "He does look like me but he has Cosmo's feet. Look how big they are for such a little guy, and he's starting to talk. He knows his name and everything. I want one of those pups for him. He loves animals. Will you part with one, Myra?"

"No, but I'll find one for you," Myra said when Little Lady's wet nose nudged her leg. She reached down to pat the golden's head to reassure her that her pups would indeed stay here at the farm and be part of her family.

Lizzie declined the dinner that Charles had kept warm in the oven. "I finally got my weight back to normal, so I have to maintain it, and I did eat on the plane. I would love some coffee, though."

Additional chairs were carried out to the terrace, where they all sat down around the large table. The girls pitched in, and within minutes, the table was clear and Charles was serving coffee.

It was a perfect evening for the beginning of August, not too warm, not too cool. A light breeze ruffled the canvas awning with little snapping sounds. The leafy branches of the old sycamores that lined the terrace whispered as the birds that nestled among the boughs prepared for the night. Jack and Ted fired up the hurricane lamps Charles had scattered around the terrace. The lamps gave off just enough mellow light that everyone looked golden and beautiful.

It was Myra who, after hearing about Lizzie's uneventful plane ride, brought the conversation around to the matter at hand. "Tell us what you think, dear."

"I've known Hank Jellicoe for a long time. Having said that, we all know that no one can ever really know someone, especially if that person doesn't want you to know their entire makeup. It's hard to believe he would do what you say he did, but I do believe you. Charles is right, too. Hank is one of the most patriotic people I have ever come across. Cosmo and I have discussed this ad nauseam, and we cannot come up with why Hank would go to such lengths to separate you. We both agreed it wasn't something Hank did on the spur of the moment; it took planning, lots and lots of planning. Cosmo thinks we need to start there to find out the why of it all. I agree with him.

"Off the top of my head, I'd say we need to go back in time to at least six weeks to two months before Hank made his offer to you to see what was going on in the covert world. Perhaps the group who hired you will be of some help. Maggie and Ted can also delve into world matters during that time. It might be something we in general wouldn't pick up on but a trained journalist will spot right away.

"Now, as to the offer the intelligence and law-enforcement services made to you. From what you all said on the phone, you want to go to work for them. I have to warn you, it's not the contractual slam dunk, where you just sign on the dotted line, that you might think it is. Look around you at your partners, and you'll know what I'm talking about. I can draw up an airtight contract, secure your monies for you in advance, but I have to tell you, your immunity with each service will only be as good as the country you are in. There is no doubt in my mind that they will pony up, collectively, kazillions of dollars to you, which I can transfer into a safe haven. If you go ahead with this, which seems to be your intention, and I know it isn't about the money, you can do a lot of good, charitable work in the world with that kind of money. I can't be certain of this, but I assume you will be working for the most part Stateside. You have no American contract here with a representative of the president, which means no blanket immunity. If you get caught, you are right back where you were before President Connor issued your pardons. You will not get a second bite of the apple this time around. It won't matter if the other leaders bring pressure to bear. Are you all following me?" Every head at the table nodded.

"Which now brings me to my next question. What is the time frame here? Do you even have one? I know you told the group you would give them your answer tomorrow; that's not the issue. I'm talking about the length of time for the mission."

"They didn't give us a time frame. But Nikki and I walked away with the impression that time was of the essence," Kathryn said. "We've been kicking this around all afternoon and came up with some ideas." She quickly outlined Maggie's idea with her two new columns in the *Post.* Lizzie nodded to show she approved.

Myra jumped in and explained about Nellie and Elias and rushed on to outline Bert's and Harry's roles. "Ted is going to start digging into the CIA and DHS. So if we get the ball rolling on all of that, we should have some news in a few days."

Lizzie nodded, but she was frowning. "How did you leave it as far as signing the contracts?"

"Ari Gold gave me a burn phone. I'm to

call him, day or night. I assume that's when he will make arrangements for us to meet again. Or do you think a video conference will suffice?"

Lizzie's frown deepened as she visualized all the things that could go wrong. "I think you should ask for both. They're the ones who came to you, not the other way around. Stand firm and don't give in to anything unless it is to your benefit. Right now, getting on a plane and meeting in some foreign country or at thirty thousand feet is not to your advantage."

"We agree," Isabelle said, as the others nodded.

"I think before we agree to anything, we should ask where Jellicoe is hanging his hat these days," Annie said. "How many days do you think it will take before our plans bear some fruit?"

Everyone started to talk at once. When they ground to a halt, the consensus was that their labors should, if things went according to plan, bear fruit in four days.

"When are you planning to meet with President Connor, Lizzie?" Yoko asked.

"We're scheduled for a late-afternoon lunch tomorrow. She squeezed me in for 2:15. She said she could give me forty minutes. In forty minutes, I should be able to find out *something.* I do not want you using that burn phone unless I'm within earshot. We need to be clear on that."

"Absolutely, dear," Myra said.

"What if the guys we're dealing with don't know or won't tell us where Jellicoe is?" Alexis asked.

"Then we'll find him on our own. Did you forget, girls, we can do anything we set our minds to?" Annie responded. "I don't know why I say this, but I think Mr. Hank Jellicoe will be coming to us. If not in person, then he'll have an emissary of some sort make contact. Do any of you care to make a wager?" No one did. Annie smiled.

Maggie and Ted stood up at the same time. "I think I'm going to head back to town. I want to do some work at the paper, so I'm good to go for tomorrow's edition. Ted will be working right alongside me."

Espinosa got to his feet, looked over at Alexis, who wagged her finger in Maggie's direction, a signal that he should follow them and she was staying at the farm.

Jack looked at Nikki while Bert fixed his gaze on Kathryn. "Go!" they said at the same time. Yoko smiled at Harry, who correctly interpreted the smile. He followed the others into the house.

Nikki looked at the gathering seated at

the table, and said, "It's just temporary. We all want to stay for a few days to unwind, to get our second wind, so to speak, and to nestle in here at our original home base. Sharing a space is what we all missed so much. Now that we have one back, we just want to enjoy it for a little while if it's okay with you, Myra."

Myra beamed and smiled from ear to ear. "I wouldn't have it any other way. This is what Charles and I so missed, too. You can stay as long as you like — forever if need be. We're family."

Hours later, the girls were still seated at the table on the terrace as they shared their tales of captivity. They talked about their relationships, the future, Little Jack, and what they would do with all the money they'd been promised. When Lizzie started to yawn, the group got up and called it a night.

Myra and Annie shooed the others inside, saying they would tidy up the terrace and the kitchen. Charles had gone below to the war room in full work mode hours ago.

When the terrace went silent, Annie and Myra sat down and looked at one another. "This would be a wonderful time to get schnockered, Myra. You know, to celebrate, but since you can't hold your liquor, would you like a glass of orange juice or a soft drink before we retire for the night? I have to admit, I don't think I'm going to be able to sleep."

"I feel so wired up, I know I won't be able to sleep, either. I have an idea, Annie. Let's take the golf cart out of the barn and drive over to Nellie's house. She never sleeps. Three heads are better than two."

"It still rankles, doesn't it, that Hank Jellicoe didn't consider you or me a threat to him? I have to tell you, Myra, that more than anything else, that really pisses me off, and excuse my language," Annie said sourly.

Myra nodded. "Isn't it weird, Annie, how people, especially the younger ones, think that because you had the audacity to grow old, you no longer count? How did that happen? I never thought that way. I always thought aging was wonderful, what with all the knowledge you garnered along the way that you wanted to share. No one is asking us for our input, did you notice that? Well, they do in a roundabout way, but it isn't the same. Back in the beginning, they used to defer to me, even later when you came aboard, to listen to what we had to say. I'm babbling here, Annie, which means I am as disgruntled as you are. So, do we go over to Nellie's or not?"

"Hell, yes, but I'm driving. Did you ever find your glasses, Myra?"

"Bits and pieces — one of the pups chewed them up. It's all right, I have a spare somewhere. Let's go, and yes, you can drive."

Thirty minutes later, Annie brought the golf cart to a stop alongside the walk-through gate that Myra had the combination to. Retired federal court judge Nellie Easter had security out the wazoo, as she put it, thanks to the taxpayers and way too many threats on her life after she retired.

"She's up! The house is ablaze with light," Myra said.

"Yes, well, you better hope she doesn't meet us at the gate with that damn gun she packs around with her. She shoots first and asks questions later. Elias just sleeps through it all."

"I heard that," Nellie said, stepping into a small pool of light next to the gate. "What in the name of God are you doing over here at this time of night? I could have shot you!"

"But you didn't, so what is the point in discussing this? We're coming in, so put that damn gun away. By the way, how are you, Nellie?" Myra asked.

"These new hips of mine are working out pretty good. I can predict the weather within minutes of a storm, rain, cold, whatever. I'm better than any meteorologist you see on TV. What the hell are you doing here?"

"Do you always have to be such a curmudgeon, Nellie? "We couldn't sleep. You *never* sleep. I rest my case," Annie snapped.

"How bad is the trouble you *think* you're in?" Nellie said, leading the way to the farmhouse she shared with Elias.

"We don't *think,* we *know.* Deep, deep, and dark brown," Annie quipped.

"Ah, that kind of trouble. I think that calls for a drink. You want to sit inside in the kitchen or outside on the deck?"

"Myra can't hold her liquor, Nellie, you know that. You should make her hot tea. I'll take some of that Wild Turkey you keep in the cabinet over the sink. The kitchen will work out just fine. Unless you think our conversation will wake up your husband."

"I can hold my liquor; don't pay attention to Annie, Nellie. I much prefer to have some of that Jim Beam with an ice cube. One ice cube. I hate diluted liquor. By the way, where is Elias?"

"Asleep, where else? I thought when I married him I was going to have companionship. After dinner he sits down and falls asleep. Then I have to wake him up at eleven o'clock to go to bed. It's a good thing I have all my cats, or I'd be starved for attention and devotion. Did I mention Elias takes a nap in the afternoon? He does. Did you marry that Fish person, Annie?"

"I did not! But I did play with him for a while. The whole experience was . . . interesting."

"In what way?" Nellie asked as she poured from two different bottles.

"I found out I still have what it takes. Don't look at me like that. I blew his socks off. Myra and I were just having a discussion on getting older. Aside from the fact that it sucks, I'm having a wonderful time," Annie said.

"Is that so?" Nellie asked as she peered at Annie over the rim of her glass. "You should maybe write an advice column. I bet that would be a big hit with the geriatric set."

"Guess that means you aren't getting *any,* what with Elias doing all that sleeping," Annie shot back. "Not to mention those two new hips of yours must limit your agility. Age is a number, Nellie, as well as a state of mind. Enough of this bullshit. We didn't come over here in the middle of the night to discuss the aging process or our sex lives. We have things we need to talk about. We're going to go back in business. The vigilantes are going to ride again. You on board or not? You do realize if you say no, I'll have to wrestle you for that gun and kill you."

"Oh, sweet Jesus, here we go again!"

Chapter 18

Most people, Lizzie thought, would be in awe of this place, but the only thing she was in awe of these days was her son, Jack. Every waking hour of the day she was in awe of the little cherub she'd given birth to. Even at night, her dreams were full of her son. She smiled now just thinking of him.

She brought her rental car to a full stop, held out her credentials, and waited for the guard to give her the okay to drive through the gates at 1600 Pennsylvania Avenue. Having worked for the president for a limited time, she knew the drill and followed it to the letter.

Lizzie was dressed to the nines, as Annie would say, which simply meant that she'd dressed for the occasion, in a manner befitting the person she'd come to see. If anything, Lizzie Fox looked more beautiful than she'd ever looked. As Annie said, motherhood gave her a whole other look, one that said, *Just you try and take me on. I'm a mother now!* Her suit was a custom Armani, the color was called Misty Mountain. The outrageously priced Jimmy Choo shoes matched the suit perfectly. She didn't carry her handbag, but it, too, matched her outfit. Her silver hair was swept back and up, and held in place with diamond-studded combs, a gift from Cosmo. It was hard to tell which sparkled more, her hair or the brilliant diamonds. No model, famous or not, could hold a candle to Lizzie Fox as she strutted her stuff. Just for fun.

She saw the smiles, heard the silent whistles, enjoyed the looks of awe and envy, the airy waves. But only for a minute. Then, in the blink of an eye, she was Lizzie Fox, Attorney at Law. And she wasn't here at 1600 Pennsylvania Avenue for a fashion show.

A Secret Service agent led her to the door of the president's personal quarters and rapped sharply. The door burst open, and Lizzie was literally dragged inside by the president, who hugged her so tight Lizzie thought she would explode. "I missed you, Lizzie. My God! How is it one person can grow more beautiful with each passing day? Damn, Lizzie, I want a gallon of whatever it is you're taking."

Lizzie laughed as she kicked off her shoes. Martine Connor was already in her stocking feet. "This is the reason," Lizzie said, pulling a slim packet of pictures out of her pocket. "This is the guy responsible for whatever it is you're seeing in the new me. Tell me he isn't the most perfect baby, the most gorgeous little boy you've ever seen. Except for his big feet. Those he got from Cosmo." Lizzie giggled.

The president flipped through the pictures, her eyes misting. "He's everything you said he is, Lizzie. God, how I envy you. He looks just like you, too. Do you think his hair will stay that silvery color?"

"The doctor says yes. He's already had a bit of a haircut with manicure scissors. His hair is thick and so curly you can't get a comb through it."

The president linked her arm with Lizzie's. "I don't have to ask if you're happy. All I have to do is look at you, and I have my answer."

"Does that mean you aren't happy, Marti? Every day I look at the mail to see if there's an invitation to your wedding, but there isn't. What are you waiting for?" she teased lightly. "How come you aren't wearing that sparkler that can light up the world, or don't presidents wear jewelry on the job?" Lizzie's tone was still lighthearted, but her gaze was sharp and clear.

"That's a whole other story, my friend. We only have forty minutes, and we have already used up five of them, and they'll be serving lunch any minute now."

"As a new mother, I can multitask. What that means, even though it isn't polite, is, I can eat and talk at the same time. Talk to me, Marti."

Martine Connor sat down at the table and waited for Lizzie to do the same thing. "There isn't going to be a wedding. There isn't even an engagement. At least that I know of. I have not seen or heard from Hank since the night he gave me the ring. I don't know why, but the press has given me a pass on it all. There haven't been any questions, no innuendoes, nothing. It's like that night never happened. Hank has not been to the White House in any capacity since that night."

"I don't understand. Why? What happened?"

"That makes two of us. I tried calling, writing. I did everything but beg. When the White House calls, most people would pick up. Not Hank Jellicoe. So my answer is, I don't know. Shhh, here's our food."

Lizzie looked down at the delectable crab

cake. It sat on a nest of baby asparagus that was nestled next to slivers of bright orange carrots, covered in cracked black pepper. She knew she wouldn't eat a thing, and she also knew the president wasn't going to eat her lunch, either.

The minute the steward left the dining room, Lizzie leaned across the table and whispered, "Where is he? I haven't kept up that much on world news, but I think Cosmo would have told me if there was a crisis somewhere in the world. Because if there was, Hank would be smack in the middle of it."

The president chewed on her lower lip as she picked at and mashed the food on her plate. Her voice was so soft, Lizzie had to strain to hear the words. "Hank Jellicoe answers to no one, not even the president of the United States, Lizzie. You know that."

"Actually, Marti, I did not know that. I thought everyone in this world had to answer to someone at some point in time. You are the commander in chief of the greatest nation on earth. One of the perks should be that you can demand an audience with him. You control the CIA, the FBI. Put the word out and bring him in. If you think they can't do it, I know some people who could do it, but there would have to be some immunity in place."

"What? So I can look like a fool in front of the whole world! I-don't-think-so! Oh, my God, do you mean . . . ? This isn't just a little lunch to show me your child's pictures, is it?"

Lizzie shrugged as she wondered where the president's indignation was. "So you're just going to do . . . nothing?"

"Well, I'm not wearing the ring. I keep moving it from place to place, and I don't know why. I have a rotten track record where men are concerned, you know that."

Lizzie did know that, but she wasn't about to mention it. "Look at me, Marti. It's just us here, me and you, and you know I can keep a secret. Can you think of any reason, outside of a personal one, why Hank would just let you hang and be humiliated like this?"

The president's face crumpled, and Lizzie knew she was close to tears. The change back to presidential mode happened so quick, Lizzie almost thought that what she had seen was a figment of her imagination. "Lizzie, you know I can't discuss those kinds of things with you. I'm sorry. Please don't take it personally."

"Absolutely not. I bet this was a really good lunch. Chesapeake crab cakes. Cosmo would go over the moon if he were here."

"The next time you come to visit, you should bring Cosmo and Little Jack, and I'll make sure we serve them even if I have to go crabbing myself to get them. Just give me a few days' notice. Better yet, we could get together at Camp David. Then again, pictures of Little Jack in the White House sitting on the president's lap might get him some brownie points along the way. Actually, Lizzie, we could do both if you have the time. If you give me a few days' notice and nothing earth-shattering is going on in the world, I should be able to arrange it."

Lizzie laughed because she knew she was supposed to laugh.

"Tell me something, Lizzie. I know you said you aren't keeping up with politics, but what about gossip? Did you or your . . . *people* hear anything about some kind of intelligence and law-enforcement world summit in midair? My staff has been buzzing about it since it hit every political blog in town yesterday. You know how the gossip flows in the summer, when everyone is on hiatus."

Lizzie felt her stomach crunch into a knot. "Not a word. I would think something like that would be pretty hard to pull off. If it was that kind of summit meeting, why wasn't a representative of yours invited? The director of the CIA or the head of the FBI? Have you asked either one about it?"

"That's a very good question, Lizzie. And, no, I haven't. Like I said, news is slow. But . . . did you see the *Post* this morning?"

"No, I didn't. Banner headline?"

"No, nothing like that. A while back they started running two new columns. I understand from my staff they are wildly successful. One is just a question-and-answer kind of thing, Dear someone or other. The other column is called Sight and Sound. People write in with sightings, and other people respond, and they blog and Twitter and do all kinds of things. Today's question was from a man who said his name was Jonathan, and he wanted to know if anyone but himself had seen Henry — Hank — Jellicoe and what they thought of his transformation? Do you think your . . . *people* would know anything about that? What does that mean, 'his transformation'?"

"I don't have a clue. Why would you think my people would know something about that, Marti?" Lizzie said as she bent down to look for her shoes before she remembered she'd left them by the front door.

The president looked at her watch, then at the food on her plate. She stood up and reached for Lizzie's plate and carried it with her own to the disposal. "By the way, we finally got it fixed," she said, indicating the garbage disposal.

"The next time we should brown-bag it," Lizzie said lightly. "I do love it when appliances work the way they're supposed to. Ditto for computers."

"How long are you in town for, Lizzie?"

"Another day or so."

"Business?" the president asked.

"It never goes away or ends, you know that. You know I kept some of my favorite clients, so I have to work from time to time."

"New business, old business?" the president asked.

"Actually, Marti, new business. I couldn't turn down the fee. I might be the only lawyer in town who will be able to buy her own country when I wrap it up."

"That lucrative, huh?" The president smiled, but the smile did not reach her eyes.

Lizzie laughed. "Well, I can see that my time is up. This was really nice, Marti. One of these days we really should eat the lunch your chef prepares for us."

At the door, the president looked Lizzie square in the eye, and whispered, "He had an agenda, Lizzie. He used me, and when it didn't work . . ." Tears glistened in her eyes, but she blinked them away. "It was nice seeing you again, Lizzie. Stay in touch, okay?"

Lizzie wrapped her arms around the president. "Marti, if you need me, just call. I'll be here as quick as I can. I promise."

"I know that, Lizzie, but thanks for saying it out loud. Give Little Jack a big hug and kiss from his godmother."

"I will, Marti. Time for you to start running the world again." The two women hugged one more time, then Lizzie was on her way back to her rental car.

The first thing Lizzie did was to call her husband. With her earbud intact, she was able to concentrate on the road in front of her, the traffic, and talk. Assured that her husband still loved her more than life itself and that Little Jack missed her terribly, Lizzie smiled. It was so wonderful to be loved. She gave him a quick update on her meeting with the president just as she realized she was in front of the *Post* building. She found a parking space, professed her undying love to her husband and son, and got out of the car.

Four men almost killed themselves as they all grappled with the elevator door to hold it for Lizzie. She offered up a dazzling smile and rode to Maggie's floor, wondering why she'd come here. Obviously to report on her meeting with the president and to see if Maggie had any up-to-date information to pass along to those waiting at the farm.

On this floor, where Maggie made things happen, no one paid any attention to Lizzie as she strode along. She stood still for a minute as she tried to comprehend what she was seeing, which was Ted Robinson texting with one hand, talking on his Bluetooth headset, working the computer with his other hand, and still managing to give signals with his feet to Espinosa, who was doing the same thing but not with Ted's speed. Now *that* was multitasking to the nth degree.

Lizzie made her way to Maggie's office and saw she was doing much the same thing. Maggie held up her hand to indicate she'd just be a minute. Then she motioned to the kitchen, which meant coffee and donuts or something else edible. Grinning from ear to ear, Lizzie made her way to the kitchen, filled two coffee cups, added two donuts and two bananas and a pile of napkins to the tray, and carried it back to Maggie's office.

Maggie was off the phone but was still tapping at her computer keys when Lizzie set the tray down on the corner of her cluttered desk. "You know what, Lizzie, I finally figured it out. All those doctors I've gone to about the way I eat said there was nothing wrong with me. Well, I now know when my adrenaline is going full blast, that's when I eat. If it's a ho-hum day, boring, nothing is going on, I don't eat. Amazing, isn't it?" she said, sinking her teeth into a frosted jelly donut. "You just came from lunch, how come *you're* hungry? You didn't eat, did you. So, did the *prez* give up anything?"

"The lady is aching a bit. She loves Hank Jellicoe, that's the bottom line. Unfortunately, Marti has a knack for picking the wrong men. She herself mentioned it."

"That's it? That's all you got?" Maggie asked in disbelief.

"That's it. When I was leaving, she did say something I thought was strange. She said Hank had an agenda, and he used her. She also reminded me she couldn't discuss White House business with me. I really didn't ask questions. Marti is smart, and she would have picked up on anything that didn't sit well with her.

"Oh, she did ask if I had read the *Post* this morning and wanted to know if I heard anything about a world summit that met at thirty thousand feet in the air. A meeting neither she nor any representative was invited to."

Maggie was about to bite into the banana. She stopped and stared at Lizzie. "I thought you said you didn't get anything. That's pretty much *something,* in my opinion."

"Ya think, Maggie?" Lizzie teased as she, too, tackled a banana. She hadn't realized how hungry she was until that very minute. "She said her staff apprised her of the meeting. She didn't say thirty thousand feet; those are my words based on what the girls said. She pretty much passed it off, at least I think that's what she was doing, as something the blogs were writing about just to stir up trouble. I went out on a limb and told her that, as commander in chief of this great country, she had the resources to pull in Hank Jellicoe. She said no, she'd be the laughing-stock of the free world. I think she really believes she was, as the young people today put it, dumped. She keeps moving the ring from one place to another, whatever that means. That's it, Maggie, the sum total of what I got out of the luncheon. Ooops, I did casually mention that I knew *people* who might want to help. She knew exactly what I was talking about and she almost, I say almost, ran with it, but then she backed off. She did mention the new columns in the paper and the story you put in about someone seeing the 'new' Hank Jellicoe. In short, Maggie, as much as she wants to trust me, she doesn't."

"Oh, boo-hoo!" Maggie snapped as she scrounged around in her desk drawer for a power bar or something to chew on.

"Have you and Ted come up with anything?"

"Ted is onto something. He's like a crazy man out there. That's how he works, and I just love it. The blogs are so busy we can't handle them. Drudge's people are hitting the blogs, but I can smell them. When are the girls calling the big boys?"

"Probably when I get back to the farm and report in. They have until midnight, unless they change their minds. What about your hacker friend, Maggie? Do you have him on this?"

"You know I do. I get sick to my stomach when I think about having to tell Annie what it's costing. That guy could retire right now and live like a king somewhere on what we've paid out to him. You should see the real estate he owns, compliments of the *Post!* Oceanfront!" Maggie snarled.

Lizzie laughed. "What would you do without him?"

"Shrivel up and die. He wrote the software for the FBI, the CIA, and the Pentagon. There is no firewall he can't penetrate, and he always writes in a back door that no one but he can find. Tell me that isn't impressive!"

"Then I guess he's worth all that oceanfront property. Has he come up with anything?"

"Not yet, but it's only been a few hours. If there's something to be found, he'll find it."

"Well, there you go; you just convinced yourself he's worth every penny you pay him." Lizzie looked at her watch. "I should get moving. It's after four, and I don't want to hit rush-hour traffic."

"Lizzie, what do you honestly think about all of this?"

"Ask me that question tomorrow after the girls make their decision, and I talk personally, one-on-one, with Ari Gold."

"How long are you staying, Lizzie?"

"As long as it takes or until I'm satisfied the girls are safe."

Maggie nodded. "I thought that's what you'd say. That's all good. It is, isn't it, Lizzie?"

"Ask me that tomorrow, too. If you need me, call."

"Do you need me to walk you to the elevator?"

Lizzie laughed out loud. "I'm a big girl, didn't you notice? I think I can find my way.

Don't work too hard."

"Never happen," Maggie said, waving with one hand. She was back in the world of blogs and Twitters and Drudge's wingnuts.

Chapter 19

It wasn't a party atmosphere poolside, but it was crowded, and the ice tea and lemonade flowed as the Sisters huddled under the awning and talked. Charles bustled about replenishing drinks and setting out snacks. The Sisters dived into a fresh batch of delicious-looking brownies that Nellie and Elias had brought with them. The only members missing were the guys and Maggie, who were knee deep in whatever sleuthing they were doing, according to Lizzie, who was just finishing cooing to her son on her cell phone.

"And the game plan is . . . ?" Annie asked.

"One step at a time, Annie. First, we need to vote one more time to accept the very generous offer that was presented to us. Second, we need to decide on a dollar amount for our services. Third, Lizzie needs to speak to Mr. Gold concerning the immunity. It has to be all across the board.

Fourth, we want and need to know where Hank Jellicoe was dropped off. After we have that information, we can make a plan. We have until midnight before we have to make our call," Nikki said. "Hopefully, by the time we make the call, Maggie and the boys will have something a little more concrete. What's our fee?"

The Sisters batted numbers around, some realistic, others over the moon. Annie finally said she'd had enough and snapped, "Fifty million! Plus expenses! Plus all of the above!"

"Done!" the Sisters said, clapping their hands.

Lizzie Fox raised her index finger to show she'd heard the decision, then she went back to the computer she was working on.

"Which now brings us to you, Elias," Myra said. "We need you to do something for us. As the former director of the FBI, I assume you are on a first-name basis with the former director of the CIA and secretary of the Department of Homeland Security. We want you to . . . for want of a better explanation, nose around and see what you come up with. The CIA director from your time, who the president kept on until she appointed the woman who now holds the post, retired around Thanksgiving of last year, if I recall correctly. Something about his wife being ill. I saw a few weeks ago in the *Post* that she passed on."

"Nellie and I attended the funeral. He's out, so what can he tell us?" Elias asked.

"I don't know. That's why we want you to pay him a condolence visit. See what you can find out. Even though he's retired, I'm sure he knew or knows what's been going on. Retirement can be deadly, even more so when one's spouse is in failing health. Brothers under the skin, that sort of thing," Myra said

"I hate the son of a bitch," Elias growled. "Everyone in the world knows the CIA and the FBI hate each other."

Myra blinked. "I didn't know that, Elias, but we can't let that stop you. Take a bottle of really good bourbon and see what that gets you. What we want to know specifically is, did or didn't the CIA pick up on the chatter Hank Jellicoe acted upon? You can say you've heard the rumors, and who's to say you haven't stayed friends with some of the leaders of the world's law-enforcement outfits. All you have to do is sound convincing. You *will* do this, won't you, Elias?"

"Yes, of course he'll do it," Nellie answered briskly for her husband. "Elias even knows where the director lives, because we went back to the house for refreshments after the funeral. It was a very somber affair, and the food was appalling. It's just about eight miles from here as the crow flies."

Elias put up an argument. "Don't you think the man is going to be suspicious? It's not like we socialized or even liked one another. I'm sure his feelings for me are the same as mine are for him."

"Ah, but you see, that was before his wife died. He's all alone now. He'll be melancholy. Feed the liquor to him and see what he coughs up," Annie said. "Was his wife nice?" she asked as an afterthought.

"Salt of the earth. A very gentle, kind soul. I don't know what she ever saw in that bastard," Nellie said. "I didn't know her well, but she went to the same church, volunteered for some of the same things I did. We called each other by our first names. Notice that I said *she* went to church, not her husband. I don't think the man ever saw the inside of a church until his wife died."

"You should go now, dear. Pick up the liquor at Save-More and hopefully you will be back here before the girls have to make that call. On the drive to the director's home, you might want to call and set up a luncheon meeting tomorrow with the secretary of homeland security," Nellie said.

Elias, a bear of a man with a shock of hair so white it looked like a snow peak sitting on top of his head, started to grumble again. "And you think these people are just waiting to see me to spill their guts and their secrets! They make appointments months in advance. At least I did. Spur-of-the-moment luncheons just aren't in the cards, but yes, I will do as instructed. Don't I always do what you say? I have to warn you, my dear, you are all going to be so disappointed when I return empty-handed. I'm going, Nellie, calm down, or your blood pressure is going to go up again."

"There you go again, Elias, selling yourself short," Nellie said soothingly.

"It's the element of surprise, Elias. It's your job to see if they're trying to hide or cover up something. They're going to be trying to figure out why you're there in the first place and what *you* know. It's going to be a game. My money is on you, Elias," Annie said cheerfully.

The Sisters gave a robust shout of approval that rang in Elias's ears long after he was tooling down the highway. He admitted to a small thrill of excitement as he wondered if he had the moxie to pull this little stunt off. If he didn't want to eat out of the trough and sleep in the barn, he knew he *had* to pull it off. He shifted his thoughts and started to work on some witty dialogue that he hoped would garner something the girls could work with.

Back at Pinewood, Annie zeroed in on Lizzie. "Dear, is your gut telling you that the president was trying to give you a clue, or was she just . . . bemoaning her love life?"

"My first reaction was she was trying to tell me something without telling me. I know that doesn't make sense, but it's what I thought at the time. And she did make the comment that she couldn't discuss White House business with me. Like I didn't know that. It's up to you all to figure out what Hank Jellicoe's agenda is or was at the time this all happened." A second later, she was engrossed with what she was doing on her laptop.

Annie threw her hands in the air. "Let's hear it, girls! What kind of agenda could a man like Hank Jellicoe possibly have? The man is King of the Hill, so to speak. From everything I've read about him, the man has no political aspirations. He likes what he does, is good at what he does, and has the money to prove it."

"Remember the first rule, Annie. Always

follow the money. I say we go back to the day the man was born and work forward," Myra said.

"That's what Maggie and Ted are doing, Myra. If we stick our noses into that, we might confuse the issue or screw it up," Nikki said.

Kathryn looked over at Isabelle. "This would be a good time for you to have one of your visions. Can you conjure one up for us?"

Isabelle sighed. "How many times do I have to tell you, it doesn't work that way, Kathryn. I can't control when they come or their intensity. They just happen. Even when I concentrate and try, nothing happens."

"Try harder," Kathryn snapped.

"Eat me," Isabelle shot back.

"Sorry. I'm just . . . I don't know what I am. I don't know what any of us are right now, this minute. We're in limbo, and I don't like it," Kathryn said.

"We're all a little antsy, dear," Myra said. "This is terribly important to all of us — life-altering, you might say. Once we see clearly what's in front of us and form a plan, the future for all of us will settle down to something we can all live with. We're at a crossroads in our lives, and we aren't certain which road we should take. I find it an awesome decision."

"Well said, Myra, well said," Annie chortled happily.

Back in the District, Harry Wong opened his *dojo,* then stepped aside for Bert and Jack to follow him inside. "C'mon, c'mon, hustle here, boys. Make me look good, and be sure you follow all my cues. Those CIA agents aren't fools. One or two of them are bound to figure out that their e-vals," Harry said, referring to the agents' evaluations, "are still two months off."

"And if they say something?" Bert said.

"Then I say I'm taking off again, and it's either now or they go someplace else and start over. When I first got back, I was in touch with my contact at the CIA and told him I had to play catch-up. They didn't have a problem, which is probably because they know I'm the best of the best."

"Nothing like a little modesty," Jack said, rolling out the workout mats. "You want me or Bert to take the class."

"I think it should be Bert. Those guys hate anyone connected in any way with the FBI. Jack, you monitor, and I'll do the e-vals. I plan to flunk them on everything, just so you know," Harry snapped.

"Whoa, little grasshopper, what's up with

the surly attitude?" Jack said.

"I hate those guys. They're cocky, they're arrogant, and they have mush for brains. That's my opinion, and I'm entitled to it. Plus, they're racist."

"Oooh, that's not good," Jack said, tying his black belt into place. "Say the word, and they won't be walking out of here with a spring in their step. You sure you really want to go with a four-hour session?"

"That's how long the video runs, and yeah, I'm sure. The powers to be want to see their agents in glorious form. I, on the other hand, do not want to see that glorious form. I want you on their asses, show them up, and do not cut them one ounce of slack. If you have to hurt them, then hurt them."

Bert laughed. Jack thought the sound was almost as evil-sounding as when Harry got really pissed over something. "So it's the FBI versus the CIA? Who you putting your money on, boys?"

"Oh, you big silly!" Jack said as he turned a somersault to limber up. "The FBI, of course, even though you're retired from the Bureau. You gonna go back there, Bert?"

"I might, but first I want them to beg me. If they beg, I'll know they really want me. In the meantime, let's just have some fun, then leak the tape to the guys at the Bureau."

"Damn, I like that. Ah, I hear the CIA van. I think your class just arrived, Master Wong," Jack said, doing a jig for Bert's benefit.

"You screw up, Jack — you, too, Bert — and your ass is grass. Remember now, no chitchat. Work them till their dicks shrivel up. No water, no tea. And . . . no liniment," Harry said as he picked up his clipboard.

"You heard the man, Bert, until their dicks fall off." Jack guffawed.

Eight men walked into the back of the *dojo* with attitude written all over their faces. All were dressed the same, all wore aviator glasses, all had high and tight haircuts. All had a spit shine to their shoes. Their attitude slipped a little when Harry said Bert, former director of the FBI, would be working the class.

Bert held out a stopwatch. "Five minutes to shed your threads, get rid of the shades, and be on the mat in single formation. Time counts," he barked.

"They're cursing Master Navarro. Mark that down. Disrespect will not be tolerated in this *dojo,*" Jack said gleefully but under his breath. Bert grinned.

Jack mentally gave each of the CIA agents

a number, because there was no way he was going to be able to remember names.

"Seven minutes. You're slugs! Those two minutes could get you dead, agents. And why are you winded? All you did was shed your clothes and get dressed. You wearing ruffled panties or maybe garter belts? Those belts are sloppy. Tie them again, and this time do it right. You're not getting off to a good start, agents," Bert said.

Jack dutifully made checkmarks on his clipboard. In the end, it would have to match Harry's for verification.

Somewhere at the end of the row, a muffled "Screw you" could be heard.

Jack walked the length of the row. He stuck his index finger in Number 7's chest, and said, "Ten points, agent. That's twelve for you in total. Fifteen, and you have to take the course over." Jack waited to see if there would be any feedback. There wasn't. The eight-man team, in his eyes, suddenly looked uneasy.

Bert blew his whistle, which he had to wrestle Harry for, and the e-vals got under way. The first hour showed how rusty the agents were as they did their best to perform. The second hour showed who had potential and who didn't. The third hour showed a strain on all eight agents. All were sweating profusely.

"Ten-minute break, agents. We're coming up to your final hour. This is where the rubber meets the road. I don't think I need to tell any of you that you aren't cutting it, which leads me to believe none of you kept up with your training while Master Wong was away. In other words, you pissants are downright pathetic. You CIA guys are wusses. FBI agents could wipe up the floor with you on their worst day in the middle of a snowstorm. For Christ's sake, you people out there at the Farm didn't even get it right where Jellicoe goes." The bait was out. He waited a nanosecond to see if anyone would pick up on it. No one did.

Jack stepped in, waving his clipboard. Harry stood on the side, looking disturbed but bored. "I heard about that fiasco. I had a beer last week with a couple of guys from the Bureau, and they said you guys screwed up big-time. They went so far as to say you were the laughingstock of the covert world, but no one needed to worry because you aren't domestic. They also said you guys at the CIA are no threat to the FBI, so no one is taking you seriously. They said you were just plain old screwups. Okay, time's up. This is your last hour, agents. Make it good, or the new course starts two days from today."

"Hold on there, Emery," Number 6 said.

"Master Emery to you, agent. Dock him, Master Wong." Harry dutifully made a checkmark on his clipboard. He looked even more bored, if that was possible.

And then all the agents were talking at once. Harry scribbled furiously, as did Jack. Bert smiled benignly.

Jack pointed to the video camera for Number 6's benefit. He looked disconcerted for a moment but decided to plunge ahead. "What the hell are you guys talking about? We didn't miss anything. And what the hell does that screwball Jellicoe have to do with the CIA? We can whip that guy's ass, his people's asses, and anyone else who gets in our way. Now, if we could advertise the way he does, things might be different. While we work to serve our country, that SOB works to make money at everyone else's expense. And damn straight, I don't like the guy or his people. So mark that down, Master Wong." The agent stepped back in line and straightened his shoulders.

"Wait a minute, let me get this straight," Jack said. "You're saying my friends at the FBI made up that stuff? That is what you're saying, isn't it? With all due respect, agent, I'd probably say the same thing you just said if my ass were on the line. What you're really saying, then, is Jellicoe, head of Global Securities, is out to get the CIA, and he made that all up. Jesus, you guys are something else, you know that?"

The second agent in line stepped forward, sweat rolling down his face. "Yeah, that's what we're saying. We have the best intel in the world. No, we don't share. I'm telling you that bullshit rumor that is going around was started by Jellicoe himself."

"Okay, duly noted. Your venom speaks volumes," Jack said. "Master Navarro, they're all yours." Jack moved over to where Harry was standing. He scribbled notes on a blank sheet of paper under the top sheet. Harry did likewise. *I think they're telling the truth,* Jack wrote.

Yeah. What now? Harry scribbled back.

They're the top eight agents out at Langley. At least one or two of them should know what's going on. We can't act too interested, Jack wrote back.

So, how do we play it? Sounds like a grudge against Jellicoe to me. Maybe we should pretend we love and adore the son of a bitch! Harry scribbled.

And the FBI. Maybe we should show them their last e-vals. They passed, didn't they?

Good idea. With flying colors. They were a

dedicated team, I kid you not, not like these buffoons.

Buffoons? Jack didn't know Harry knew the meaning of the word, much less actually knew how to use it in a sentence. Jack shrugged and walked away, his eyes on the massacre going on in front of him. Bert was right, it was pitiful.

The moment the fourth hour was up, Bert blew his whistle. "Let me put you out of your misery right now, agents. Unless Master Wong saw something that I didn't see, you all failed. Not only did you fail, but you failed miserably." He pointed to the video camera. "It's all there in glorious color, agents. It will go out with your e-vals tomorrow. We'll be seeing you here the day after tomorrow. Master Wong, do you have anything else to add?"

Harry held up his hand. "I think this is one of those times when a picture, in this case, video, is worth a thousand words. Front and center, agents. Watch!"

Jack, Harry, and Bert watched the eight agents wince, cringe, and bite at their lips. Harry was right, these pictures depicted the FBI's lean, mean fighting machines. "That's how it is supposed to be done. You might as well have been wearing tutus and ballet slippers. Not one of you came close to meeting the e-val requirements. We all know what that means. You don't go back to the field, you go back to the Farm for additional training. These e-vals will be part of your permanent record."

"Unless . . ." Bert said.

The eight agents pounced on the single word like white on rice. "Unless what?" they said in unison.

Chapter 20

Maggie Spritzer rubbed at the back of her neck. It was late, and she should have gone home hours ago, but her gut — more importantly, her reporter's instinct — was telling her to stick with what she was doing. She blinked, rubbed the grit from her eyes, then drained her coffee cup. She needed a refill, but it would just have to wait. She sifted through the pile of printouts for the fifth, or maybe it was the sixth, time — she really couldn't remember. These were the blog comments she'd printed out because they sounded more legitimate than the others. She dropped to her knees and spread them out on the floor behind her desk. Then she put on her hateful reading glasses and stared at the neatly lined-up, printed comments. One stood out above the others. Written by someone named Emma Doty, whose blog name was Sparkle. Maggie frowned. What kind of idiot would not only sign her real name but offer up her personal e-mail address on a blog? A real idiot, that's who. All the blog said was she had information, but she wasn't putting it on a blog. Maggie picked up the printout, swiveled around, and opened her e-mail program. She quickly typed in a message before she could change her mind. She identified herself, typed in her cell phone number, and asked for the recipient's phone number, saying she would call her when she got the number.

Maggie swiveled back around and again dropped to her knees to pick up and move the papers in front of her. She wondered if all the people who blogged were crackpots looking for five minutes of fame. She rubbed at her eyes again. She really needed to go home.

Maggie quickly weeded through the scattered printouts. She immediately tossed three of them when she saw they were sightings of Hank Jellicoe, one by the Space Needle in Seattle, the second in downtown Atlanta, and the third one riding a horse in Jackson Hole, Wyoming. All sent within five minutes of each other. She rocked back on her haunches just as her cell phone rang. Thinking it was Ted, she growled, "I know, I know, I'm leaving now."

"I beg your pardon," a sweet-sounding

voice said on the other end of the line. "This is Emma Doty, and I would like to speak to Miss Spritzer. If I dialed the right number, that is."

Maggie's fist shot in the air. "You did. I mean, you dialed the right number. I was . . . I thought you were my boyfriend. It's late, and I'm still here at the office."

"I can always call you back tomorrow, Miss Spritzer. I'm two hours behind you time wise. I live in Prairie City, Idaho, a small town, two thousand or so people. I just received your e-mail. I thought you must be anxious to know information to send out an e-mail this late. I want to help if I can."

"Oh, I do, I never sleep; well, hardly ever," Maggie said, yawning. "I would love to hear whatever it is you think I should know. I'm wide-awake," she said, yawning again.

"Well, I read your paper online every day. I lived for many years in the Chesapeake area. When my husband passed away a while back, I came home to where he and I grew up. We were childhood sweethearts. I'm disabled and housebound these days, so my life is pretty much my computer. Don't you go feeling sorry for me, now; my children take real good care of me. Now, the reason I did the blog was because the man you appear to want to know about, a Mr. Henry or Hank Jellicoe, that isn't going to happen. Well, you might find him, but he isn't real. The reason I say that is, that's not his real name. His real name is Andrew Graverson. I went to school with him. He was Andy Graverson back then."

Maggie's heart started to pound in her chest. "Mrs. Doty, how can you be so sure?"

"I'm sure because my husband was sure. That man never made a mistake in his life, and the first time we saw a write-up about how successful Mr. Jellicoe had become, Matt, that's my husband, did a little poking around. Went to our old school on a vacation visit home one year, checked out the senior-class picture. Back then we didn't have yearbooks in our schools. It was Andy, all right. But if you need more proof, I have a picture of Andy, Matt, Joey, and Will all showing off a tattoo they got in their senior year when the Fireman's Carnival came to town. They're all gone now but Andy. And of course me and Will and Joey's widows. We all belong to the same quilting group. Most times it's here at my house because it's hard for me to get out. One of these days I'm going to get a van that's wheelchair equipped. One of these days." She sighed, knowing full well it wasn't going to happen.

"We all have pictures. I'd be more than happy to overnight them to you if you think it would help. The boys were inseparable best friends back then."

Maggie could hardly find her tongue. "Do you have a scanner?"

"Lord, no, child. I'm lucky I have this ancient computer that's on its last legs. The profits from our next quilt come to me. I'm hoping to make enough to at least put a down payment on a new computer. But that's not till Christmas, when the church raffles it off at the bazaar."

"Okay, overnight everything you have that you think will prove Andy Graverson is Hank Jellicoe. I'll send you a check to cover the mailing if you give me your address. Do you know why he changed his name?"

"No idea at all, Miss Spritzer. Matt and the boys wrote him a couple of letters maybe fifteen or so years ago when he was becoming famous, and they all came back as undeliverable. I guess he had his reasons."

"When and why did he leave Prairie City?"

"After graduation, and for the same reason we all left. No work in our little town. I think Andy went to Boise. Matt went to Colorado, and when he got a job and was settled, he came back for me. Will and Joe lit out for Nevada. We all stayed in touch except for Andy. There were no jobs in Prairie City, like I said. Summers we all picked potatoes, and no one wanted to make a career of doing that. I'm not complaining; we all had good lives. Why are you trying to find Andy, if you don't mind me asking?"

"I wish I could tell you that, Mrs. Doty, but right now I can't. I promise I will tell you when it's the right time. I don't know how to thank you."

"My thanks will be your telling me I'm right. I just hate it when people think because you're getting up there in years, you can't remember anything. I remember everything."

Maggie laughed. "I'll look forward to receiving the pictures. By the way, where is the tattoo on Andy, and what does it say?"

Emma Doty laughed out loud. "It was a silly thing, really. Like I said, we all picked potatoes. They make sour mash from potatoes. It kind of foamed, so they had the words *spuds and suds* tattooed on the back of their left hands. I hated it; so did Matt as he got older. I think all the boys regretted it, but by then it was too late. When we would go to a social event, I always made Matt wear a Band-Aid on his hand. Your Hank Jellicoe has the same tattoo, unless he had it removed at some point, which is entirely possible since he could certainly afford to have it done. If there's nothing else, Miss Spritzer, I'll say good night. My son will send off the pictures to you tomorrow."

"Thank you, Mrs. Doty."

The moment Maggie powered down, she thought she was going to explode upward and hit the ceiling. "When you want something done, call on a woman!" she shouted to the empty room. Now that she wasn't the least bit sleepy, she powered up her cell phone and called Ted. "What do you have?"

"Nothing. I'm sleeping."

"Well, I have something, and if you can't match what I have, you are fired, so get your tail out of bed and get to work."

Maggie's next call was to Abner Tookus, who was awake but cranky. "Do you have anything?"

"Jesus, Maggie, I just got on all of this. What's with you, anyway?"

"Yeah, well, you're going to be begging me to take all that oceanfront property off your hands for a song, because I've only been on it for forty minutes, and I hit the mother lode. You better have something for me by morning, or I'm going to be a real-estate mogul. Chew on that, Abner Tookus!"

Now she could go home.

■ ■ ■ ■

Fifty miles away, with only twenty minutes to go before the clock struck midnight, the Sisters hovered around the conference table with Charles and Lizzie Fox.

Annie stretched her arm so that she could slap her hand down in the middle of the table. "This is it, girls, the clock is ticking. It's either yes or it's no. We vote *now!*" Without a moment's hesitation, Myra's palm came down hard on top of Annie's. The Sisters followed suit.

Lizzie drew a deep breath. "That makes it unanimous. Who has the phone?"

Nikki looked at Kathryn, who was rummaging in the pocket of her jeans. She laid the phone carefully in the center of the table. "Ari Gold said all you have to do is power up, hit the number one, and we'll hear his voice."

Charles Martin felt like he should voice an opinion of some kind, but one look at the women's faces told him that was not the way to go. He didn't think he'd ever been as frightened in his life as he was at that moment.

All eyes turned to Lizzie, who reached for the phone. The silence in the room was so total, the click of Lizzie hitting the number one sounded like a thunderclap.

"What time is it in Israel?" Alexis whispered.

"Who cares?" Annie hissed, just as Lizzie introduced herself on the phone. They were in awe of the silver-haired, silver-tongued lawyer as she laid out their demands, then proceeded to rattle off questions, to which she made squiggly notes on a yellow legal pad that no one but her could or would understand. The silence continued, broken only when Lizzie asked a question or made a comment. The gel point pen she was using made no sound as she made notes.

"Since you agree with me on all fronts, Mr. Gold, the next thing we need to do is schedule a video conference for tomorrow morning. Ten o'clock our time. Of course I trust you and the others, Mr. Gold. About as much as you trust me and the ladies of Pinewood. Just so we're clear on this, blanket immunity all across the board. Total. The monies are to be wired into the account number I gave you earlier. I will expect confirmation from the bank when we begin our video conference. Which now brings me to my last question. If you can't or won't cooperate on this point, all of what we've agreed to is moot. The ladies want to know where you dropped off Mr. Jellicoe."

The Sisters leaned forward, hoping to hear Ari Gold's response. They could hear nothing coming through the phone but Lizzie's wide-eyed look of surprise stunned them. "And how do I know this is true? Yes, yes, a video of his departure will do nicely. Yes, of course I understand that you and the others wanted proof of his departure. Then, Mr. Gold, I think that concludes our business for the evening. Ten o'clock tomorrow morning."

Everyone started talking at once. "What? Did we commit? Are we . . ."

Lizzie placed her pen in the middle of the legal pad. "It's a go all around. They agreed to everything, even to interceding with the powers that be in Washington. Don't put too much faith in that promise. If you dissect it, it means that any one of those guys will guarantee you a safe harbor for the rest of your life. Providing you can get there. They agreed to your monetary demands, and the money will be offshore by ten tomorrow morning, at which point we will move it again to an even safer place." Lizzie stopped long enough to take a deep breath and a long swallow of the coffee Charles had just poured for her.

"Hank Jellicoe?" Nikki asked tightly. "Did

they give that up?"

"Yes, Nikki, they did. Mr. Gold said Hank got off the plane right behind you. He followed several of the maintenance people and entered the terminal through a different door. He's here, or he was here. Mr. Gold said they had video of him walking down the steps and across the tarmac. He said he understood your haste and desire to reach the terminal and that there was no reason for any of you to look back."

"But we did look back. We even talked about the fact that no one got off the plane and that Gold's group was heading right back," Kathryn said.

"Be that as it may. I can only report on what he said. He did volunteer to show the surveillance video they took from the plane tomorrow morning when we do our video conference. As far as proof, that should be sufficient to prove it's the truth. Ask yourself why he would lie about something like that at this stage. By the way, Mr. Gold is the spokesperson for the entire group. That, too, will be verified in the morning. Lord, it is morning already."

"Did his words ring true, Lizzie?" Isabelle asked.

"They did, but remember this, first and foremost, important or not, the man is a high-ranking professional intelligence officer. They always sound truthful until you catch them in a lie. If everything goes off on schedule, you all sign on, I take the early-evening flight to London, hand-deliver the contracts so each country's seal can go on them, then I fly home the following morning. Don't worry, they are paying my fee" — she grinned — "and they're sending a private plane for my trip, and it will fetch me back. That's a win-win in any book."

Lizzie started to gather up her papers and stuff them in a battered briefcase. "If you all don't mind, I'm going to call it a night. I want to call home and tell Cosmo I won't be home for a few more days. He's going to love having Jack all to himself."

"Run along, dear," Myra said. "Cosmo and Little Jack are more important right now than sitting here hashing and rehashing all this. What time is breakfast, Charles?"

"Seven," Charles said smartly. Lizzie saluted and, moments later, was gone.

"I guess that means we're back in business," Alexis said in a jittery-sounding voice.

Without missing a beat, Charles said, "When do you plan on telling your significant others that you are . . . ah . . . back in business?"

Kathryn reared up, her eyes sparking,

"Speaking strictly for myself, Charles, when I get around to it. Bert does not own me. We're not married. We are not even engaged. I am a free agent, which means I am accountable to no one except to the people in this room, and that's by my choice."

"You articulated that just perfectly, dear," Myra said, her voice ringing with steel. The others high-fived each other, the signal that Charles had better not ask any more questions or voice any opinions. He didn't.

"I think it is time for all of us to retire. It's after midnight," Yoko said. The others agreed. They all said good night to Charles, who was at his workstation. He gave a halfhearted wave and continued with what he was doing.

Back in the city, Maggie Spritzer was just about to open her front door when her cell phone rang. She powered on, not even bothering to see who her caller was.

"This is Emma Doty again, Miss Spritzer. I hope it's not too late to be calling you, but I just thought of something. Well, that's not exactly true. After I hung up from speaking with you, I called my friend Alice, she's Will's wife. She told me something I totally forgot about, and while it might not mean anything, I thought you might like to know."

"I do, Mrs. Doty, and don't give the time another thought. What is it that you remembered?" She was inside now, kicking off her shoes and tossing her backpack into the corner. She headed straight for the fridge in the kitchen.

"Alice asked me if I remembered the year the Graversons inherited a piece of property in Florida. She said it was our junior year in high school, and Madeline Graverson's grandparents, who lived in Florida, died and left her the house. It's on some waterway. Neither of us can remember the name of it. It was really a big deal back then for someone in Idaho to inherit Florida property. That summer, when school was out, Gerald Graverson, that's Andy's father, decided the family would vacation in Florida. Of course, Andy went with them. We were all jealous. But he did bring us back plastic palm trees and jars of Florida sand. Maybe Andy still has the property, and if he's gone missing, he might be there. We just can't remember the name of the waterway."

Maggie was so excited she could hardly breathe. "Could it be the Intercoastal?"

"I'm sorry, dear, I just don't remember. Alice did remember Andy's parents' names, though. Madeline and Gerald Graverson. Maybe you could check property records or something. And I spoke to my son, who said he could do as you asked and scan the pictures for you from where he works in the morning. Have I helped?" Emma Doty asked anxiously.

"Mrs. Doty, you have no idea. If you were here right now, I'd give you such a hug you'd squeal for mercy. I'm going to make this up to you. Thank you so much."

Maggie's fist shot upward. A second later she had Annie on the phone. She talked so fast that Annie had to shout in her ear to slow down and start over, which she did.

In the kitchen, the phone to her ear, Annie motioned for Myra to stay behind when the others trooped off to the second floor.

Annie continued to listen, getting more excited by the minute as Maggie continued to rattle on. Finally, she said, "Of course, dear, whatever it takes. Absolutely, I agree with you. Everything she wants. Yes, yes, I understand she doesn't want anything. What I meant was, everything *you* think she needs. Uh, yes, scanner, printer, laptop, desktop, iPhone, iPod, BlackBerry . . . whatever. Outfit the van with everything top-of-the-line. Pay the insurance for three years. We'll revisit that at a future date. Oh, and send her some flowers. Lots and lots of flowers. I'm sure they're in scarce supply in

Idaho. Then again, maybe not. Just bill everything to the paper. I'll have Conrad take care of it tomorrow. Thank you, Maggie. Thank you so very much."

Myra nervously fingered the pearls at her neck as she listened to Annie's end of the conversation. "Don't just stand there, what did Maggie say? Every word, Annie. You look just like the cat that swallowed a canary. What's up with all the high-tech communications stuff you were talking about, and who is it going to?"

"Myra, listen to me. Stop with the damn pearls already, okay? Those things that you and I fight over all the time are because we don't want anyone to know we don't know what they're talking about . . . because . . . we're too old and everyone knows you can't teach an old dog new tricks."

"What are you trying to say, Annie, that we're too old?"

"The word you're looking for is *obsolete,* Myra. And if that's true, then Hank Jellicoe was right in thinking we're no threat to him."

Her pearl lifeline forgotten with Annie's startling words, Myra stomped her foot. "Bull*SHIT!*"

"Attagirl, Myra. That's about as good as, 'Obsolete, my ass,' which was what I was going to say! I'm beginning to think you just might have the makings of a *cougar.*"

Myra, a wicked look on her face, moved a little closer to Annie. "Well, what are we going to do about it, Annie?"

"I'm thinking, Myra, I'm thinking."

CHAPTER 21

Elias Cummings let his mind drift as he tooled along. He wished he hadn't caved in to his wife and the ladies. It wasn't that he was a *wuss,* because he did get a thrill when things got dicey with the ladies, and they called on him for his expertise. Not a small thrill, a rather big thrill, to be precise. He grinned when he thought about all the things the girls — better to call them "girls" than the vigilantes — had done even when it was just in his private thoughts. He could have used their chutzpah when he was director of the FBI. Not that he would ever admit it. He almost laughed out loud when he remembered the day that Nellie had finally confided that she was *one of them.* He'd almost blacked out, which didn't say much for him when she admitted to aiding and abetting the vigilantes. Retired federal court judge Cornelia Easter, Nellie to her friends, an honorary *active* member of that elite little group.

He literally did choke when he found out his acting director, Bert Navarro, was not only active in the group but a full-fledged member. Which explained more than he cared to know back then. He guffawed aloud inside the car when he recalled the day he'd gone to the White House to announce his retirement and plead Bert's case to the president. And it had worked. With all the Bureau's foibles and bad press, Bert had turned things around so that it was no longer the laughingstock of Alphabet City. Then just when things were looking up, Bert had thrown in the towel, along with all the others. Now, that was a black day at the Bureau for sure. Elias had lost count of the calls he'd gotten to pitch in and help, all of which he'd declined by saying Nellie needed him. And once again, the workforce inside the Hoover Building was floundering. The new director was a pissant who didn't know his ass from his elbow. Maybe Elias should do some serious lobbying to get Bert back in the fold.

The GPS on his dashboard started to talk to him. He had one more turn, and he would be at his destination, which was the residence of the retired director of the CIA.

Elias turned the corner of a very pleasant, old, tree-lined street, where the houses, most of them Federal style, were set back from the street. One-acre, treed lots, lovely green grass, and shrubs that were well tended. Retired people mostly, he surmised. When he'd been here the last time, after the director's wife's funeral, he hadn't really paid too much attention to his surroundings. Calvin Sands had lived here with his family for more than forty years. Elias couldn't remember who had told him that or if had heard it at the funeral. Not that it mattered. All in all, a pleasant home in a pleasant neighborhood. The GPS squawked one more time before Elias cut the engine and reached for the gift-wrapped bottle of Kentucky bourbon. He had a silly moment as he reached for the package because he didn't know whether Calvin Sands was a drinker. Considering the job he'd held for so many years, the odds were in favor of at least a snort now and then.

Elias took a quick look at his reflection in the side mirror before he began his trek up the flower-bordered walk-way that led to the front door. He rang the bell and was rewarded with a ten-note musical chime that was not unpleasant. He heard footsteps on the other side of the door, then it opened.

Elias blinked and so did the man staring at him.

"I suppose I could say I was in the neighborhood, but that would be a lie. I made the trip out here to talk to you, Calvin." Elias held out the bourbon, and Sands took it. He motioned for Elias to follow him into the house.

Nothing looked familiar to Elias as he followed Sands down a foyer, through a dining room, then through the kitchen to an outside deck covered with a brightly colored awning. Again, the retired director motioned for Elias to take a seat at a wooden table full of newspapers, mostly unread from the look of them, and a frosty pitcher of lemonade. Cookies and sandwiches sat under a glass-domed cover. *Almost,* Elias thought, *like he knew I was coming.*

"So, you weren't in the neighborhood, but here you are. What can I do for you, Elias?"

"I don't know. Maybe nothing. Maybe something. I'm sorry for your loss, Calvin. It's hard to lose a spouse after so many years. I went through it. I have to be honest with you, nothing helped. You have to take it one day at a time."

Calvin Sands shrugged and spoke softly. "I think Helen was glad to . . . go. Before . . .

before she got bad, we talked quite a bit, probably more than we talked during our whole married life. She didn't like me at the end, Elias. In fact, I think she hated me. I was never here. I didn't contribute to anything emotionally or physically because I was married to the goddamn job. Helen did it all. She raised our children and did a fine job of it. They let me know it, too, in no uncertain terms. Not one of them, and there are four, have been out here since . . . since the funeral. I don't expect to see them anytime soon, either. But that's not the worst. I have three grandchildren I have never even seen. Even I know that's pretty damn bad."

"Yes, Calvin, it is. Like I said, I traveled that road. Time helps, but it won't make it right. To this day, I ask myself every single damn day, was it worth it? The answer in my case is no. Did you come up with an answer, Calvin, or don't you want to know?"

"I know. Instead of this lemonade, why don't we just hit this fine bottle you brought out here with you. I usually start around now and drink myself into a stupor, and my housekeeper, who also hates me, puts me to bed."

"That bad, eh?"

"Yep, that bad. I always hated you and

those pussies over at the Bureau. No offense."

"None taken. I hated you and those Neanderthals at the Farm, too. I'm sure you have some redeeming qualities, Calvin?"

"Not a goddamn one, Elias. Do you have any?"

"I'm kind to animals and women," Elias said, sipping from his glass. Sands downed his in two long swallows and wiped his mouth with the back of his hand. "We're just two old codgers these days. Life's too short to hate each other."

"You think? It's in our blood. Short of a full-body transfusion, I don't see either one of us running a mom-and-pop grocery store. Unless they sell AK-47s and Uzis in the back room."

In spite of himself, Elias laughed. "Listen, let's cut right to the chase here. What do you know about Hank Jellicoe, and what's the real story on all that buzz about some cell wanting to take down this administration?"

"What the hell are you talking about, Elias? What cell? As for Jellicoe, that bastard should burn in hell. He's been a thorn in the CIA's side for twenty years. He thinks he runs this country. Not only does he think it, he fucking believes it. What the hell has he done now?"

"I think he disappeared. Seems he got the leaders of the world's other major intelligence and law-enforcement services into a snit over that — MI5, the Sûreté, Mossad, Scotland Yard, and Interpol."

Sands poured another two inches of bourbon into his glass. He looked at it before he brought it to his lips. He took a mighty gulp. "What's the time frame you're talking about?"

"Eighteen, maybe nineteen months ago."

Sands closed his eyes. "I was still working. Helen hadn't been diagnosed then. Wasn't that about the time your boy at the Bureau cut loose and went with Jellicoe? That sure as hell caused a stir, I can tell you that."

"Yes, right around that time. Did something happen? Do you know?"

"Well, no, nothing I heard of. Certainly nothing to do with covert chatter or mystery cells trying to take down the administration."

It was true, liquor did loosen one's tongue. Before giving it a second thought, Elias poured another two inches of the amber fluid into Sands's glass.

"Assuming . . . I said assuming . . . I know something you don't know, and if I tell you, what are you going to do with the information?"

"I don't know, that's the God's honest truth. I'm thinking it might help some pretty wonderful people, but I don't know that for sure. What do you have?"

"Well, and I don't know if this is anything you're interested in, but starting about eight months later, Jellicoe's people screwed up. Remember those seven contractors that were killed over there in the sand?" Elias nodded. "Well, Global was the firm hired to protect those men. There wasn't a real *big* fuss, but there was a fuss. His image got tarnished, and he wasn't able to polish it back to its original shine. Jellicoe was on it like white on rice for all the good it did him. 'Allegedly' was the buzzword during that period. There were hearings, task forces, the whole nine yards, but for some reason the press cut him more than one break and played the whole thing down. In other words, it never grew legs. The widows and families went nuts at first, then, all of a sudden, they dropped off the grid. *Allegedly,* they were paid off handsomely. Our people went after him, and his people, but we couldn't make anything stick. It's a blight on Captain America's record. Everything else has been whitewashed. The man has some very powerful friends, and he's got more fucking money than . . . what's that woman's name who was one of those vigilantes? Well, whoever she is, he has either more money than her or almost as much."

Elias thought his blood was starting to boil in his veins. Somehow he managed an offhand shrug. "And that means, what?"

"I don't know, Elias, you tell me. You came here to pick my brain, and that's all I have to give you. My people thought he was derelict; the families thought so, too. Trust me when I tell you, we went after him, but we were stonewalled every step of the way. We started to dig, and we dug deep. Do you know how many civilian American deaths we came up with? Men that Jellicoe's people were trained and hired to protect? Sixteen, that's how many. Twenty-three if you count the last seven. And come to think of it, those deaths started right around the time you were asking about. Maybe a month or so after your guy joined his outfit. That's twenty-three too many. He never answered to anyone for even one of those deaths. He said it was collateral damage and a war was going on."

"He's disappeared is what I'm hearing. He went off the grid around that time," Elias said, pouring more bourbon into

Sands's glass.

"As Helen would say, good riddance to bad rubbish." Elias thought Nellie used the same term from time to time, because he'd heard it before. He didn't say anything but waited. He didn't have long to wait. After a long pull on his drink, Sands said, "What's the son of a bitch done now?"

"He disappeared. Word was he retired. People like Jellicoe never retire, you know that. The bastard is a mercenary, and like you said, it's in his blood. But he didn't do it until after he practically started a war with the leaders of the world's intelligence and law-enforcement services. That's pure scuttlebutt, Calvin. You know, kind of like 'alleged' back during your stint."

"Why would he do something stupid like that?"

Elias shrugged. Sands was slurring his words now, but he still made sense. "We're good, Elias, you have to admit it. My people did not *miss* anything. We'd know. Hell, I'll give the devil his due and say you guys at the Bureau would have picked up on something. Maybe after we did, but you would have picked up on something. DHS would have been on our asses the second they heard any kind of chatter. You know how that works. So, what's his game? How the hell could someone like Hank Jellicoe disappear? Maybe the son of a bitch is dead," he said, an evil smile on his lips.

"I was hoping you could tell me what his game is. He's not dead, that's for sure. Do you think you could ask around, get in touch with DHS and see what they have on him?"

"Sure, but don't hold your breath. Those boys and girls at Homeland Security don't like to share. By the way, didn't that crud get engaged to the president? Wasn't it around that time? Yeah, yeah, that's when she pardoned the vigilantes. Then poof . . . nothing. What's up with that, Elias?"

"I don't know."

Sands waved his arms about. "There you go, just goes to prove my point, you pussies over there at the Bureau don't know squat. When you want to know something, you have to come to us."

Elias leaned across the table jabbing at the air with his index finger. "And you don't know anything, either. That means that son of a bitch is better than both the Bureau and the CIA. Chew on that one, Calvin."

Calvin Sands couldn't chew on anything because he was sound asleep. Elias shook his head before he took the bottle of bourbon and poured what was left of it over the railing of the deck. He did the same with his glass and Calvin's glass. "Thirty-five bucks shot to hell!" he muttered as he made his way through the house to the front door. He was halfway to the door when he decided to go back and leave his card under the bourbon bottle. Maybe when the retired director woke up, he'd give him a call if he remembered anything else. He looked across at the slack-jawed man and winced. "Been there, done that."

On the drive back to the farm, Elias ran his visit with Calvin Sands over in his mind. He didn't like the man any better than he had before, even though Sands was vulnerable now and he could relate to that vulnerability. As much as he disliked his colleague, he felt sorry for him. As he reviewed their verbal exchange, he couldn't come up with anything that sounded like a lie. For whatever it was worth, he decided Sands had leveled with him. Maybe it was wishful thinking or just professional courtesy. All he knew for certain was when he reported in back at Pinewood, he would be telling the women something fishy was going on, and they were the ones who had to get to the bottom of it. But that meant they would be spinning their wheels, not him. If the CIA said there was no impending threat to the

White House or the current administration, then as far as he was concerned, there was no threat.

He wondered what the girls would do when he shared the information Sands had given him on the dead contractors under Jellicoe's watch.

Elias crossed the Key Bridge and drove until he found a generous shoulder to pull over and park. His assignment wasn't over. Nellie said he was to call Donald Frank, the secretary of the Department of Homeland Security, and make an appointment to see him. He dialed the number and was put through to Frank's secretary. He gave his name and phone number and asked that the secretary call him when he returned to the office. Done!

Elias waited for a break in traffic before he peeled onto the highway. He was going home and damn glad he didn't have to worry about the world anymore.

Chapter 22

The Sisters sat around the conference table in the war room waiting for Charles and Lizzie to say the big shots they were going to deal with were available for the video conference the girls had worked on tirelessly for the past few hours. Pings and dings and whistles could be heard as faxes and e-mails poured into Charles's workstation. The women looked up when Charles whistled softly and waved a confirmation slip in the air. "The money has been deposited. And now . . . it's gone to an even safer haven." The Sisters clapped their hands.

Lizzie grinned from ear to ear when Charles held up a second confirmation slip indicating that Lizzie's exorbitant fee was just as safe as the Sisters' money. She was rewarded with a whoop of approval from the Sisters.

With five minutes to go until the video conference began, Charles took a call, listened, and then held up his hand for silence. "That was Elias. Donald Frank, secretary of the Department of Homeland Security, swore on his mother, his wife, all the saints in heaven, and his dog Zip that there is no threat now nor was there a threat to the current administration eighteen months ago. Elias said his bullshit meter was turned on high, and the man was telling the truth."

Annie looked around the table. "We can talk that one to death after the conference. Just so you know, girls, when we corner Mr. Marvelous, also known as Henry, call me Hank, Jellicoe, Myra and I get first crack at him. I absolutely will not take no for an answer."

"Then you will have to fight me," Yoko said with a wicked glint in her eye. "He's *mine!*"

"You did call it first the other day, dear," Annie said, opting to take the high road. "But you will let us senior citizens *play* with him a little first, right?"

"But of course, Annie."

Myra's and Annie's faces lit up like Christmas morning. Up at his workstation, Charles shivered at the evil laughter he was hearing wafting his way. Lizzie just smiled.

"Showtime, girls!" Lizzie said.

No one knew quite what to expect, and when it was over, with Lizzie promising to deliver the signed contracts to London the next day, the Sisters sat back and looked at each other, their faces puzzled.

Kathryn, always the most vocal of the group, asked, "Now what? Our side is saying nothing is going on. Their side says there is. Where the hell are we supposed to start? I think we just screwed ourselves into a corner."

"*Au contraire,* Kathryn. Ladies, take a look at this, compliments of Maggie and her brilliant column, Sight and Sound, and one Mrs. Emma Doty from Prairie City, Idaho."

"Where they grow all the potatoes, *that* Idaho?" Alexis asked.

"The one and only," Charles said, trying to hide his dismay that Maggie had come up with something his people had missed. Heads were going to roll.

"Jellicoe is really this Andrew Graverson person?" Myra said, shock ringing in her voice. "How did he manage to get away with an assumed identity all these years? The man was vetted six ways to Sunday by Washington. I distinctly remember reading that in his biography."

"I'm guessing no one looked that hard. You really should read more spy novels,

Myra. There are ways, then there *are ways,* to get around everything. One just has to learn the navigation rules. Obviously, Hank found a way that worked for him and covered his tracks. Until he was eighteen, he was just a kid. No one goes back that far when they dig," Annie said.

"The Bureau does, Annie. Bert told me they go back to the day someone is born when they do a full-fledged background check."

"Jellicoe is sixty-six, right, according to this paperwork? Forty-eight years ago there was no real security to speak of. Certainly nothing like it is today, or even twenty years ago. I can see how he got away with it," Nikki said. "He's off the rails now, and my guess would be he's holed up at that property in Florida. I'll bet even his own people don't know about that property. Oh, it is *sooo* hot in Florida at this time of year."

"We aren't certain yet, Nikki," Charles said. "Maggie has Ted and Espinosa on it as we speak." The girls all started to babble at once. Lizzie moved closer to the huge plasma screen and clicked a few buttons. A moment later, her son appeared on the screen. Lizzie beamed, her eyes misty. "Good morning, Jack," Lizzie said, blowing the cherub a kiss that he returned. The little guy started to jabber nonstop.

"What's he saying, Lizzie?" Isabelle asked.

"That he loves me!"

Lizzie was waving her arms and blowing air kisses to the little guy. "Watch Mommy, Jack. I'm sending you a kiss and a hug around the neck. Give Daddy a big hug for me." The little boy leaned forward and hugged his dad.

"That's a carrot he's eating," Lizzie said proudly. She did some more waving and blew another kiss before she addressed her husband. "I'm taking a Gulfstream to London this afternoon, Cosmo. I'm leaving Pinewood now. I'll stop off at my office and the house. I'll call you when I board, then when I land in England. Tomorrow afternoon, I'll be on a private jet headed for Vegas and home. See you day after tomorrow. Love you guys."

Lizzie turned back to the girls. "I'm outta here, ladies, Charles. We did good, girls, real good. Keep me in the loop." A round of hugs and kisses, trailing perfume, and Lizzie Fox Cricket was gone, and the room immediately lost some of its luster.

"All right, girls, it's time to start *plotting,*" Annie said, rubbing her hands together in gleeful anticipation.

■ ■ ■ ■

Back in town, Maggie Spritzer marshaled her army of two. "Listen up, both of you, because I, meaning me, am going to blow your socks off. Me! While you two were diddling around with whatever you were diddling with, I got the goods. I really got the goods. I'm not saying it is a hundred percent, but my reporter's instinct is telling me it's 99.9 percent on the money, and boys, it just dropped in my lap, and I ran with it like a good reporter does. You're still wearing your socks, why is that?"

"Because you haven't told us what this super-duper news you have is," Ted snarled. He was still miffed that Maggie had him in dry dock. He looked down at his feet and realized he wasn't wearing socks with his sneakers. Neither was Espinosa. So much for blowing off his socks.

"I just want to make sure the two of you *know* I am the best of the best. Take a seat and tell me who you think the man in these pictures is," she said, handing over the photos Emma Doty's son had sent an hour earlier. Maggie didn't realize she was holding her breath until Ted and Espinosa both said, "It's Jellicoe. What, is this some kind of game?"

Maggie leaned in closer. "How sure are you?"

"Damn sure. I spent eighteen months hating that son of a bitch. I'd know him in a dark room. I know everything there is to know about him that's ever been printed," Ted barked.

Espinosa rolled his eyes. "Yeah, ditto for me on everything Ted just said. He's younger, but that's him. I'm telling you this with a photographer's eyes."

"That's good enough for me. I just wanted to be sure. The problem is, guys, this is not Henry, call me Hank, Jellicoe. This man, boy, whatever you want to call him, is Andrew Graverson, who was born and raised till the age of eighteen in Prairie City, Idaho. Big potato country."

Ted looked at Espinosa, then threw his hands in the air. "So, that makes us stupid, is that what you're saying?"

"No," Maggie said kindly. "If I said yes, that would make me stupid, too. None of us are stupid. Look, a very nice lady named Emma Doty blogged on the Sight and Sound blog yesterday and I e-mailed her and then we spoke on the phone. I told you, it fell in my lap, and I ran with it. She went to school back in the day with Andy Graverson. Andy Graverson was one of her husband's best friends. Seems there were four best buds back then. Small town, no job opportunities, so they all lit out after graduation for greener pastures. Graverson was the only one who never stayed in touch. The others remained friends until the men died off. The widows are still friends. Oh, I almost forgot. Many years later, when Jellicoe hit the big time, the little group realized it was him. They wrote him a few letters, but he never responded.

"Mrs. Doty is handicapped and housebound. She spends most of her days, and probably nights, on the computer. I guess it's a lifeline of sorts to the world when you can't get out and about. That's why she responded to the blog. She lived with her husband in this area for a period during their married life, and always read the *Post*. When her husband passed away, she moved back to Prairie City to be with her friends, and she reads the *Post* online. In other words, she loves us and our paper."

"And . . . ?" Ted asked. "Why do I have the feeling you left the best for last?"

"Ah, you know me so well, Teddie. I did leave the best till last. Mrs. Doty called back last night just when I got home. Apparently she called her friends after our conversation, and one of them remembered something that Mrs. Doty had forgotten, but when the friend brought it up she started to remember. Mrs. Graverson, Madeline was her name, Andy's mother, inherited a house on some waterway in Florida. They think it was during their junior year in high school. That summer the Graversons and Andy went to Florida to check it out. Mrs. Doty said they were all jealous because they knew none of them would ever be able even to go to Florida, much less own a second house there. Not that this is important, but Mrs. Doty said Andy brought them all back plastic palm trees and jars of Florida sand."

"What's the name of the town where the house is?" Espinosa asked.

"None of them can remember, and they can't remember the name of the waterway. It was a long time ago, guys. I'm thinking the Intercoastal. Possibly Fort Lauderdale. No clue, really."

"We could do a search?" Ted said.

Maggie made a very unladylike sound. "Listen, Ted, if that guy is as smart as he thinks he is, and he kept that place, it isn't in his name, that's for sure. He's managed to bug everything in sight that has to do with us. What makes you think he wouldn't have done the same thing where that piece of property is concerned? He's got himself covered every which way. It's just pure dumb luck we know what we know. We can't go there, wherever *there* turns out to be. We can't access the public records for fear he's paid someone off to watch them. We need a hacker. And we need to talk to Mrs. Doty again, or else you two have to make a trip to Prairie City, Idaho, and get the lay of the land. You could talk to some of the older folk, check out the library, check out the Graversons' old house, see who lives there now. If it's the same owner, they might know something. It's all we have, so we need to work it to death. Talk to me and make it good, guys."

Ted shrugged. "Book us tickets, Maggie, but make sure they're first-class. Don't even think about asking us to bring you back some spuds. Idaho! Damn! Okay, okay, we go to Idaho. What are you going to be doing?"

Maggie smiled sweetly. "What I do best, getting to the bottom of it all. But there is something . . . I can't quite put my finger on it, something about Florida. Tell me what it is I can't remember, guys."

Espinosa grimaced. "The bike rally on Alligator Alley for the benefit of the Juvenile Diabetes Foundation. I think it's coming up soon, or maybe it's passed already, but for some reason I think it's next week. We can check."

"Thank you, Espinosa. That's exactly what I couldn't remember. Now, think about how we can make that work and coincide with what we have to do."

"You figure it out, Miss Smarty Pants. Espinosa and I are going to frigging *Idaho.* Nobody goes to Idaho in the summer. For sure they don't go in the winter, spring, or fall, either. Just us. We're going to frigging Idaho. What's wrong with this picture?"

"Boo-hoo! Get going. Your tickets will be waiting when you get to the airport. Catch the first flight you can get that will land you anywhere near your destination. Go!"

The moment the door closed behind Ted and Espinosa, Maggie's finger hit the speed dial on her phone. "Abner, honey, sweetie, I need some additional help here. You're being cranky, and I do not like cranky. I don't have time to negotiate with you right now. You need to drop everything you're doing, even if it is my work. I want to find out about a piece of property in Florida. I don't know where it is or whose name it's listed under. All I know is that it is on some waterway. Or at least it was fifty years ago."

"Oh, a piece of cake, darling. There must

be at least three million or more dwellings in the state of Florida, and they all have owners. Like I said, a piece of cake," Abner snarled.

"I expect to have that information to you by tomorrow. Right now, though, I want you to do any kind of search you can do on a Madeline and Gerald Graverson. Probably born and died in Prairie City, Idaho. I think they're deceased; in fact, I'm almost sure of it. So start there. Find out everything you can, and don't leave any trails that lead back to you or that anyone watching can find. This is probably the most secretive thing you've ever done, Abby. You are listening to me, right? If you aren't, all that lovely beachfront property is *mine,* buddy. You can probably Google a lot of this stuff. No, I'm not trying to tell you what to do. It was a suggestion, sweetie. Now, I am going to give you an order. Track Hank Jellicoe's bank accounts. I'm sure they are all offshore, but he has to have working capital here Stateside. You're the one, Abby, who always told me, follow the money. Well, I want you to find it and follow it." Maggie listened for a few minutes, and said, "Of course I'm going to steal it. Why else would I want to know? Too much information, I know. So, how long is it going to take you?" Maggie blinked, then blinked again when she realized the connection was broken. Then she laughed.

CHAPTER 23

"Why are you looking at me like that, Jack? You didn't have to agree to make the trip. You could have said no," Ted said over his shoulder as he loped behind Espinosa to the private plane sitting on the tarmac.

Bert weighed in. "Why does Maggie think it is going to take five people, I repeat, five people to traipse around some damn town in Idaho to try and get fifty-year-old information? Isn't that why we have all those state-of-the-art computer systems?"

Harry sprinted ahead, his sandals making slapping sounds on the tarmac. He zeroed in on Espinosa, who was known to never put up an argument. "Well?" he said menacingly.

Espinosa raised an eyebrow. "Did any of you think for even a minute that the girls want us out of their hair. Idaho is about as far away as you can get, if you are asking my opinion."

Ted whirled around as he walked backward. "First, it was just Espinosa and me going. Then the flights were so screwed up we wouldn't have gotten there till tomorrow with all the stops and layovers and the last-minute ticketing, not to mention the cost. Yeah, I know, the private jet costs more, but Maggie said time was the issue, so here we are, gentlemen, so suck it up and enjoy the flight. It's not snowing there. Yet."

"What the hell are you talking about? It's just the beginning of August. It doesn't snow in August!" Jack said.

Ted laughed. "You ever been to Idaho, Jack? I didn't think so. I rest my case. I do know that we will be served filet mignon and lobster aboard this flight. And Boston cream pie."

"And that's supposed to make me feel better. I can cook that myself," Jack grumbled.

Ted came to a stop at the portable stairway that led to the open plane door, where the pilot and hostess were waiting, welcoming smiles on their faces. "Last chance, Jack. Back out now or shut up."

Harry moved a step forward and sent Ted spiraling up the stairs at the speed of light. The others followed. "That was so rude, Harry. Now the pilot and hostess are going to think we're a bunch of ill-mannered thugs." He stepped backward the moment he saw Harry wiggle his foot. "Move! What are you guys waiting for, a bus? The sooner we get airborne, the sooner we'll get back here. Probably with a ton of potatoes in the cargo hold. You can keep potatoes in a cool, dry place for almost a year, did you know that, Harry?"

"Yeah, Jack, I do know that. Like you can keep pumpkins . . . you know, those orange things you love so much, till Easter. Don't talk to me, Jack. I hate you right now."

"Damn, Harry, you're nasty this afternoon. Why can't you be like the rest of us and be happy that we're going to Idaho? How many people get to go to Idaho on a nice August day in the middle of summer where it might or might not be snowing? Not many, that's how many. Think of all those russet potatoes, and they have some newfangled potato called a fingerling or something like that, tiny little morsels of goodness that will light up any dinner table. Different colors, too."

Harry looked like he wanted to cry when he took his seat and buckled up per the hostess's instructions. The moment she was out of earshot, Harry shot Jack a withering look, and said, "Fuck you, Jack."

"Potty mouth." Jack sniffed as the hostess

appeared with a bottle of champagne.

"Does anyone want information on Idaho to broaden his mind?" Ted asked. "I am a virtual encyclopedia of information. Espinosa can do a color show on his phone, if you like."

"Will you please shut up, or I will see to it that you sleep for the entire trip to wherever it is we're going, Ted," Harry said as he shook his head, declining the champagne. He held up a little bag of ground tea and instructed, "Let it steep for ten minutes. I prefer a cup with no handles."

"Of course, sir," the hostess said sweetly. So sweetly, Jack thought he was going to gag.

"Not that I care, Ted, but why was it so difficult to get tickets to Idaho? I thought no one went there," Jack commented.

"Some potato festival, Maggie said. Gourmet cooks from all over the country are making the trip. Everyone wants to win a gold potato on a pedestal. And it was a last-minute booking. You complaining, Jack?"

"Nah, just making conversation. I have to admit I am a little perturbed that the girls don't want us around. What's up with that?"

"They always have a reason for what they do," Espinosa said, authority ringing in his voice."

"Yeah, and you know this . . . how?" Jack said sourly as he finished off the champagne in his glass.

"I know because Alexis talks to me. We discuss *everything.* That's what couples do. I probably know more than all of you put together. Just because I don't blab my business to you . . . because none of you can be trusted to keep a secret, doesn't mean I don't know what's going on."

They were on him like fleas on a dog. Alarmed, the hostess backed away with her champagne bottle, muttering something about dinner at thirty thousand feet.

Espinosa clamped his lips shut, his signal that he wouldn't be parting with any information anytime soon. Even Harry's threat — "Don't worry, when we land, I'll kill him. I'd do it now, but I don't want to be the first man to kill someone in midair on a private plane" — kept Espinosa's lips clamped shut.

Bert, who had been quiet throughout the exchange, sat upright. "You know, Espinosa, if you know something we should know, it's not going to do you a bit of good to withhold that information. We're brothers under the skin. A team, I thought. If I had information, you guys would be the first ones I would share it with."

Espinosa thought about it for a moment, then said, "The girls don't know what to do."

"That's it! The girls don't know what to do!" Jack said in disbelief.

"Yeah. They signed on, Lizzie did it all, and she's on her way, or will be shortly, to London. Elias says the CIA and DHS say nothing is going on on our turf. Of course, Elias did not let on that the big shots in the foreign intelligence and law-enforcement worlds contacted the girls. But our side is saying there is no threat to the administration, nothing covert is going on or has been going on, which brings it all back to Hank Jellicoe, who started the whole thing in the first place. That's why we're going to Idaho, back to *his* beginning. The girls are waiting and depending on us to come up with some workable information."

Harry stirred, which was never a good sign. "Then why didn't you say that in the first place? Then I wouldn't have had to issue my threat to kill you," he complained, one eye open and one eye closed.

"Because I don't take kindly to threats. Alexis wouldn't let you go free if you killed me. She loves me."

"Oh, yeah, well, she's no match for Yoko," Harry blustered.

"Enough with the pissing match, boys. We now have the information we need, which is, the girls *need* us. 'Need' is the operative word here. Are you all following me? In addition, I think we should all thank Espinosa for clueing us in."

Before anyone could comment either way, the hostess appeared carrying dinner trays. They managed to use up an hour cutting, chewing, and mumbling about the gourmet dinner. When coffee was poured, they went back at it, but not with any real intensity. Smarting from their lack of knowledge, Ted zeroed in on Espinosa. "And why were you picked to get this information and not us?"

"Maybe because your phones were off? Well, I *was* supposed to share it with you, but you were all so belligerent, I just didn't feel like it. You know now, so just shut up. I have nothing more to say."

"I'll pray for you," Jack said solemnly. Bert and Ted agreed to do the same. Harry slept.

Three hours later the plane landed in Boise, Idaho. Ted spoke at length to the pilot, tapped some numbers into his phone, and was the last off the plane. "We have a rental car waiting. We have a two-hour drive ahead of us, so who wants to take the wheel?" Jack volunteered, and they were on the road in less than twenty minutes.

"Okay, Bert, you're my navigator. Type in the address and let the GPS do our work."

"Where are we going, Ted?"

"The only address I have is Emma Doty's." He rattled it off. "I guess we should start there. How big can a town with a population of thirty-six hundred be?"

"I thought you said the population was two thousand," Harry said. "I hate falsehoods. And the people who tell them."

"It's two thousand if you don't count the people who live outside the town limits. Do we really care what the hell the population is?" Not bothering to wait for a response, Jack answered the question. "No, we do not care. Let's all just kick back and think about our mission here and how the girls are depending on us to come through for them. Now, sit back and think pleasant thoughts."

By local time, it was the dinner hour when Jack drove the rental car down Main Street. "Here we are, boys, Mayberry, USA, or Prairie City, Idaho, which is also in the good old U. S. of A. There's the town square to the left. That's town hall next to it. I know this because there's a sign on the lawn. To the right is Saint Albans Church — not sure what the denomination is. Let's just go with religious and be done with it. That brick building is the post office. There's a sign on the door saying UNITED STATES POST OFFICE. Ah, here's a hardware store, a drugstore, and Miss Eva's café. To the right of Miss Eva's is Waddell's Emporium. The sign says they sell everything. I guess that means a toaster or a pair of socks. Looky there, on my left is the PO-LICE station. Hiram Sherman sells all kinds of insurance to fit your needs right next door. Cody's Beauty Shop does discreet waxing in a back room if you're interested," Jack said, enjoying his witty monologue. "Farm Bureau is coming up on the left, right alongside McBride's one-stop shopping. Groceries," Jack clarified.

"In case none of you noticed, there are no traffic lights. Ah, here's a STOP sign, so I am stopping. You know what, I like this little town. Look at all these trees, and the sidewalks with benches. All the stores have flowers, probably donated by the Garden Club. Make a note, Harry, so you can tell Yoko. Better yet, take some pictures and send them to her. She loves flowers."

Two ladies in flowered dresses carrying string bags stopped in the middle of the road to stare at them before they moved on.

"Oh, shit, they made us. Strangers from out of town. Now the cops will be trailing us, and before you know it, we'll be locked up. I saw that in a movie once," Espinosa said in a jittery-sounding voice. "Nobody came for them. They were rotting away before they were found, and none of them were ever the same again."

"Relax, we're going to see Emma Doty, and she won't let anything happen to us," Ted said.

"Hold on, Jack. Look, there's a funeral home. James Dial and Sons. What better place to start than there. We can go to Emma's after we pay a visit. Looks quiet, so probably no customers. It's worth a shot," Bert said, excitement ringing in his voice.

"Yeah, let's see what they can tell us, if anything." Jack made a right turn and parked behind a shiny black hearse. "You can do the honors, Bert, since this was your idea."

Inside the mortuary, it was dim and cool. The decor was burgundy walls, dark blue carpeting, and cherrywood. The sickening smell of flowers was everywhere. Somber music played in the background. There was no one behind the shiny cherrywood desk, so Bert rang the little bell sitting on a pedestal. A door opened; the scent of flowers grew stronger. A balding youngish man in a three-piece suit, who looked more like one of his customers, extended a snow-white hand. He had polish on his nails. "Marshall Kelly. How can I be of service to you and your loved ones?"

Bert debated just a second before he reached for his wallet, flashed his retirement badge, and hoped Kelly didn't look too close. He didn't. "We're working a cold case, and our leads have brought us to this beautiful little town of yours. We need some information on a couple who used to live here a long time ago. I'm sure before your time, but you must keep records."

Marshall Kelly's Adam's apple bobbed up and down. He would have so much to talk about at the next Rotary meeting if he could last that long. The FBI right here in his mortuary in Prairie City. "We have records dating back to the day my grandfather opened this mortuary. I'm sure they're somewhere. To be honest, I couldn't say where they are at this precise minute. Tell me who it is, and possibly my father might know, and we won't have to go through all that digging. No pun intended. It's rare that I get to use mortuary witticisms." He laughed.

Bert winced. "Madeline and Gerald Graverson."

"I've heard the names. Dad's napping in the back. Let me fetch him and see what he has to say."

"Napping in the back," Ted hissed. "You don't think he naps in a . . ."

"Do not go there, Ted," Jack hissed in return.

Five minutes went by, then another five minutes. Finally, Marshall Kelly and a white-haired, suited-up senior came through a burgundy leather door that didn't make a sound. Introductions were made all around. Tea or coffee was offered and declined.

Marshall Kelly Senior motioned the men to sit in a row of dark burgundy leather chairs. "It was sad; Gerald passed first, then Madeline six months later. They both looked lovely. We get so many compliments on our work, that's why people elect to come to James Dial and Sons, opposed to going out of town. There's the travel, the caskets are discounted, the satin is tacky." He shuddered to show what he thought of such places.

"How was the turnout?" Harry asked bluntly.

Both Senior and Junior Kelly looked at Harry as though they'd never seen a live oriental. And they probably hadn't if they'd never left Prairie City. "And you are?"

"Harry Wong," Bert said.

"He's our resident terrorist," Jack said.

Harry stared at the two men until they looked away.

"Well," Mr. Kelly Senior said, "Everyone in town came to pay his or her respects. Funerals and wakes bring out the best in people. There was an overabundance of flowers, as I recall, but with no name attached to the cards at either funeral. That's the only reason I remember it. People sign their names to gifts of flowers. Both Madeline and Gerald are buried in St. Albans Cemetery. It's two miles down the road, right off our main street."

"Any family members attend?" Bert asked.

"As I recall, there was no family, just friends and neighbors. The Graversons had a son, but no one knew where he was to notify him. We tried. We held the bodies an extra week, just in case we were able to locate him. I'm sorry to say we never did."

"Who paid for the funeral?"

The elder Kelly held up his hand. "Now, that was very strange. A bank draft came in for a large amount of money. It paid for the cemetery plots, top-of-the-line Springfield caskets, the minister, our fee of course, and the refreshments that were served afterward at our home. Actually, I think there is still fourteen hundred dollars in an escrow account we set up. I'm sure the interest has accumulated nicely. We would be more than happy to turn it over to the son if you can locate him for us."

"We don't know where he is, either," Jack said.

"Their home, what happened to it?" Ted asked.

"Nothing, as far as I know. It's still standing. I believe the neighbors boarded up the windows and doors. I do know their cars are still in the garage. I'm sorry, but I don't remember who told me that."

"That's okay," Bert said. "Who pays the taxes on the property?"

"I really don't know for certain. You could ask at the town hall. I would assume they were paid ahead, possibly by the son, or else there was money in an account. This is a small, friendly town, gentlemen. I'm sure if there wasn't enough money, the townspeople would have chipped in. We're not talking a huge amount of money for property taxes — less than $200 a year. Ask for Ellie at the bank. There are no secrets in this town. There will be records."

"Did the Graversons own any other property anywhere?"

The elder Kelly slapped playfully at his forehead. "How could I have forgotten that? It was all this little town talked about when

Madeline inherited a house in Florida. The land of sunshine and oranges. They went there once a year, and they even posted a bulletin at the church saying that anyone wanting to go to Florida could stay there for a vacation. I don't think anyone ever took them up on the offer, but it just goes to show how kind the Graversons were."

"What is all this about?" the younger Kelly asked.

"We think they were witnesses to something that happened in Florida a long time ago. As I said, we're working a cold case. It's probably not going to go anywhere, but we have to check every possibility. I don't suppose you have an address for the property?" Bert said.

"Shouldn't you have that if, as you say, something happened there? I certainly don't know it. Maybe Pastor Homes has it, I really can't say."

"No problem, it's in our files someplace."

"Good record keeping is as good as a good memory. It's a mark of a successful businessman, but then, the government is not known for good record keeping, considering the mess the world is in today," the Senior Kelly said.

"Dad! These men are from the government." What he didn't say was, *Shit, now we're going to be audited.* The old man tossed his mane of white hair and turned to leave. He didn't offer to shake hands.

"Thank you for your time, Mr. Kelly," Bert said.

"I hope we were some help. Dad gets cranky at this time of day for some reason. I'm sorry if you think he was rude."

"Not a problem. Thank you for talking with us, and, yes, you were helpful," Bert said as he followed Marshall Kelly to the door. They all heard the snick of the lock falling into place.

Back in the car, everyone started to talk at once. Jack let loose with an earsplitting whistle. "We can bat this around later; next stop, Emma Doty's house. Bert, turn on that GPS, and let's get this show on the road. Jesus, I'm never going to get the smell of that place out of my nose!"

A ripe discussion followed, with an agreement that when they died, no one wanted flowers at their wake.

CHAPTER 24

It was going on six-thirty when the GPS announced they had reached their destination. It was a small house, more like a cottage of possibly a thousand square feet. It was painted white and looked like it was in good repair. There were four rocking chairs and pots of colorful flowers arranged neatly on the old-fashioned front porch. Two lush, green ferns hung from the rafters. A coiled hose was nestled in a rack of sorts behind one of the rockers. Something that looked suspiciously like a keg was sitting next to a huge clay pot of bright red geraniums. Jack led the way to the front door, which was painted a dark hunter green. The main door was open behind the screen door, which didn't have even one hole in it. The screen was stretched taut and looked new. Jack pressed the doorbell. It rang, one loud bong that didn't interfere with the sounds coming from the back end of the house, probably a television. "Come in, come in!"

"Small-town people are hospitable," Espinosa said.

They heard the sound before Emma Doty appeared around a corner in a motorized wheelchair. She didn't miss a beat when she said, "Hello, what can I do for you?"

"I guess it never occurred to her we might be Jack the Ripper's apprentices," Jack mumbled under his breath.

"Jack the Ripper doesn't know where Prairie City, Idaho, is," Bert mumbled back. He had his badge in his hand and held it out.

"No need for that, young man. Miss Spritzer said you would be stopping by. She called earlier this afternoon. Now let me see if I can identify you from what she told me about all of you. She said you five were the finest human beings to ever walk the earth. People only say that about their friends. I'm Emma Doty. You must be Jack, and you're Bert. You, young man, are Joseph, and the man next to you is Ted. So this handsome man is Harry. Not that you aren't all handsome, mind you, but Harry stands out for some reason." Harry blushed.

"Maggie said I should use her given name. I don't want you to think I'm being forward. She asked me to talk to my friends to see if any of us could remember something that we might not think is important but you would. Please, come in and sit down. Can I offer you anything to drink?"

"We're fine, ma'am. Did you come up with anything?"

"No, I'm sorry to say. Perhaps if you ask me questions, specific questions, it might help to jog my memory. My friends are standing by in case I have to call them to confirm something."

"Mainly what we need to know is where the Florida property the Graversons inherited is located. We stopped at the funeral home on our way here, and Mr. Kelly Senior told us what he could remember. He said the house is boarded up, someone has paid the taxes, the son Andy didn't attend either parent's funeral, but there was an abundance of flowers with no name on them, and a bank draft arrived that paid for all the funeral expenses," Bert said.

"I wasn't living here then. Neither were my friends. The Graverson house is boarded up. It's just two streets over. It's not like it's a blight on the neighborhood. The neighbors maintain the lawn and flower beds and rake leaves in the fall and shovel the snow in the winter. Prairie City is a lovely little town of people who care for one another."

"Is there anyone in town who might know where the property in Florida is? Mr. Kelly mentioned a notice the Graversons posted at the church offering their property for free to anyone wanting to vacation in Florida. He also said someone named Ellie at the bank might be of some help. Do you know Ellie?"

"Son, I know everyone in Prairie City. Ellie belongs to my quilting group, and she's the one who brought me all those lovely plants on my front porch. Pastor Homes is relatively new to our church. He's only been here about twenty years, give or take a few. I doubt he would know about that particular posting, but Bertha might remember. If she's having a good day, that is. Would you like me to call them, or would you rather visit with them? Bertha, now, she's getting up there in years, and her memory isn't as sharp as it used to be."

"Records?" Jack said lamely.

"Son, I doubt there is a record of a posting about a vacation home, but what do I know? Let me call first. No sense you traipsing all over the place if a phone call will work. Just you all relax, and I'll make my calls."

Minutes later, Emma Doty smiled. "Ellie is on her way; it will only take her ten minutes. She's going to pick up Bertha on the way. We'll sit on the porch and drink beer after you leave. That's a perk for me. I don't get too many visitors, so I thank you for that. Ellie's son makes his own beer — some new thing he's into. It's quite good for home brew."

Whoa, Jack thought.

Emma was as good as her word; exactly ten minutes later, they all turned when a cheery "Yoo-hoo" came from the door. A buxom redhead and an aproned little lady with snow-white hair came into the room. Introductions were made and everyone sat back down, Ted and Espinosa giving up their chairs to the ladies.

Ellie took the floor, and within minutes the little group knew the exact amount of money in the Graversons' account. "It's still open; it was never put to bed. We pay the taxes from the bank and for the fuel in winter, that kind of thing. We keep impeccable records in case Andrew Graverson ever comes back and wants an accounting. It probably isn't legal, but we do it this way anyway."

It was Bertha's turn next. She had a squeaky voice and played with a knotted hanky as she peered at the men watching her. "Of course I remember the posting. It was the only one we ever had. Pastor Blandenship and I used to talk about it all the time, wondering if anyone would take the Graversons up on their kind offer. No one ever did."

Jack leaned forward. "Do you remember where in Florida the property is, Bertha?"

"Right by the water. Madeline said they had a dock but no boat. That's just plain foolish to have a dock and no boat. They said they were never going to buy a boat, because neither Madeline nor Gerald could swim."

"Do you know the name of the town?" Jack asked again.

"Florida. How many towns are there? Maybe if you mention a few I might remember."

Jack sucked in his breath. "Fort Lauderdale, Miami, Pompano Beach, Lantana, Lighthouse Point, Palm Beach."

Bertha shook her head. "It could be any of those. I do remember the name of the street, though," she said proudly.

Hot damn! "And that would be . . ." Jack said.

"Dolphin Drive. I only remember it because Pastor Blandenship and I talked about living on a street like that and wondered if there were dolphins in the water.

Wait, now, let me think. There was another street that was either next to it or close to it that . . . it also had a happy name. Oh, let me think. You know, Emma, a glass of beer right now might help me think a little better."

"The beer's for later, Bertha, when we visit on the porch. If you don't come up with a name, you're going home without any," Emma snapped.

"Flipper Way! After that dolphin named Flipper. Now can I have that beer!"

"Bertha, you can have the whole damn keg!" Emma said happily. "Does that work for you, gentlemen?"

"It does, Emma, and thank you, and thank you, ladies."

The three women beamed as everyone said their good-byes.

"You think they're gonna get schnockered?" Bert asked when they were in the car and headed around the corner for a look-see at the Graversons' house so that Espinosa could take pictures.

"Are you kidding! Did you see the size of that keg on the front porch?" Jack grinned.

"Okay, Ted, where is it?" Jack asked twenty minutes later.

Ted stopped texting and yelped in delight. "Maggie says it's between Pompano Beach and Fort Lauderdale, and it is right on the Intercoastal. Every homeowner on both streets has a dock. She did a Google Earth check. She wants us to go to the airport and head for Florida. We are to wait for further orders. She's on the phone now with the pilot. Annie okayed it."

Bert was driving this time, and Jack was keying in the location for the airport in Boise. "I'm feeling pretty good, boys. We came through for the girls. See, they really do need us. And all it took was a keg of homemade brew we didn't even have to pay for."

"Dolphin Drive has seven houses on it, and it's a cul-de-sac. Flipper Way runs parallel, and there are nine houses on it. Maggie's on it, but it is late back home, so she's got her snitch working it. By the time we get to the airport, she should have some info for us. She did say we are not to make a move until the girls okay it. If Jellicoe really is holed up there for whatever reason, we can't tip him off," Ted said.

"Now, gentlemen, would be a good time to have a sing-along. How about if I start off, and the rest of you join in?" Harry's arm snaked out, and before Jack could blink, he was sound asleep.

■ ■ ■ ■

Maggie wasn't the least bit surprised to see Myra's farmhouse lit from top to bottom even though it was two o'clock in the morning. She pressed in the security code, waited for the gates to open, then drove Ted's battered Mustang to a parking space on a wide concrete apron. The screen door from the kitchen opened, and three huge dogs rushed at her. "Hi, guys. Yep, that's your mortal enemy you smell on me, but that's okay." She took the time to fondle each dog behind the ears before they escorted her, quite regally, she thought, to the kitchen door, where everyone was waiting for her.

"Girls, you are going to shower me with undying love! I got it. Well, the guys got it, I just ran with it! You got anything to eat?"

Food appeared like magic on the kitchen table — ham, turkey, roast beef, homemade bread, lettuce, tomatoes, and a giant bowl of cut-up fruit that the girls hastened to provide for the bearer of what they knew was going to be invaluable information. They did their best to contain their excitement while Maggie scarfed down the food in front of her. When she decided she couldn't eat another bite and had seriously deleted today's lunch, she leaned back and started to talk. The Sisters sat by, their jaws slack as Maggie rattled on and on and on.

"You got all this information in the last few hours, while Charles has been digging and digging and can't come up with anything?" Nikki asked, her voice full of awe.

Maggie beamed with pleasure. "You know what they say, it's not what you know, it's *who* you know. Throw in a big dose of a reporter's gut instinct, and we're rocking, girls!"

"I'm almost afraid to ask how you got Jellicoe's bank information," Kathryn chortled gleefully.

"Then don't ask. The less you know, the better off you are. The man is *wealthy!*"

Annie was miffed, but just for a few moments. "There is so much need in the world today. I'm sure when we deal with Henry, call me Hank, Jellicoe, he won't mind if we relieve him of such a burden. So much need," she prattled on. The girls laughed. Nikki flexed her fingers, then laughed the loudest. It was always Nikki who did the money wire transfers on a mission.

"So, let's go over it again to make sure we all understand," Myra said. "All the houses on Dolphin Drive are rented by snowbirds. Allegedly. As are the houses on Flipper Way.

Allegedly. According to the records, the houses are sold through one corporation to another, but they all come back to one main holding company. All the houses are empty save one. All are maintained, all are furnished, all taxes, utilities, and other such bills are paid on an individual basis. There are no neighbors to complain because there are no neighbors. We assume the lighting is on timers, which makes sense. We do not know this for sure, but your source thinks the house at 123 Dolphin Drive is always occupied by at least one person. Your source calculated the water bill, and somehow he was able to figure out that water usage, at times, indicates three persons. Showers and doing laundry, I assume. The water bills on the other empty houses can be explained away by irrigation systems. Just in case some nosy person decided to do a little checking."

"The man has a brain," Alexis said sourly, "but I am liking what I'm hearing. Do you know how long ago he bought up the other properties?"

"The original property, 123 Dolphin Drive, was inherited by the Graversons in 1959. A Florida room was added in 1968 and the open-air carport converted into a regular two-car garage. The building permit says the walls were Sheetrocked and a wood floor was laid down. No one puts a wood floor in a garage. Tongue and groove, no less. That was 1979. In 1980, the house was sold to a corporation called Andover & Sons. It sold four more times in the next seven years. The tax rolls say that John and Gertrude Solomon are the current owners. I sense a streak of nepotism here. Do you see the JGS? Jellicoe Global Securities, which was what Global Securities was named when John and Gertrude bought the house. John and Gertrude also own two houses at 125 and 121 Dolphin Drive. In other words, the houses on either side of him. For privacy, I assume. All but 123 are rental properties that are never rented. Ditto for Flipper Way," Maggie said.

A disgruntled Charles spoke up. "What about an aerial video of the Intercoastal and the two streets. Just one flyby, no return, in case Hank is really staying there, which I doubt."

Myra pounced. "Why on earth would you say that, Charles? This all makes so much sense it's mind-boggling."

"I say it because this is not how Hank Jellicoe operates. Think about it for a minute. Think of the details, the outlay of cash, the maintenance, the cover-up. Hank was, is, all over the globe during those years. Who took care of all the details? Particularly the last eighteen months. I'm not saying it isn't possible, but I think it's a stretch even to think along those lines. Another thing, what is Hank's motive for such . . . I don't even know what word to use."

"Well, I for one don't think it's a stretch of any kind. Now, if anyone is interested, I think I can tell you who took care of all those pesky details and made his plan work," Annie said smugly.

"Who?" the Sisters shouted as one.

"Fish and Stu Franklin, that's who!"

"Oh, my God, Annie, you're right! That would certainly explain so many things," Isabelle stormed. "And it also would explain one of those . . . visions I had. I told you about it when I first got here. I saw Stu, Jellicoe, and Fish fighting for their lives. There was so much gunfire, I thought I was going to lose my hearing. In the end, I was afraid of Stu."

Annie snorted. "I was never afraid of Fish, but I think he was afraid of me. He said more than once he couldn't depend on me, that I was like mercury. I took that as a compliment."

"And well you should have, dear. Being mercurial is a wonderful attribute," Myra said. The Sisters agreed, and Annie basked in their praise.

"I cannot wait to get my hands on that weasel," Annie said. "I want you to know right now that I am declining any and all help when it comes to Fish."

"Point taken and noted," Kathryn said, giggling.

"What else do you have, Maggie?" Nikki asked.

"It's really only been a few hours, girls. I'm sure my source is working diligently on getting more, but for now, that's pretty much it. Do you have anything sweet?"

Yoko scurried to the fridge and brought out half a coconut cream pie. "Just eat it out of the pie plate. There's only enough for you." Maggie obliged.

Even though the hour was late, and no one had had any sleep, the girls trekked down to the war room, where they went to work, Alexis with her list for Charles to fulfill for the mission that was just days away. Charles's eyebrows shot upward, but he didn't say a word. He tried to shift his mind into the neutral zone, but it refused to budge. He cringed when his wife looked at him, and she said, "It's admirable to stick up for one's friends; it's another thing not to have an open mind. You can't always be right, dear. And last but not least, we're women. You seem to have temporarily forgotten that. We haven't failed yet, and we won't fail now. I just want you to know we are not going to hold this against you in any way, dear," Myra said. "Are we, girls?"

Charles strained to hear the Sisters' responses, but none were forthcoming. His insides felt like an army of ants on the march.

"You did, dear, but don't dwell on it now. We're closing in," Myra said soothingly as she patted Isabelle's arm.

Chapter 25

The strip, as it was called, which was actually A1A in Fort Lauderdale, teemed with tourists, locals, and thousands of men and women who were gearing up for a show of solidarity for the ride up the eighty-mile stretch of Alligator Alley for the benefit of the Juvenile Diabetes Foundation.

Jack Emery — decked out in what he called Florida gear, an outrageously colored shirt covered in palm trees, a straw hat with strings hanging all over it, sunglasses, cutoff short shorts, and sandals — looked at his posse and burst out laughing. "Someone really should take our picture, especially old Harry here." Harry's middle finger shot into the air. Espinosa clicked away.

"You're looking bloody silly," Avery Snowden said, coming up behind the five men. "Silly because I could have taken you in the blink of an eye."

"Aren't you supposed to say 'over and out'

or something equally stupid, Snowden?" Jack pointed to Snowden's outfit and burst out laughing. "You are never going to pass for a biker dude, *dude!* You look like you've been embalmed, and they forgot to tell you. My advice is to go out there in the water, get soaking wet, then roll around in the sand so you don't look so *new.* I don't think I ever saw anyone ride a Harley with a spit shine on his biker boots. Plus, you look just like what you are, law enforcement," Jack said, adding insult to injury.

"And you all look like something the cat dragged in, then realized she'd made a mistake," Snowden shot back.

"Now you're getting it, you asshole. That's the look we were shooting for. It makes us belong. We're beach bums, locals. You did notice how people are crossing the street so they don't have to walk past you, right?"

"I don't like you," Harry said quietly. Jack and the boys stepped backward against a window display of colored beach towels that were two for twelve dollars. The scent of coconut suntan lotion wafting out the open door was overpowering.

"Well, ask me if I bloody well care," Snowden snapped.

"You should care," Harry said, "because there is no more room on my list of dislikes."

Jack and the boys watched as Snowden tried to process Harry's words. When he couldn't, he turned and motioned to four of his men. "This is no time for personalities, Mr. Wong. We're here to do a job. If you want to take me on when it's over, come ahead."

"That makes sense, Harry. Now you have something to look forward to," Jack said. "If you're stupid, that is."

Harry slid his sunglasses down over his nose. "As usual, Mr. Emery, that makes a modicum of sense. Thank you for your input."

"Anytime, Harry, anytime." Jack cackled.

"Let's go over there to the Anytime Bar and Grill and talk this through to make sure none of us screws up, Snowden," Bert said. "We have plenty of time, thirty-six hours to be exact, before the bike rally starts. We've been here twenty-four hours already, so I think we have a good bead on things."

Seated around a scarred wooden table, the party of ten ordered burgers and draft beer. To order anything else would have been suspicious, Bert said. "How did the flyby go?" he asked.

Snowden smirked. "Well, 123 Dolphin Drive is occupied by three people as of seven o'clock this morning. We know this because of the heat sensors in the plane. They flew low, so let's not get into the technical end of things or a bunch of questions. We have a video of the neighborhood. It was one flyby, and by now I'm sure your guy has called the airport and checked the tail numbers. Before you can ask, the plane is registered as a trainer, and the log shows a student going up at 7:17. No blowback there. The video was uploaded to Charles the minute the plane landed. We're waiting for further instructions."

"Annie called us a half hour ago and said the girls think Fish and Stu Franklin are with Jellicoe," Bert said.

"Makes sense. Beautiful day — the waterway will be busy today. I have guys out there. If Jellicoe has been hiding out here for as long as you all think he has, his guard might be down, what with nothing happening. Has anyone said how the girls plan to . . . infiltrate . . . 123 Dolphin Drive?" Snowden asked.

Jack and his boys laughed. "Surely you jest, Snowden. We won't know that till the last minute. I do know this — they're on their way. Annie said there are twelve of you, right? That makes us a party of seventeen. Our own little biker gang," Bert said.

Snowden chomped down on his burger,

ketchup dribbling down his chin. He swiped at it. "I spent four hours yesterday in the records department here in Fort Lauderdale. I checked all of the building permits, and I think it's accurate to say 123 Dolphin Drive is about as safe as Fort Knox. The doors are steel, but there's a mahogany veneer on them. The building permit just says mahogany doors, but with the high-powered binocs, I could tell. And those garage doors, they're just doors — but there's a solid wall behind them. These lenses can see through everything but three layers of steel. What the hell is this guy afraid of?"

"Beats the crap out of me," Jack said. "Then again, maybe it's the fear of those five guys from the intelligence and law-enforcement services coming down on his ass. That would scare the hell out of me."

Snowden leaned across the table. "What the hell did he do?"

"Like we know! Something, obviously. We just don't know *exactly* what it is."

"And for some unknown reason, we are taking this guy out?"

"Yeah. Interesting, huh?" Ted said, speaking up for the first time. "Technically speaking, we aren't taking him out, the girls are. We're just backup."

"What now, Snowden?" Jack asked.

"We're quartered a half mile up the strip at the Seashell Motel. Our bikes arrived last night. We signed up to take part in the rally, although why is still a mystery to me. I guess it goes under the category of nitpicking details. We have creds that say we belong. Your bikes should be arriving in" — Snowden looked at his watch — "thirty minutes. We have just enough time to pay the check and hoof it back to the motel. I registered you guys last night, so all the details have been taken care of. You plan on riding in those silly getups?"

"Uh-huh," Harry said.

Bert paid the bill and mumbled something about $192 being a rip-off.

"With or without the tip?" Espinosa asked.

"Without," Bert snarled as he pocketed the receipt, wondering who he could turn it in to for reimbursement.

As they walked along ogling the nubile sunbathers, Ted decided it was time to vent his frustration. "This . . . this mission smacks of a few past missions where no plan was in place. Is anyone seeing this but me?"

"If that snide comment was directed at me, *Teddie,* eat shit! I'm not in charge of anything and, like you, I'm here because I was ordered to be here. Look at the bright side. We got some new duds out of the deal," Jack said, referring to the beachwear they'd purchased at a thrift store for pennies on the dollar. "The even brighter side is when you and Maggie finally tie the knot, and you take her to Hawaii on your honeymoon, you won't have to shop for island wear."

"What are you guys babbling about?" Snowden demanded.

Jack didn't think Ted's voice or tone could get any surlier, but it did. "I was just mentioning it would be nice if there were a plan in place. Or is this crap NTK?"

"It is need to know, Robinson. First and foremost, never question orders; just obey them."

"I don't like your attitude, Snowden. Furthermore, I don't work for you, so that means I don't take orders from you. I'm with Harry. I don't like you. In addition to all of the above, you are going to look pretty damn stupid in those biker duds sitting poolside with us *while we wait for orders.*"

"Wiseass! My men and I will *not* be sitting poolside with you clowns. We will be tinkering with our Harleys. That's what bikers do; they tinker every minute they aren't riding."

Harry inched closer to Ted and hissed,

"Would you like me to kill him now or later?"

"I heard that! I heard that! You and what army, Wong? Hope you aren't counting on those four *wusses* behind you."

Harry laughed. Jack thought it was a delightful sign of mirth. For certain it was a harbinger of evil things to come. Snowden must have thought the same thing, because he moved away to take a call that was coming in on his cell.

"Well, boys, I think we have arrived at the Seashell Motel," Bert observed, pointing to an ugly square structure painted pale purple, yellow, and pink.

Espinosa reared backward. "This looks like one of those places that rents rooms by the hour. I am not staying here. And I am not going into that pool. Just look at that murky water. There's no telling what is breeding in it."

"Well, then, I guess we should start tinkering on our bikes. I do believe those five Harleys sitting on the side belong to us, at least temporarily. And they come equipped with helmets, thank you very much. These people drive like drunken cowboys here in this fine state. What do you think, Harry?"

"I do believe you're right, Jack. However, if these bikes are compliments of one

Charles Martin, my advice would be to *pretend* to tinker. 'Pretend' is the operative word. These machines are delicately honed to respond to their drivers. I read that; I don't know it to be true, but it is always best to err on the side of caution, do you agree, Jack?"

"I do, Harry, I absolutely do. So it's okay to sit on it and have Espinosa take my picture? For Nikki. I'm sure she'd like a glossy eight by ten."

"You're ahead right now, Jack, so quit."

"Okay, Harry."

Snowden took that moment to end his call. "Okay, listen up. I have some temporary orders, so pay attention. First, though, I have to go inside and see if I can upload some info and print it out for you cruds."

"I have a better idea, Snowden." Harry's palm slapped at the side of Snowden's face, and he dropped to the ground. His men rushed to his aid while Jack and the boys watched. Harry bent down and picked up the cell. "I'll do the uploading and printing out."

"Well, that certainly works for me, Harry!" Jack said cheerfully. "There is absolutely nothing like a man of action. Is there, boys?"

"Nope, nothing," they all agreed.

Harry was back in fifteen minutes. "Hard

to believe this dump has wireless. If you'll notice, I collated everything and stapled it for your reading pleasure, and it cost me twenty bucks. So, here it is in a nutshell. In other words, *THE PLAN!*"

Kathryn settled herself behind the wheel of the eighteen-wheeler, Murphy on the passenger side. "You know what, Murphy, I feel like I died and went to heaven. I can't tell you how much I've missed this rig. I can't wait to get on the horn to see if my old buddies remember me."

Murphy tossed his head back and howled, Kathryn's signal to blast the horn. The horn blast meant they were going on the road. "This is as good as it gets, Murph. Just you and me, baby, until we get to Georgia to pick up the girls. Settle in with that cheese bone while I check out who's on the road in case we need some unexpected help along the way."

Hours later, Kathryn was about to give up when she tried one more time to locate her old trucking buddy, Jesse Sturgen, also known as Big Bear. "Hey, Bear, you copy? This is Little Sis." It finally dawned on Kathryn that most of her buddies had probably gone high-tech while she was gone and none of them used their CBs any longer.

But, not Big Bear. With fingers like tree trunks, Bear would definitely forgo texting. Besides, he loved talking to people.

Disgruntled, Kathryn finally accepted the fact that if she was going to continue to be a trucker, she had to keep up with what was going on.

An hour outside of Georgia, her CB came to life. "Yo, Little Sis, this is Bear. Where you been, Sweet Cheeks? Got seven calls saying you were looking for me. Had to catch a little shut-eye, so I didn't hear the squawk."

"You telling me you don't know about my nefarious past? God, it's good to talk to you, Bear!" Kathryn said, happiness ringing in her voice.

"Nah, I was being polite. Where are you?"

"An hour outside of Jacksonville, where I'm meeting up with some . . . ah . . . friends. Where are you?"

"Forty minutes from Hobo's. You want to meet up for some good old trucking food?"

Kathryn did some quick mental calculations. "Yeah, sure, I'm making good time. What are you hauling, Bear?"

"Kitchen sinks for Home Depot. Got one that's about ready to fall off the truck in case you need one."

"Got all the kitchen sinks I need, Bear.

Thanks for the offer." It was a joke, pure and simple.

"Whatcha hauling, Sis? You back to trucking full-time or are you . . . ah . . . working your own gig?"

"Jet Skis. Or I will be when I hit Jacksonville. Top-of-the-line, latest models, not in stores yet. Not sure about full-time, but I sure am enjoying the road again. Life's a little uncertain these days."

"Yeah, I know what you mean. Listen, Sis, we were all on your side, every damn trucker from California to Maine. And their families. We all waited for calls in case you needed us."

Kathryn felt a lump form in her throat. "That's nice to know, and, Bear, I did know that. I just didn't want to involve any of you with what was going on. But tell me this, when do you have to deliver those sinks?"

Kathryn heard a booming laugh. "Whenever I get there is when. You need me, I'm yours."

"Know anyone who will be in the Fort Lauderdale, Florida, area tomorrow with a little spare time?"

"Let me check. I'll have the info for you when we get to Hobo's. You get there first, order for me and tell them to keep it warm. If I get there, I'll do the same for you. You got Murphy with you?"

"You bet. Two rib eyes should do it for him, and a lettuce and green bean salad. He needs his greens."

Kathryn was rewarded with a booming laugh before she signed off.

"I think we just got an addendum to Plan A, Murph." The shepherd raised his head, gave a short bark, then went back to his cheese bone.

"Oh, yeah." Kathryn laughed. Just for fun she blasted her air horn. A couple in a red Toyota waved as she cruised by.

"Nothing like the open road, Murph."

CHAPTER 26

Kathryn gave the air horn a long blast as she swung into Tom Turtle's Truck Stop, which professed to have the best goulash in the entire country. Someone had crossed out the word *country* on the sign and wrote in the word *world.* She'd eaten the goulash many times, and so had Murphy. It was that good. Too bad she was full from her early dinner with Bear.

The Sisters stepped out of a van parked next to a rig with a Wisconsin license plate. The van said it belonged to someone named Handyman Mike, whose logo was, IF YOU WANT IT DONE RIGHT, CALL HANDYMAN MIKE. It wasn't that the Sisters were traveling incognito; they weren't. Charles said it would look better with a labeled truck so no one would give them a second glance. They were, after all, famous or infamous depending on who was doing the talking. He'd gone on to say they were definitely recognizable, even more so in a group.

Truckers, Kathryn said, as a rule, minded their own business, which meant no one in the lot or inside the restaurant would pay attention to them. "I have some news — good news, girls. I personally recommend the goulash if you haven't already eaten. I'll have some coffee with you."

"Is it better than Charles's goulash?" Myra asked.

Kathryn laughed. "Way better, but don't tell him I said that. Do you have any news? Are we on target? What's the latest? Stay, Murph. Watch the truck," she called over her shoulder as she walked with the Sisters into Tom Turtle's.

Kathryn beamed with a pleasure that didn't go unnoticed by the others when four truckers eating at the counter welcomed her with open arms, hugs, then peppered her with questions, all of which she expertly dodged. The final parting shot was, "Glad to have you back on the road, Sis. You need us; you know what to do." Kathryn waved, her eyes damp. Yoko reached up to wipe a lone tear ready to trickle down her cheek.

"They mean it, too," Kathryn said as she took a seat at a large round table in the corner of the room.

"Of course they do, dear, they're your colleagues," Myra said, remembering the one road trip she'd taken with Kathryn and the camaraderie she'd personally experienced among her friends.

"Don't even look at the menu, just order the goulash, and they serve fresh homemade bread with the yellowest butter you've ever seen in your life."

The women gave their orders to a perky, ponytailed youngster, Tom Turtle's daughter. The moment the girl was out of earshot, Kathryn said, "Talk to me. What's the plan? We have a plan, right? Because I have something to add to the plan. Let's just call it an addendum for now. But later on, if we want to call it Plan B, that's okay, too."

"Jack and the boys are at the Seashell Motel in Fort Lauderdale. Counting Snowden's men, they number seventeen. Their cover is the bike rally, which starts tomorrow morning at ten. The plan is to go cruising early in the morning and hit the neighborhood where Jellicoe is holed up. You know, just a fun ride, up and down the different streets. We have to synchronize our times because we're coming in by water on the Jet Skis. We hit the beach, so to speak, at precisely 7:00 A.M. We've been online the whole trip down here, and this rally is big stuff. It's on all the news stations, headlines in all the papers. It's legitimate, so good old Hank won't think too much about a bunch of motorcycles cruising a street that no one but him lives on. At least we hope not," Nikki said. "And, there's a private Jet Ski cove not far from John U. Lloyd Park, where we're going to launch the Jet Skis. I'm sure Jellicoe has scoped it all out on a regular basis. It is just what it seems. He can't control the waterway, so it's fair game. He can't control the county roads in the development where he lives, either, so that's fair game, too.

"And as sure as I am of that, I'm also just as sure that the man has the street booby-trapped. By that, I mean a warning system. The worst-case scenario is he holes up, and we can't get inside to get him. He will then call the police, and we're dead in the water. Charles said they might be able to jam all the frequencies to and from the house, but he wasn't sure. Therefore, we assume it can't be done and work from there," Nikki said.

"This is where I come in," Kathryn said quietly. "Lean closer, girls, and tell me what you think of what I'm about to tell you. Now, bear in mind, Charles said Snowden reported in that Hank has fortified 123 Dolphin Drive with steel doors and God knows what else. I'm assuming he thinks no one can gain entry to his fortress. With whatever warning system he has in place, he can have local law enforcement out there in the blink of an eye. Home invasion, that kind of thing. You get hung up in that, and you never see the light of day again."

"And your point is . . . ?" Isabelle said.

"My friends have offered to help me with no questions asked. The only thing I had to promise was to pay for any damage done to their trucks. I promised," Kathryn said, looking at Annie for support.

"Whatever it takes, dear." Kathryn sighed with relief.

"So, what's the plan?" Yoko asked.

"This will have to be your decision. Either I go with you on the Jet Skis, or I drive the truck, the truck that will go right through that steel door of Mr. Jellicoe's. The four rigs behind me will successfully block off the street cutting off any plans he might have for using a vehicle to hoof it somewhere. That leaves the water as his only means of escape. I don't remember who said it, Maggie maybe or Ted, but there's a cigarette boat tied to the dock. Those babies are built for speed, so when you girls pull into the dock, you're going to have to find a way to disable it somehow. Or, how about this — the guys ditch the Harleys and go in the water by Minnow Lane? It's two streets down from Dolphin Drive. Hank can't control that. There are four extra Jet Skis in the rig. I won't be needing mine if I drive the truck. That means five guys can come up behind you girls and guard the waterway and disable the boat. I'm sure one of them knows something about boats."

"Is this where we get to say, 'Gotcha, you son of a bitch'?" Annie asked, just as the waitress appeared with steaming bowls of goulash that smelled heavenly. Annie held up her hand, and announced, "We need to vote if Kathryn drives the rig or a Jet Ski?"

All were in favor of Kathryn driving her rig through Hank Jellicoe's front door.

"Yep, ladies, that's the moment," Kathryn said, holding up her coffee cup for a refill.

"Damn, we're good!" Myra said, surprising everyone with the glee in her tone.

"You girls go ahead and eat while I text the boys and Maggie. Guess I better bring Charles up to date, too," Kathryn said.

Forty minutes later, the waitress cleared the table and offered red velvet cake for dessert, which they all declined.

"I don't think I'll ever be able to eat Charles's goulash again without thinking about this place," Myra said happily. "Whoever changed the sign out front was right on the money." The girls all agreed.

"Now what?" Alexis asked.

"Now we head down to Fort Lauderdale and John U. Lloyd Park to meet up with the guys. We are free until the early hours of tomorrow morning. I have to unload these Jet Skis and their trailers. I sure can't do it alone, so we need the guys for that. Charles said he used every sort of pressure he could exert to get us rooms at the Whale Harbor Inn, which is less than a mile from the launching site. He said, and I don't know how he knows this, but he said there are biker parties, tailgate parties, everywhere. This bike rally is really a big thing. They hope to raise a million dollars. Did you know most of the entries in the rally are doctors, nurses, lawyers, and dentists? Anyone can enter, but they are the majority, and if you can believe this, for the weekend, the state of Florida is turning over the $2.50 toll on Alligator Alley to the JDF.

"Here's something else I didn't know. They're having a rally on the boardwalk in Atlantic City, one on the strip in Vegas that you sponsored, Annie, and didn't even know about. Your buddy Fish okayed it back in March. They're having them all over the country, with the ultimate goal of raising a total of ten million dollars. There's even talk about doing another rally in the spring for Breast Cancer Awareness. I plan to ride in that one," Kathryn said.

The others agreed that they, too, would ride with Kathryn in the spring if they weren't in jail.

"Don't even go there, girls," Annie said, her eyes sparking dangerously. "We *will* ride in that rally."

Out in the parking lot, the girls said goodbye — Kathryn to head to the warehouse where she was to pick up the Jet Skis, the girls to John U. Lloyd State Park.

An hour later the girls had registered at the Whale Harbor Inn, where no one paid the least bit of attention to them. Satisfied that they were as anonymous as they were going to get, the group headed poolside, ordered fruity drinks, and started to text. Myra and Annie glared at one another. "Too bad we don't have anyone to text," Annie grumbled. "I suppose I could text Fish, but I've never done that before, and he might get suspicious."

"I would *call* Charles, but I'm sure he's busy," Myra said.

"Myra, you do realize, don't you, that we would not be here if all this wasn't about to go down? Ironic, isn't it? Seeing that article in the paper, getting to the farm and your agreeing to take part in the rally with me. We might have been bored if we were just participants. You know what they say, everything happens for a reason. Listen, I could call Fish and blast him for something. You know, ask him where he is, that kind of thing. No, better to leave sleeping dogs lie," Annie said, deciding against her own suggestion.

Myra agreed. "The only thing that is bothering me . . . well, actually several things are bothering me. One, Charles probably can't jam the airwaves or whatever so Hank gets a chance to call the police, and one getaway boat. I'm not boo-hooing, Annie, but I think I'd like to know more about the safeguards he has in place. You know Murphy's Law, what can go wrong, will go wrong."

"What bothers me, Myra, is we don't know why we're doing this. I mean why . . . oh, hell, you know what I mean," Annie fretted.

Myra played with her pearls. "Well, I'm sure once we're inside, we'll manage to get the details out of him. Do you think he's going to put up much of a fight?"

"Oh, yeah," Annie drawled. "So will Fish and Stu Franklin. Three baddies is how we have to look at it."

"You're dealing with this very well, Annie. I hope you feel the same way when Fish is no longer on your radar screen."

Annie started to laugh. "There are more fish in the stream, Myra, no pun intended." Myra burst out laughing. "That whole relationship thing . . . that didn't work for me. I totally understand Kathryn's refusing to get married to Bert even though she says she loves him. Alan was her one true love, her true soul mate. That's how I feel about my husband. That doesn't mean you can't love someone else, or care about him a great deal. You can. For me it would be betrayal, disloyal to marry again. I didn't make a promise because I didn't have time. Kathryn made a promise to her husband and, to her credit, she's honoring her promise. I applaud the dear girl for that. That's something you would do, Myra."

Myra thought about it for a moment, then said, "Yes, Annie, that is something I would do. I think that would be classified as old-school or something like that. I applaud you, too, Annie. I love that you have honor, and yet you're a free spirit. I know that some days you hurt inside so badly with the memories, but you never let it get you down. I wish I was more like you."

"Oh, Myra, no, you don't. I don't ever want you to change. If you ever lost those damn pearls, I'd cry a river for you."

The girls turned around when Annie and Myra went into peals of laughter.

"They're up to something," Nikki whispered to Yoko.

"I know. Isn't it great? Our little team would be nothing without those two. Oh, Nikki, this is what I missed so much. All of you are the family I never had. As much as I love Harry, he can't be all of you."

Nikki squeezed Yoko's hand. "I know — boy, do I know."

It was eleven o'clock when Kathryn appeared. She looked tired but exhilarated. "Jet Skis are docked. My truckers are parked a mile down the road. I hitched a ride here. The Whale Harbor Inn does not allow eighteen-wheelers in their parking lot. You'll have to drop me off in the morning. I'm going to hit the sack. When's our wake-up call?"

"Five o'clock," Alexis said. "I'm with you. One more of these silly umbrella drinks, and I'm going to fall over. Just for the record, I checked the wet suits — all our gear is set to go, so all we have to do is roll out of bed and hit the road. I sure hope we have good weather."

Myra yawned. "Weren't you paying attention when the weather came on, dear?" She pointed to a wide-screen TV perched over the tiki bar. "Typical August weather, sweltering hot, high humidity, and eighty-degree waters. I think we're good to go."

"Then let's all say good night. It's automatic checkout, so we don't have to worry about that," Nikki said, stifling a yawn. "I just checked with Jack, and they're turning in, too. He said two of Snowden's men did a walk through the neighborhood with a stray dog they found. And yes, they're keeping the dog. He said there are lights on in the house, and it's buttoned up tight.

"Sweet dreams, everyone."

Annie and Myra continued to sit by the pool. There were no other guests to be seen, and the tiki bar had just lowered its shutters and called it a night.

"I'm not the least bit sleepy, Myra. I hate hotel rooms. I think I'll sit out here for a while, but if you want to go to bed, don't worry about me."

"I'm not tired, either. I'll keep you company. We can talk."

"Talking is for old people. Let's just bitch and moan and groan."

"But, Annie, we really don't have anything to bitch, moan, and groan about. We have wonderful lives compared to others. We are so blessed, it would be sinful to complain. Annie, I want the truth now; how upset are you that Fish is part of whatever it is that's going on?"

Annie sniffed. "Well now that you ask, Myra . . . not one little bit," she replied, laughing. "What upsets me is how obsessed he is with Hank Jellicoe. It borders on . . . way beyond unhealthy. Isabelle said she feels the same way about Stu. She also said it was over between the two of them some time ago, but she just couldn't get out of it. That's pretty much how I felt, too. Does that answer your question?"

"It does. There's no kick to this ginger ale, Annie."

"What was your first clue, Myra?" Annie chuckled.

The two old friends continued to talk and laugh as they rehashed old memories and their newest memories, until Annie pointed to a large clock hanging from the thatched roof of the tiki bar. "In thirty minutes it will be five o'clock. Are you as excited as I am, Myra?"

"I am. This will be the first time we've gone on a mission not knowing the why of it. I hope it doesn't work against us. What do we do if we can't beat it out of Jellicoe?

Does that mean we should have agreed to stand down until we figured out the reason for it all?"

"We'll get it out of him, Myra, one way or the other. Depends on how much he can stand. Fish and Stu are altogether different now. I'm thinking if Hank stays buttoned up, one or the other of them will spill what they know. We're pretty good at winging it, don't you think?"

Myra's phone chirped. Startled, she looked at Annie, who appeared just as startled. "You need to answer that, Myra."

Myra flipped the cell phone and brought it to her ear. "Charles! Do you know what time it is?"

"Of course I know what time it is. I'm looking at the clock as I speak with you. My question to you would be, why aren't you sleeping? You need to be in top form for your ride down the Intercoastal, my dear. I am assuming you are sitting poolside with Annie."

"You assume right, Charles. Why are you calling other than to wish us luck?"

"Because I know the *WHY* of it all."

Myra's jaw dropped as Annie huddled closer to better hear what was being said. "Are you going to tell me, or are you going to make me guess?"

"Neither, my dear. Go inside to the office and wait for my fax, which will be coming through in about seven minutes. I also want to apologize to you, Annie, and the others for my misguided loyalty."

"Where did you come by this information, Charles?" Myra asked, as she scooted along behind Annie. She didn't know why she even bothered to ask the question, knowing what the answer would be.

"That, my dear, is something you do not want to know. Not now, not ever. It is completely on the up-and-up, though, as you will see when the fax comes through."

"This is what is called taking it right down to the wire. Annie and I were just discussing what we were going to do if Hank refused to give it up. Do you mind telling me why it took so long to come by this information?"

"Because it was under seal. My informant's only condition aside from a boatload of money, which is seriously going to deplete Annie's coffers, was that he and his family had to be relocated and given immunity. That has now happened. Lizzie just put the deal to bed a short while ago. Good luck. Watch those gators."

"You had to say that, didn't you, Charles?" Myra heard his chuckle as the connection went silent.

The pimply, spiked-hair desk clerk playing solitaire behind the counter looked up as Myra and Annie approached. "We're here to wait for a fax. It should come through any minute now."

"There's a five-dollar charge for a fax and a dollar for each page," he said, just as the fax machine came to life. "It says six pages are coming through. That's eleven dollars. Plus tax."

"Just charge it to Room 216," Annie snapped, just as the first page rolled out of the machine.

If the clerk thought it strange that two old ladies were getting a fax at almost five in the morning, it didn't show. He tapped the charge into the computer, handed over the faxed pages, and went back to his game.

Annie and Myra literally ran to a far corner of the lobby, where there was a grouping of chairs and better light. They sat down together and read the pages. Neither said a word until Myra folded the pages into a tight square and stuck it in her pocket. She looked up at Annie, a wicked smile on her face. "I think this takes us out of the *obsolete* category, don't you? I say we keep it to ourselves and spring it on everyone when they least expect it. What say you, Annie?"

"It works for me. I have to tell you, Myra, that never would have occurred to me. You?"

"Never."

"I think we should keep Charles on our payroll. It takes a good person to man up when all the chips are gone. Plus, he is your husband, and you're stuck with him."

"There is that," Myra agreed. "Come along, Annie, let's wake the girls. Suddenly I cannot wait to reach 123 Dolphin Drive."

Chapter 27

Fifteen minutes later, the girls were in the Handyman Mike van and headed for John U. Lloyd Park. They dropped Kathryn off and waited until she picked up Murphy from one of her trucker friends who had elected to sleep in the back of his cab. Satisfied that all was well in that arena, Nikki drove off just as Avery Snowden and his posse of cyclists stood at attention.

"If no one has any questions, it's time to ride!"

The roar was that of a supersonic jet breaking the sound barrier as all seventeen Harleys came to life. There was a drill-like precision to their exit that even Harry marveled at. They were back at the Seashell Motel at 6:20 as scheduled.

"Good work, men!" Snowden said smartly. "Okay, Emery, you're up. You guys head down to the park and join the girls. Don't worry about the bikes. I have it covered. You'll see us when you see us."

"Aren't you supposed to say, 'Godspeed, boys, over and out'?" Jack said, straddling his Harley.

"No, this is where I say, 'Your ass is mine if you screw up.' "

Jack made kissing motions with his lips and yelled to be heard over the roar of the Harley, "I just love it when you sweet-talk me, Snowden. Over and out, you asshole!"

With little to no traffic at that hour of the morning, the boys rode two across, with Espinosa bringing up the rear. They passed the four-truck convoy. Even over the roar of the cycles, they could hear Murphy's joyous bark. When Kathryn blasted the air horn, the others sounded off in sequence. Jack waved and forged ahead.

They arrived at the park just as the girls were pushing the Jet Skis away from where they were tethered. The boys parked the Harleys, tossed their helmets down, and leaped on the skis the girls were holding for them.

"Who's got the time?" Nikki shouted.

"I do. We're on schedule. Move, move! That means you, too, Harry!"

Harry moved. Not for the world would he admit he'd never been on a Jet Ski. Nor would he admit he was scared shitless of water because he couldn't swim. How hard could it be?

Sensing his distress, Jack brought his Jet Ski as close to Harry's as he could, and said, "Just do what I do. Turn the damn key, ease out, and stay right behind me. If you fall off, it shuts off. Just get back on. Don't worry, she thinks you're a pro. Besides, she's up front and won't see you making an ass of yourself. Don't let the gators get you. Look, it's a straight run. By the time we get there, you're gonna want to do this every weekend."

Nikki and Alexis were in the lead, the others close behind. Eight minutes ahead of schedule, Nikki pushed in the throttle and roared past the dock at 123 Dolphin Drive. Four minutes later, she swung the machine around and headed back to the dock, the others so close she could smell them. She throttled back just as Bert slid off, dove underwater, and jammed a drill bit through the fiberglass bottom of the boat. He did the same thing three more times before he surfaced.

There were Jet Skis everywhere, bobbing in the furious wake that hadn't died down. One by one, their riders were hauling themselves up onto the dock. Jack had his arm braced under Harry as he boosted him up. "You owe me for this one, big-time."

They heard the crash, then they saw the cab of Kathryn's rig sticking outside the back door of 123 Dolphin Drive. Then they saw Kathryn and Murphy streaking inside the wide gap the eighteen-wheeler had left. They followed, Myra and Annie in the lead.

"Surprise! Surprise!" Annie said, elation ringing in her voice.

"If either one of them moves, Murphy, bite his dick off!" Kathryn ordered as she raced to what remained of the steel front door. She waved, grinning from ear to ear to her trucker friends. When they waved back, she sprinted back to what remained of the kitchen.

"Grab those phones. See if they called anyone," Nikki said.

Isabelle snatched them up, clicked and clicked. "They tried, but they didn't get through. Yay, Charles. Well, helloooo there, Stu! Imagine meeting you here." In the blink of an eye, her knee shot upward and made contact with Franklin's crotch. He doubled over just as Isabelle's foot lashed out to strike him in the neck. He fell backward to land next to the passenger-side wheel of Kathryn's rig. No one rushed to his aid. Gasping for breath, Stu struggled to talk.

"I can't be sure, but it certainly sounds like he thinks you crushed his larynx," Myra said.

"Thinks! He *thinks* I did that. I *know* I crushed it," Isabelle said, giving his prone body one more vicious kick in the side. "Now I cracked your ribs. You won't have to think about it." The Sisters clapped their hands in approval.

"Guard, Murphy. If he twitches, you know what to do. Doesn't matter whose dick you bite off. Show him those beautiful teeth, big guy." Murphy let out a happy bark and planted his two front paws on Franklin's chest, his fangs bared.

"Weapons? Where are they?" Annie asked as she went nose to nose with Fish. "Don't even think about lying to me and my friends. You lie to me and I'll peel the skin right off your face."

The group watched Fish's eyes narrow to slits as he tried to figure out whether or not Annie was serious. He saw something in her eyes that didn't sit well with his sense of self-preservation. "They're in every room in the house."

Annie's arm whipped backward, and a second later Fish was looking down the barrel of the gun in her hand. "I know that. Be precise. Like in as when we find them, then we find one you forgot to mention, I start peeling." To prove she meant business she stepped back, aimed, and fired, first at his right foot, then his left. "So much for those snakeskin boots you love and adore so much."

Fish crumpled to the floor as he stared at the blood oozing from his favorite boots. He cursed loudly and often as he started to rattle off the places where the guns were. The boys moved like greased lightning as they gathered the arsenal of weapons and tossed them into Kathryn's rig.

"Annie, dear, I hesitate to mention this, but perhaps you should have aimed a little higher," Myra said.

"Do ya think, Myra?"

"I do, dear. He can still crawl around. We simply cannot have that."

"You are so right, Myra. What was I thinking?" To everyone's delight, Annie did a little jig, then lifted her leg, her arm, and gun straight out. Two rapid shots could be heard.

"You took his ear right off. Excellent shooting, Annie!" Alexis said.

"I do believe you shattered his left shoulder. That's really a lot of blood, dear!" Myra said.

"Fucking bitch!" Fish bellowed.

"You were ahead, Fish. You should have stayed there. Now I'm going to have to tell everyone gathered here for this soiree that you're addicted to Viagra. One more peep out of you, and I *will* peel the skin off your face."

Bert's face was white as he stared at his beloved, who returned his look with steely-eyed amusement. Jack leaned against the front of Kathryn's rig as he waited for round two to get under way.

Espinosa was dizzy with delight as he snapped and snapped, then uploaded the pictures he was taking to Maggie Spritzer. Ted was so busy texting Maggie that he had trouble keeping up with what was going on. Harry went silent, his eyes on his wife. He smiled.

All eyes turned to Henry, call me Hank, Jellicoe. He looked just the same as he'd looked on the plane — the dreadlocks were in place, his skin was still dyed an outrageous shade of burnt umber, and he was in his boxer shorts and tee shirt. His feet were bare. And he was in the clutches of Yoko, unable to move.

"Well, hello there, Mr. Henry, call me Hank, Jellicoe. Or should I say Andy Graverson. Fancy finding you in John and Gertrude Solomon's home. How kind of them to let you borrow it."

"You're good, I'll give you that!"

"Tell us something we don't know. Your turn, you piece of crap. We saved you till last because we've been fighting among ourselves. Each of us wants a piece of you. Guess who won the lottery?" Nikki said.

"You!" Jellicoe said.

"I wish. Nope," Nikki said. "The little china doll holding you captive won the honors," she said, pointing to Yoko. Yoko, embarrassed, bowed. Harry smiled.

"Whenever you're ready, dear," Myra said.

"I'm ready, Myra," Yoko said. Harry smiled.

"Well, if Yoko is ready then, girls, wire up Mr. Jellicoe!" Myra said.

They were on him faster than Typhoon Tillie. Off came his shirt, down went his boxers. Strong hands pinned Jellicoe's arms behind him. Espinosa clicked away as Ted's fingers started to blister. Harry smiled.

"Alexis, dear, the electrodes. I know, I know, it's flaccid, but do your best. Use the duct tape. Homeland Security recommends it so highly," Myra said.

"You aren't saying anything, Mr. Jellicoe. Why is that? Girls, this man has been way too silent. Other than admitting we're *good,* he hasn't said a word, not even when we took out his two 'best' men. I find that classification debatable, but that's for another time. I want him to talk."

"Well, Annie, why didn't you say so?" Nikki singsonged.

Jellicoe lifted his leg to kick out at Annie, but Murphy leaped and sank his teeth into the fleshy calf. Jellicoe howled as Murphy hung on, waiting for the command he knew was coming. When it did, he relaxed his hold and went back to what he had been doing as he listened to the praise all around him. He let loose with two sharp barks to show he was grateful for it.

"Wow, there's a lot of blood flowing here," Jack said. "You getting all this, Espinosa?"

"Every last drop!"

"Jack him up against the cab and tie his legs. The man, if you believe his press, can tolerate unbelievable amounts of pain," Nikki said. "But everyone has a breaking point, so let's get to his so we can report back to the heads of the world's various intelligence and law-enforcement services, the very people Mr. Jellicoe decided to dupe into helping take a year and a half of our lives away from us. Not to mention foisting Stu Franklin and Fish on two of us. Those same individuals are anxiously awaiting results. Yoko, it's your call. Do you want to go to work on him or should we give him a chance to talk?"

Harry smiled. Yoko smiled at her husband, puckered her lips, then blew him a kiss. "He's not going to talk; he's stupid. I say you let me fry his ass right now, then if he wants to talk, *if* he can talk, we'll listen."

Jellicoe slowly and deliberately looked around and said, "You're all dead. Maybe not today or tomorrow, but my people will take all of you out one by one. Guaranteed."

"I don't think so, Mr. Jellicoe," Myra said. "It was all a big hoax. I have to give you credit for conning the people who have contracted with us to bring you down. Your people are the ones responsible for the chatter that so wired them up. You couldn't make it stick here in America, though. You had us jumping through hoops there for a while, but we finally figured it all out. Would you care to expound to our little group here about what got your boxers in a knot nineteen months ago? No, I didn't think so. Yoko, he's all yours!"

"That's really pretty clever, don't you think, Bert? Who would have thought wiring some guy's dick, then shocking him to hell and back would make him turn white like that? I didn't know that, did you?"

"Jesus, look at their faces, Jack. They're

enjoying this."

"Yeah, they are. I am, too. I think the question is, why aren't you enjoying this?"

"Because, you dumb-ass, I can see Kathryn trying this out on me the next time I piss her off. You might want to give that some thought, Mr. Emery."

"I prefer not to think about it, Bert. Besides, I'm married, and you aren't."

"So?" Bert shot back.

"If you do it again, Yoko, I can catch him in midbounce even though he's tied. Oooh, that's good!" Espinosa cackled.

"Maggie said she doesn't think the *Post* can print these pictures because it's a family newspaper."

"That's true, but she can put them out there on the Internet. For the whole world to download!" Annie said. "Honey," she said, addressing Yoko, "ask him if he's ready to talk."

Instead of doing as Annie asked, Yoko hit the plunger again. Jellicoe bounced in the air.

Then he sagged into a crumpled heap. The Sisters looked at one another, worried expressions on their faces. Jack leaned over and cut him loose. "He's still breathing," Jack said, happiness ringing in his voice. "I don't think he'll ever be the same again, though."

"Where's his computer, Fish?" Nikki asked as she pulled a piece of paper out of her wet suit. "I'm going to relieve him of all his funds. As in like *now!*"

Curses, words they'd never heard before, rang out in the room as Jellicoe tried to sit up. "You leave my goddamn money alone. I earned that!"

"Sure you did, and now we're taking it." Nikki laughed. "Fish?"

"Upstairs, middle room. Everything is password-protected."

"Wanna bet?" Nikki laughed as Jellicoe attempted to lunge for her legs. Yoko was on him in a nanosecond. She yanked his head backward, her knee in the small of his back. She leaned over, picked up his head, and slammed it on the tile floor. "Don't worry, he's not dead," she trilled.

Harry beamed with pride. His little lotus blossom had rendered the big bad wolf harmless.

"This is a real mess," Jack said. "Are we sure we got all the weapons?"

"Got pictures of everything, Jack. We need to think about getting out of here and quick. We've already been here an hour. It's full morning; people start moving around. Someone is bound to see all those trucks out there, and this one in particular."

Jack looked over at Kathryn. "Are you going to have any trouble backing this rig out of here?"

"Not one little bit. My guys have me covered, so don't worry about me. I know the drill. I drive to the drop-off point, and Snowden's people take care of the rest. Meaning, of course, that all three of them will be loaded on the plane sitting on the tarmac in Fort Lauderdale, which will take them back to where our employers will deal with them in their own way. Our job here is done. Well, almost done."

Upstairs in the middle room, Nikki worked the computer. "Okay, Alexis, what do we want to do with all of Hank's sizable fortune?"

"Send it to the same place our fifty million went. We can divvy it up later. We need to get out of here. This is some place," Alexis said, looking around.

"Yeah, it is. Done! His money is now *our* money. Billions with a B, baby!" Nikki said, printing out copies of her wire transfers. She unzipped her wet suit and stuck the papers inside.

"You know what, Alexis, that bastard didn't lie about one thing."

"Yeah, what's that?"

"He said we were good."

"Oh, yeah," Alexis drawled. The two women high-fived each other before they bolted for the steps. They stood watching as Kathryn started to back the rig out of the house as the other truckers outside guided her movements.

Back in the kitchen, which was no longer a kitchen, the group stared at one another. "And we still don't know the why of it all," Isabelle mumbled.

"Oh, but we do know, dear," Myra said, as she spread open the six-page fax. "I'll give you the short version. Later on, we can all read this and talk it to death."

"You know?" the Sisters chorused as one.

"Of course. Just because Annie and I are . . . up there in years doesn't mean we can't hold our own. It's really quite simple. Nineteen months ago the Pentagon decided not to renew Global's contracts. They had their reasons; most of them can't be divulged because of national security. Very valid reasons. His contracts had twenty-two months to go, then he was out in the cold. Oh, he made money from foreign governments and from private corporations, but the billions he earned every year came from the Pentagon. The bottom line was, he was no longer the Golden Boy. He couldn't and wouldn't accept that.

"So, he decided to start a campaign to re-ingratiate himself with the Pentagon. But first he had to make sure the vigilantes couldn't be used to come after him and expose what he was doing. So he courted Martine Connor, subtly helped to get her to grant our pardons, then convinced our current employers that we needed to be neutralized in order to allow Global to go after the group Jellicoe had made up out of whole cloth.

"Once they agreed and kicked in money to bribe our guys, he set up the murders, and that is the only word that fits, of twenty-three contractors who the Pentagon and some private corporations had paid Global to protect, starting in February and culminating in the murders, just before Thanksgiving, of the seven contractors that Elias learned about from Calvin Sands.

"And, I'm sorry to have to say this, but Isabelle and Annie, if you can reconstruct the eight months from that February until last Thanksgiving, I think you will find that Stu Franklin and Fish were gone at precisely the times the contractors Global was supposed to protect were murdered."

There were gasps all around, and Isabelle

and Annie looked as if they were ready to faint.

"According to Charles's informant, who is now a very rich man, thanks to Annie's money, for which she will be reimbursed from the funds we just liberated, Jellicoe hoped to 'expose' the plot against the murdered contractors, blame the supposed assassination attempt on the same people, and get back in the Pentagon's good graces. And since all the alleged plotters would be killed in the attempt to apprehend them, no one would be the wiser."

"But why," Jack interrupted, "did he pretend to retire and have Bert and me take over the reins of Global Securities? Didn't that risk our finding out about what was going on? It doesn't make sense."

"Doesn't it?" Nikki asked. "Think about it. Did you ever hear about the deaths of the first sixteen contractors? Did you? Of course not. We heard only about the seven killed around Thanksgiving when it became front-page news around the world. The only information you got was what Jellicoe wanted you to have. And the same went for Bert, didn't it?"

"I guess," Jack said, looking thoroughly dismayed.

"There's one other important thing

Charles learned," Myra continued. "After the murders started, Jellicoe decided that if things went badly, and Global was blamed for the failures to protect the murder victims, he would pin the blame for lax security on Jack and Bert's cost-cutting efforts. So even if his grand strategy failed to get the intended results, his risk of exposure was basically zero."

"Wait a minute," Bert objected. "I didn't get involved in any cost-cutting efforts. Did you, Jack?"

"Not on your life. Hell, all I ever did was read papers my secretary put on my desk. I knew as much about what was really going on as Bush did about New Orleans."

"Jack," Myra asked pointedly, "how much do you want to bet that any investigation of your computers would turn up conclusive evidence that you and Bert were engaged in a sustained program of cutting corners in the area of contractor security?

"Never mind, you don't have to answer. Anyway, I think it's safe to say it was never really about the money with Hank. He believed he was infallible. He or his people had started making mistakes. He tried to cover them up, and things went downhill to the point that he became desperate. That's when he came up with that wild story about the chatter, the bogus threat, and managed to convince everyone but our own government because they knew. They knew. I think they might even send us a thank-you letter once they find out we took care of business for them," Myra said.

Wide-eyed, jaws agape, everyone looked at Myra and Annie in stunned amazement.

"And you found this out . . . how?" Nikki demanded.

"We didn't find out till just before five o'clock this morning. I did tell Hank that we knew the whole story just before they loaded his sorry ass into the truck. He tried to spit on me, but Annie knocked him out."

"Way to go, ladies!" Jack said.

"Obsolete my ass," Annie hissed in Myra's ear. Myra laughed as she led the parade out what was once a back door and down to the dock.

"Hey, Harry, why don't you ride with Yoko. One of Snowden's men is staying behind, and he needs the Jet Ski."

Harry's fist shot in the air as Jack blew him a kiss. Harry winked as he slid onto the ski behind Yoko.

No one looked back as the Jet Skis shot forward.

Eleven minutes later, the support beams at 123 Dolphin Drive collapsed, and the house crumpled to the ground. It stayed that way for thirty-six hours until a Coast Guard helicopter spotted the wreckage, by which time the Sisters were on the deck at Pinewood, toasting each other on a job well done.

Epilogue

Christmas Eve
Pinewood, Virginia

Outside the old farmhouse in McLean, Virginia, there wasn't an evergreen to be seen that wasn't festooned with colorful Christmas lights. Inside the house, which was lit from top to bottom, giant twelve-foot balsam firs, resplendent with colored lights and heirloom Christmas decorations, were tucked into every corner of every room. The scent was delightful. Delicious, heavenly aromas wafted from the kitchen, where Charles, wearing a decorative Christmas apron, held court.

He and the guys had rehashed for the umpteenth time the events of last summer and had moved on to speculating about how Hank Jellicoe had managed to escape from Avery Snowden and his men. All anyone knew was that when Jellicoe was to be turned over to the big shots who had hired the Sisters, he was gone.

Despite their disappointment, the intelligence and law-enforcement chiefs had been sufficiently relieved to learn that all the chatter about assassination plots was nothing more than a con job by Jellicoe that they had agreed to take care of Stu Franklin and Fish. From what the Sisters had later heard, the two murderers were now permanently, as in for eternity, located near a place with one of those funny-sounding names in the deserts of the Middle East. Nothing further had been heard from Jellicoe, though no one took the threats he had made against the Sisters lightly.

All the persons near and dear to Myra's heart were there for the Christmas festivities. They'd all arrived three days before Christmas to help with the extensive decorating Myra, Charles, and Annie insisted on. Garlands were strung, mistletoe hung, and fragrant balsam wreaths hung from each window and door. As Nikki put it, and the others agreed, "We need to make up for not being here last year." And make up for it, they did.

"I don't think I've ever been happier in my whole life," Myra said as she looked around at her little family, which wasn't so little anymore. Everyone was present and accounted for except Lizzie, Cosmo, and Little Jack, who were on their way from the airport via a horse-drawn sleigh that Jack and Bert had arranged for. Their ETA was any minute now, depending on the horse's gait.

The seven dogs, wearing antlers and red collars with bells on them, pranced and danced around, enjoying all the activity. Even the pups, who were no longer little. They were still named One, Two, Three, and Four, and as Myra said, "I don't see me changing their names anytime soon."

The dining room table was set for twenty. A high chair that had more bells and whistles than a top-of-the-line sports car sat in the middle of the row and did not seem out of place. The table was set with the finest china and crystal, and silver that Myra and Annie had washed and polished for days. The tablecloth was more than a hundred years old, threadbare in some spots but carefully mended along with the napkins, which were equally worn and soft to the touch. In the center of the table, flanked by red candles, sat a gorgeous evergreen centerpiece on which Annie and Myra had worked for hours. Red berries and scarlet poinsettias added all the color that was needed to the magnificent table arrangement.

A finely crafted serving tray sat on the buffet, another of Myra's heirlooms, filled with crystal wine flutes and several bottles of Cristal champagne.

Outside, a fine snow was falling, perfect weather for this exceptional Christmas Eve.

In the living room, in the center of the floor, sat the most exquisite Christmas tree that Myra's farm had to offer. Underneath were mounds of presents, all gaily wrapped, waiting for Little Jack's busy fingers to unwrap.

The dogs heard the sleigh bells first, then they all ran to the kitchen. "Lizzie's here! Lizzie's here!" Myra opened the door, and they all rushed outside to see the sleigh driven by a man decked out in a red suit, a curly white beard, a stocking hat with a big white fur ball on the end, and shiny black boots. A.K.A. Avery Snowden. Next to him was a huge red velvet bag full of surprises.

Cosmo Cricket hopped down from the sleigh and reached for his son, whom he handed off to the man in the red suit. He held out his hand for Lizzie, who was dressed in something that looked like white ermine, and probably was.

Snowden let loose with a few "ho ho ho's" for Little Jack's benefit before driving the sleigh to the barn, all seven dogs hot on his trail. Fifteen minutes later, sans costume, he was in the kitchen with the other guys, having his usual "friendly" colloquy with Harry.

The dogs took one look at Little Jack, who was no longer in his bulky snowsuit, and nosed him forward. They barked happily as they led the way into the living room to where the giant Christmas tree waited for the little one. The dogs circled him, tugging at his pant leg. The toddler looked around, his eyes bigger than saucers as he squatted, then sat down. The dogs were on him in a second, rolling around and tussling with one another, as he squealed happily.

Charles whistled. The dogs immediately came to attention, even the pups. Little Jack got up and wobbled over to his mother. Lizzie picked up her son, and said, "Everyone, I want you to meet my and Cosmo's son. We call him Little Jack. If you all stand back, kind of in a line, I'm going to put him down so he can go to you when I call your name. He knows all of you because . . . because you're our family. While we aren't here on a daily basis to see you all in person, Cosmo and I have shown him videos and pictures."

As Lizzie called out each person's name,

Little Jack waddled up to that person for his hug and kiss. When only one person whose name hadn't been called remained, Lizzie said, "Jack, where's that one special person Mommy told you about?" The toddler turned around, his eyes going from person to person until he found Jack Emery. In his haste to get to that special person, he stumbled and fell, but Murphy reached down, straightened him up, and set him on his way. Lizzie's eyes sparkled with glistening tears when Jack held out his arms, and the toddler stepped into them. "Me Jack!" One chubby finger jabbed Jack in the chest. "Big Jack!" The same chubby finger then jabbed at his own chest. "Me Lil Jack! Luff you!"

"Yeah, yeah, I love you, too," Jack said, tears rolling unashamedly down his cheeks. He hugged the little boy hard to his chest. Nothing in the whole of his life had ever felt this warm, this good, this perfect, this right.

Little Jack started to jabber, but it was hard to keep up with what he was saying. Jack looked at Lizzie, who whispered, "He's trying to say you're his mommy's White Knight, and he's thanking you for letting me be here. I told him our story the day he was born, and I've told it to him every night ever since. It's his favorite bedtime story."

Jack swiped at his eyes, a lump the size of a golf ball in his throat. All he could do was nod.

Sensing something different in the air, something the dogs didn't understand, they barked, and the moment was gone, though it would never be forgotten.

Charles stepped forward. "I do believe it's time for dinner."

Hours later, when the table was cleared and Little Jack was sleeping upstairs in Nikki's old bed, Charles served coffee, and everyone retired to the living room to sing some carols and wish one another a joyous Christmas.

Eventually, as the clock was about to strike midnight, they all ran to the window. It was snowing harder. A truly white, wonderful Christmas.

"I wonder where we'll all be next year at this time," Nikki said.

Annie and Myra linked arms, mysterious smiles on their faces. In unison, they both said, "Right where we want to be, where we all belong."

"That's it, that's all you're going to say?" Kathryn grinned.

"For now, dear. For now."

ABOUT THE AUTHOR

Fern Michaels is the *USA Today* and *New York Times* bestselling author of the Sisterhood series as well as *Up Close and Personal, Fool Me Once, Picture Perfect,* and dozens of other novels and novellas. There are over seventy million copies of her books in print.

Fern Michaels has built and funded several large daycare centers in her hometown, and is a passionate animal lover who has outfitted police dogs across the country with special bulletproof vests. She shares her home in South Carolina with her four dogs and a resident ghost named Mary Margaret. Visit her website at www.fernmichaels.com.

We hope you have enjoyed this Large Print book. Other Thorndike, Wheeler, Kennebec, and Chivers Press Large Print books are available at your library or directly from the publishers.

For information about current and upcoming titles, please call or write, without obligation, to:

Publisher
Thorndike Press
295 Kennedy Memorial Drive
Waterville, ME 04901
Tel. (800) 223-1244

or visit our Web site at:

http://gale.cengage.com/thorndike

OR

Chivers Large Print
published by BBC Audiobooks Ltd
St James House, The Square
Lower Bristol Road
Bath BA2 3SB
England
Tel. +44(0) 800 136919
email: bbcaudiobooks@bbc.co.uk
www.bbcaudiobooks.co.uk

All our Large Print titles are designed for easy reading, and all our books are made to last.